STILL THE TIGERY PROWLED

"I am thinking, I am thinking . . ." Abruptly he halted. He drove the knife into a bole so that the metal sang. "Yes—a twisted path—but we must needs hurry, and not give the Zacharians time to imagine we are crazy enough to take that way."

Beyond the last concealment the forest afforded was a hundred-meter stretch. A link fence enclosed a ferrocrete field. Service buildings clustered and a radionic mast spired at the far end. Of the several landing docks, two were occupied. One craft Diana identified as interplanetary, new and shapely.

It was an instant and a century across the clearing. Men ran from the terminal, insectoidal at their distance, then suddenly near. She saw pistols in the hands of some; heard a buzz, a thud. Diana opened fire.

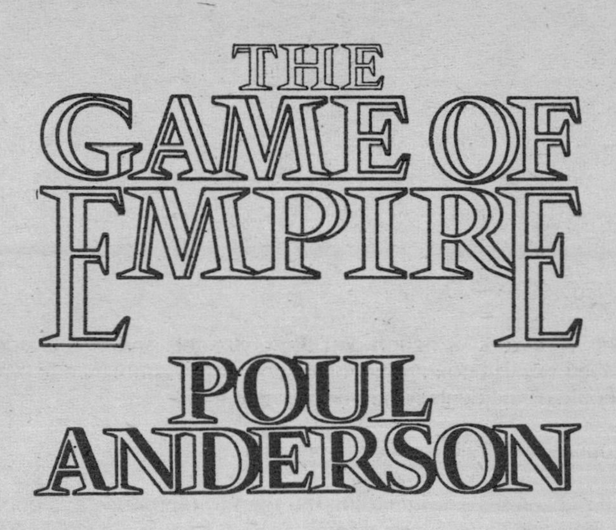
THE
GAME OF
EMPIRE
POUL
ANDERSON

BAEN
science fiction
BOOKS

THE GAME OF EMPIRE

This is a work of fiction. All the characters and events portrayed in this book are fictional, and any resemblance to real people or incidents is purely coincidental.

A Baen Book

Baen Enterprises
8-10 W. 36th Street
New York, N.Y. 10018

First printing, May 1985

ISBN: 0-671-55959-1

Cover art by Victoria Poyser

Printed in the United States of America

Distributed by
SIMON & SCHUSTER
MASS MERCHANDISE SALES COMPANY
1230 Avenue of the Americas
New York, N.Y. 10020

To James P. Baen

Writers aren't supposed to say anything pleasant about editors or publishers, but the fact is that in both capacities Jim has done very well by me, and been a good friend into the bargain.

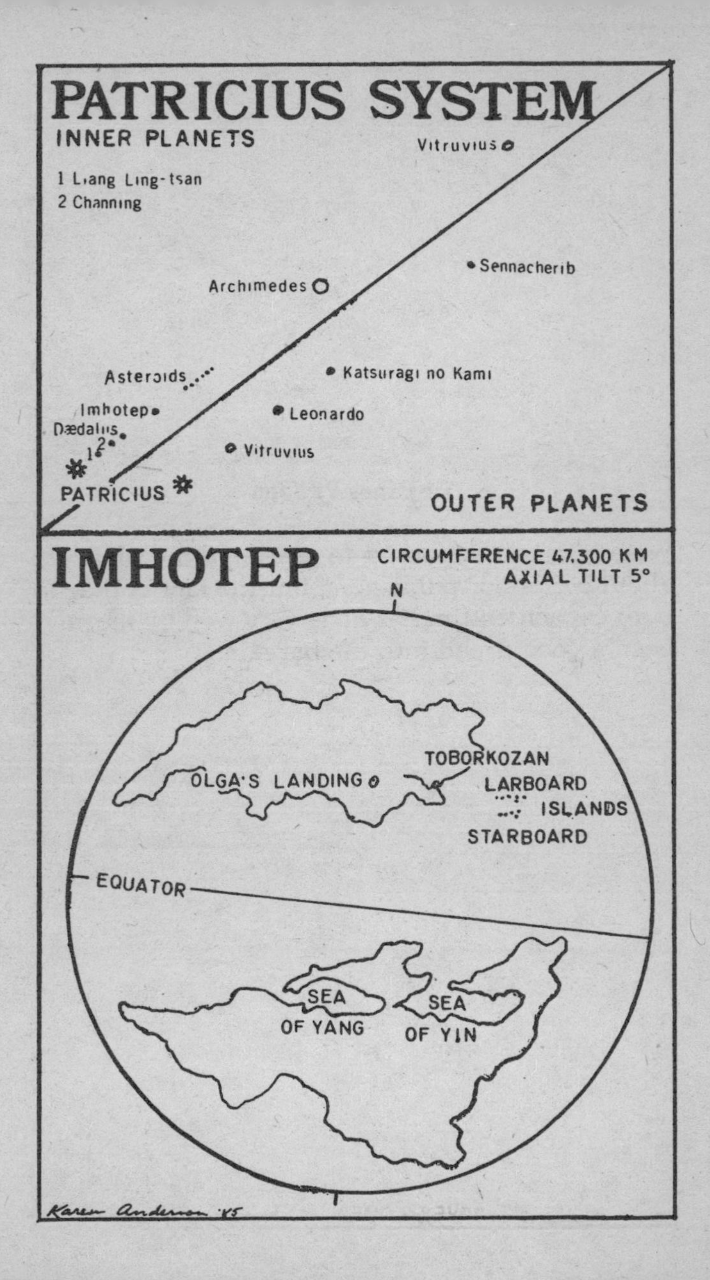
PATRICIUS SYSTEM
INNER PLANETS
1 Liang Ling-tsan
2 Channing
Vitruvius
Sennacherib
Archimedes
Asteroids
Katsuragi no Kami
Imhotep
Leonardo
Dædalus
Vitruvius
PATRICIUS
OUTER PLANETS
IMHOTEP
CIRCUMFERENCE 47.300 KM
AXIAL TILT 5°
N
TOBORKOZAN
OLGA'S LANDING
LARBOARD
ISLANDS
STARBOARD
EQUATOR
SEA
OF YANG
SEA
OF YIN
Karen Anderson '85

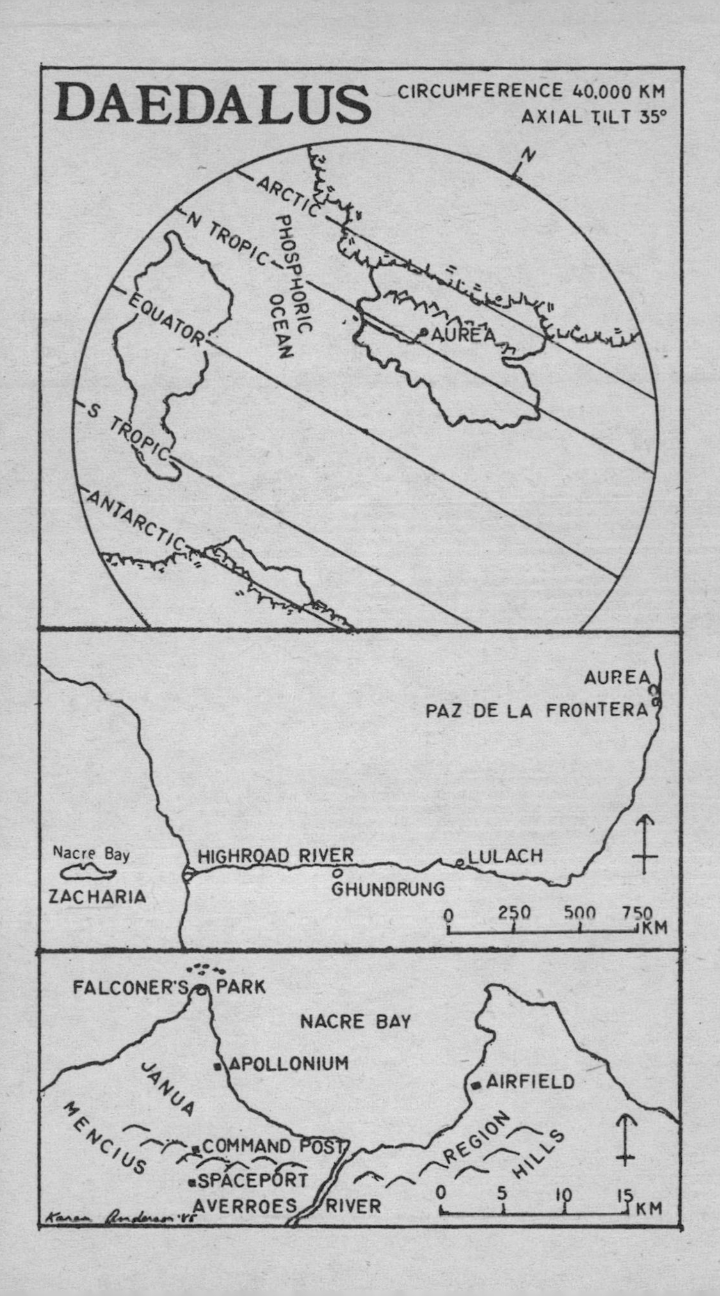
DAEDALUS
CIRCUMFERENCE 40,000 KM
AXIAL TILT 35°
N
ARCTIC
N TROPIC
EQUATOR
S TROPIC
ANTARCTIC
PHOSPHORIC OCEAN
AUREA
AUREA
PAZ DE LA FRONTERA
Nacre Bay
ZACHARIA
HIGHROAD RIVER
GHUNDRUNG
LULACH
0
250
500
750
KM
FALCONER'S PARK
NACRE BAY
APOLLONIUM
JANUA
AIRFIELD
MENCIUS
COMMAND POST
SPACEPORT
AVERROES
RIVER
REGION
HILLS
0
5
10
15
KM
Karen Anderson '85

Chapter 1

She sat on the tower of St. Barbara, kicking her heels from the parapet, and looked across immensity. Overhead, heaven was clear, deep blue save where the sun Patricius stood small and fierce at midmorning. Two moons were wanly aloft. The sky grew paler horizonward, until in the east it lost itself behind a white sea of cloud deck. A breeze blew cool. It would have been deadly cold before her people came to Imhotep; the peak of Mt. Horn lifts a full twelve kilometers above sea level.

Westward Diana could see no horizon, for the city had grown tall at its center during the past few decades. There the Pyramid, which housed Imperial offices and machinery, gleamed above the campus of the Institute, most of whose buildings were new. Industries, stores, hotels, apartments sprawled raw around. She liked better the old quarter, where she now was. It too had grown, but more in population than size or modernity—a brawling, polyglot, multiracial population, much of it transient, drifting in and out of the tides of space.

"Who holds St. Barbara's holds the planet."

That saying was centuries obsolete, but the memory kept alive a certain respect. Though ice bull herds no longer threatened to stampede through the original exploration base; though the Troubles which left hostile bands marooned and desperate, turning marauder, had ended when the hand of the Terran Empire reached this far; though the early defensive works would be useless in such upheavals as threatened the present age, and had long since been demolished: still, one relic of them remained in Olga's Landing, at the middle of what had become a market square. Its guns had been taken away for scrap, its chambers echoed hollow, sunseeker vine clambered over the crumbling yellow stone of it, but St. Barbara's stood yet; and it was a little audacious for a hoyden to perch herself on top.

Diana often did. The neighborhood had stopped minding—after all, she was everybody's friend—and to strangers it meant nothing, except that human males were apt to shout and wave at the pretty girl. She grinned and waved back when she felt in the mood, but had learned to decline the invitations. Her aim was not always simply to enjoy the evershifting scenes. Sometimes she spied a chance to earn a credit or two, as when a newcomer seemed in want of a guide to the sights and amusements. Nonhumans were safe. Or an acquaintance—who in that case could be a man—might ask her to run some errand or ferret out some information. If he lacked money to pay her, he could provide a meal or a doss or whatever. At present she had no home of her own, unless you counted a ruinous temple where she kept hidden her meager possessions and, when nothing better was available, spread her sleeping bag.

Life spilled from narrow streets and surged between the walls enclosing the plaza. Pioneer buildings had run to brick, and never gone higher than three or four stories, under Imhotepan gravity. Faded, nearly featureless, they were nonetheless gaudy, for their doors stood open on shops, while booths huddled everywhere else against them. The wares were as multifarious as the sellers, anything from hinterland fruits and grains to ironware out of the smithies that made the air clangorous, from velvyl fabric and miniature computers of the inner Empire to jewels and skins and carvings off a hundred different worlds. A sleazy Terran vidplay demonstrated itself on a screen next to an exquisite dance recorded beneath the Seas of Yang and Yin, where the vaz-Siravo had been settled. A gundealer offered primitive home-produced chemical rifles, stunners of military type, and—illegally—several blasters, doubtless found in wrecked spacecraft after the Merseian onslaught was beaten back. Foodstalls wafted forth hot, savory odors. Music thuttered, laughter and dance resounded from a couple of taverns. Motor vehicles were rare and small, but pushcarts swarmed. Occasionally a wagon forced its way through the crowd, drawn by a tame clopperhoof.

Folk were mainly human, but it was unlikely that many had seen Mother Terra. The planets where they were born and bred had marked them. Residents of Imhotep were necessarily muscular and never fat. Those whose families had lived here for generations, since Olga's Landing was a scientific base, and had thus melded into a type, tended to be dark-skinned and aquiline-featured. Men usually wore loose tunic and trousers, short hair, beards; women favored blouses, skirts, and braids; in this district, clothes might be threadbare but were raffishly bright. Members of the armed services on leave—a few from the local garrison, the majority from Daedalus—mingled with them, uniforms a stiff contrast no matter how bent on pleasure the person was. They were in good enough physical condition to walk fairly easily under a gravity thirty percent greater than Terra's, but crewpeople from civilian freighters frequently showed weariness and an exaggerated fear of falling.

A Navy man and a marine passed close by the tower. They were too intent on their talk to notice Diana, which was extraordinary. The harshness reached her: "—yeh, sure, they've grown it back for me." The spaceman waved his right arm. A short-sleeved undress shirt revealed it pallid and thin; regenerated tissue needs exercise to attain normal fitness. "But they said the budget doesn't allow repairing DNA throughout my body, after the radiation I took. I'll be dependent on biosupport the rest of my life, and I'll never dare father any kids."

"Merseian bastards," growled the marine. "I could damn near wish they had broken through and landed. My unit had a warm welcome ready for 'em, I can tell you."

"Be glad they didn't," said his companion. "Did you really want nukes tearing up our planets? Wounds and all, I'll thank Admiral Magnusson every day I've got left to me, for turning them back the way he did, with that skeleton force the pinchfists on Terra allowed us." Bitterly: "*He* wouldn't begrudge the cost of fixing up entire a man that fought under him."

They disappeared into the throng. Diana shivered a bit and looked around for something cheerier than such a reminder of last year's events.

Nonhumans were on hand in fair number. Most were Tigeries, come from the lowlands on various business, their orange-black-white pelts vivid around skimpy garments. Generally they wore air helmets, with pressure pumps strapped to their backs, but on some, oxygills rose out of the shoulders, behind the heads, like elegant ruffs. Diana cried greetings to those she recognized. Otherwise she spied a centauroid Donarrian; the shiny integuments of three Irumclagians; a couple of tailed, green-skinned Shalmuans; and—and—

"What the flippin' fury!" She got to her feet—they were bare, and the stone felt warm beneath them—and stood precariously balanced, peering.

Around the corner of a Winged Smoke house had come a giant. The Pyramid lay in that direction, but so did the spaceport, and he must have arrived there today, or word of him would have buzzed throughout the low-life parts of town. Thence he seemed to have walked all the kilometers, for no public conveyance on Imhotep could have accommodated him, and his manner was not that of officialdom. Although the babel racket dwindled at sight of him and people drew aside, he moved diffidently, almost apologetically. Tiredly, too, poor thing; his strength must be enormous, but it had been a long way to trudge in this gee-field.

"Well, *well,*" said Diana to herself; and loudly, in both Anglic and Toborko, to any possible competition: "I saw him first!"

She didn't waste time on the interior stairs but, reckless, scrambled down the vines. Though the tower wasn't very tall, on Imhotep a drop from its battlements could be fatal. She reached the pavement running.

"Ah, ho, small one," bawled Hassan from the doorway of his inn, "if he be thirsty, steer him to the Sign of the Golden Cockbeetle. A decicredit to you for every liter he drinks!"

She laughed, reached a dense mass of bodies, began weaving and wriggling through. Inhabitants smiled and let her by. A drunk took her closeness wrong and tried to grab her. She gave his wrist a karate chop in passing. He yelled, but retreated when he saw how a Tigery glowered and dropped hand to knife. Kuzan had been a childhood playmate of Diana's. She was still her friend.

The stranger grew aware of the girl nearing him, halted, and watched in mild surprise. He was of the planet which humans had dubbed

Woden, well within the Imperial sphere. It had long been a familiar of Technic civilization and was, indeed, incorporated in Greater Terra, its dwellers full citizens. Just the same, none had hitherto betrod Imhotep, and Diana knew of them only from books and database.

A centauroid himself, he stretched four and a half meters on his four cloven hoofs, including the mighty tail. The crown of his long-snouted, bony-eared head loomed two meters high. The brow ridges were massive, the mouth alarmingly fanged, but eyes were big, a soft brown. Two huge arms ended in four-fingered hands that seemed able to rip a steel plate in half. Dark-green scales armored his upper body from end to end, amber scutes his throat and belly. A serration of horny plates ran over his backward-bulging skull, down his spine to the tailtip. A pair of bags slung across his withers and a larger pair at his croup doubtless held traveling goods. Drawing close, Diana saw signs of a long life, scars, discolorations, wrinkles around the nostrils and rubbery lips, a pair of spectacles hung from his neck. They were for presbyopia, she guessed, and she had already noticed he was slightly lame in the off hind leg. Couldn't he afford corrective treatments?

Why, she herself was going to start putting money aside, one of these years, to pay for antisenescence. If she had to die at an age of less than a hundred, she wanted it to be violently.

Halting before him, she beamed, spread arms wide, and said, "Good day and welcome! Never before has our world been graced by any of your illustrious race. Yet even we, on our remote and lately embattled frontier, have heard the fame of Wodenites, from the days of Adzel the Wayfarer to this very hour. In what way may we serve you, great sir?"

His face was unreadable to her, but his body looked startled. "My, my," he murmured. "How elaborately you speak, child. Is that local custom? Please enlighten me. I do not wish to be discourteous through ignorance." He hesitated. "My intentions, I hope, shall always be of the best."

His vocal organs made Anglic a thunderous rumble, weirdly accented, but it was fluent and she could follow it. She had had practice, especially with Tigeries, who didn't sound like humans either.

For an instant, she bridled. "Sir, I'm no child. I'm nine—uh, that is, seventeen Terran years old. For the past three of those I've been on my own, highlands and lowlands both." Relaxing: "So I know my way around and I'd be happy to guide you, advise you, help you. I can show testimonials from persons of several species."

"*Hraa* . . . I fear I am in no position to, m-m, offer much compensation. I have been making my way—hand-to-mouth, is that your expression?—odd jobs, barter—at which I am not gifted—anything morally allowable, planet to planet, far longer than you have been in the universe, chi—young lady."

Diana shrugged. "We can talk about that. You're in luck. I'm not a professional tourist herder, chargin' a week's rent on the Emperor's favorite palace to take you around to every place where the prices are quasar-lofty and expectin' a fat tip at the end." She cocked her head. "You could've gone to the reception center near the Pyramid. It's got an office for xenosophonts. Why didn't you?"

"*Gruh*, I, I—to be frank, I lost my way. The streets twist about so. If you could lead me to the proper functionaries—"

Diana reached up to take him by the rugged elbow. "Wait a bit! Look, you're worn out, and you don't have a pokeful of money, and I can do better by you than the agency. All they really know is where to find you the least unsuitable lodgings. Why don't we go in where you can rest a while, and we'll talk, and if I only can steer you downtown, so be it." She paused before adding, slowly: "But you aren't here for any ordinary purpose, that's plain to see, and I do know most of what's not ordinary on Imhotep."

He boomed a chuckle. "You are a sprightly soul, no? Very well." He turned serious. "It may even be that my patron saint has answered my prayers by causing me to blunder as I did. M-m-m . . . my name is Francis Xavier Axor."

"Hm?" She was taken aback. "You're a Christian?"

"Jerusalem Catholic. I chose the baptismal name became its first bearer was also an explorer in strange places, such as I hoped to become."

And I. The heart jumped in Diana's breast.

She had always sought out what visitors from the stars she could, because they were what they were—farers through the galaxy—O Tigery gods, grant that she too might someday range yonder! And, while she agilely survived in Old Town's dog-eat-dog economy, she had never driven a harder bargain with a nonhuman than she felt that being could afford, nor defrauded or defaulted.

Orders of magnitude more than she wanted any money of his, she wanted Axor's good will. He seemed like a darling anyway. And possibly, just barely possibly, he might open a path for her. . . .

Business was business, and Hassan's booze no worse than most in the quarter. "Follow me," she said. "I'm Diana Crowfeather."

He offered his hand, vast, hard, dry, warm. Wodenites were not theroids, but they weren't herpetoids either; they were endothermic, two-sexed, and viviparous. She had, however, learned that they bred only in season. It made celibate careers easier for them than for her species. Thus far she'd avoided entanglements, because that was what they could too readily become—entanglements—but it was getting more and more difficult.

"An honor to meet you," Axor said. "*Hraa*, is it not unusual for such a youthful female to operate independently? Perhaps not on Terra or its older colony planets, but here—Not that I wish to pry. Heavens, no."

"I'm kind of a special case," Diana replied.

He regarded her with care. Neither of her parents having been born on Imhotep, and both being tall, she was likewise. The gravity had made robust a frame that remained basically gracile; muscles rounded the curves of slim hips and long legs. Weight had not yet caused the small, firm bosom to sag. Her head was round, the face broad, with high cheekbones, tapering down to the chin; a straight nose flared at the nostrils, and the lips were full. Her eyes were large, gold-flecked hazel, beneath arching brows. Black hair, confined by a beaded headband, fell straight to the shoulders. A thin blouse and exiguous shorts showed most of her tawny-brown skin to the sun. Belted at her right side was a little purse for oddments, at her left a murderous Tigery knife.

"Well, but let's go," she laughed. Her voice was husky. "Aren't you thirsty? I am!"

The crowd yielded slowly before them, turbulent again, less interested in the newcomer now that he had been claimed than in its own checkered affairs.

Inside, the Sign of the Golden Cockbeetle amounted to a room broad and dim. Half a dozen men, outback miners to judge by their rough appearance, were drinking at a table with a couple of joygirls and a bemusedly watching Tigery. The latter sipped from a tube inserted through the chowlock of her air helmet. The whine of its pumps underlay voices. While oxygills were far better, not many could afford them or wanted the preliminary surgery, slight though that was. Diana didn't recognize the individual, but it was clear from her outfit that she belonged to another society than the one around Toborkozan. The group gave Axor a lengthy stare, then went back to their talk, dice, and booze.

The Wodenite ordered beer in appropriate quantity. His biochemistry was compatible with the human, barring minor matters that ration supplements took care of. Diana gave a silent cheer; her commission was going to be noticeably higher, percentagewise, than on distilled liquor. She took a stein for herself and savored the catnip coolness.

"Aaah!" breathed Axor in honest pleasure. "That quenches. God bless you for your guidance. Now if you can aid my quest—"

"What is it?"

"The story is long, my dear."

Diana leaned back in her chair; her companion must needs lie on the floor. She had learned, the hard way, how to rein in her inquisitiveness. "We've got all day, or as much more as you want." Within her there hammered: *Quest! What's he after, roamin' from star to star?*

"Perhaps I should begin by introducing myself as a person, however insignificant," Axor said. "Not that that part is interesting."

"It is to me," Diana assured him.

"Well—" The dragon countenance stared down into the outsize tankard. "To use Anglic names, I was born on the planet Woden, although my *haizark*—tribe? community? tuath? —my people are still comparatively primitive, nomads in the Morning Land, which is across the Sea of Truth from the Glimmering Realm to the west where the Terrans and the civilization that they brought are based. My country is mostly steppe, but in the Ascetic Hills erosion has laid bare certain Foredweller ruins. Those were long known to us, and often as a youngster did I regard them with awe. In the past generation, news of them has reached the cities. Watching and listening to the archaeologists who came, I grew utterly fascinated. A wish flowered in me to learn more, yes, to do such delving myself. I worked my way overseas to the Glimmering Realm in hopes of winning a merit scholarship. Such is common among the literate Wodenites. Mine happened to come from the university that the Galilean Order maintains in Port Campbell."

"Galilean Order—hm—aren't they, um, priests in the Jerusalem church? I've never met any."

Axor nodded in human wise. "They are the most scientifically minded organization within it. Very fitting that they should conduct studies of Foredweller remains. While under their tutelage, I was converted to the Faith. Indeed, I am ordained a Galilean." The slow voice quickened. "Father Jaspers introduced me to the great and holy thought that in those relics may lie an answer to the riddle of the Universal Incarnation."

Diana raised a palm. "Hold on, please. Foredwellers? Who're they?"

"They are variously known on the worlds as Ancients, Elders, Others—many names—The mysterious civilization that flourished in the galaxy—apparently through far more of it than this fraction of a single spiral arm which we have somewhat explored—vanishing millions of years ago, leaving scanty, glorious fragments of their works—" Dismay quavered in the deep tones. "You have not heard? Nothing like it exists anywhere in this planetary system? The indications seemed clear that here was a place to search."

"Wait, wait." Diana frowned into the shadows. "My education's been catch-as-catch-can, you realize, but—M-m, yes. Remnant walls and such. Rumors that the Chereionites built them once, whoever the Chereionites are or were. But I thought—um, um—yes, a spaceman from Aeneas told me about a lot of such sites on his planet. Except Aeneas is small, dry, thin-aired. He figured the Old Shen—that was his name for them—they must have originated on a planet of that type, and favored the same kind for colonization."

"Not necessarily. I venture to think that that is simply the kind where remnants are best preserved. The materials were as durable as the structures seem to have been beautiful. But everything in our cosmos is mortal. On airless globes, micrometeoroids would have worn them down. On planets with thick atmospheres, weather would do the same, while geological process wrought their own destructions. However, sometimes ruins have endured on terrestroid worlds, fossilized, so to speak. For example, a volcanic ashfall or a mudslide which later petrified has covered them. Something like this happened in the territory now covered by the Ascetic Hills of Woden. Since, the blanketing soil and rock have been gnawed away by the elements, revealing these wonders."

Axor sagged out of his excitement. "But you know of nothing anywhere in the Patrician System?" he finished dully.

Diana thought fast. "I didn't say that. Look, Imhotep is a superterrestrial planet, more than a third again the surface area of Daedalus—or Terra—not much less than that next to Woden, I'll bet. And even after centuries, it's not well mapped or anything. This was just a lonely scientific outpost till the Starkadian resettlement. Tigeries, explorin' their new lands—yes, they tell stories about things they've seen and can't account for—But I'd have to go and ask for details, and then we'd prob'ly have to engage a watership to ferry us, if some yarn sounded promisin'."

Axor had recovered his spirits. "Moreover, this system contains other planets, plus their larger moons," he said. "I came here first merely because Imhotep was the destination of the tramp freighter on which I could get passage. The colonized planet sunward, Daedalus?"

"Maybe. I haven't been on Daedalus since my mother died, when I was a sprat." Diana considered. Resolve thrilled along her nerves. She would not knowingly lead this sweet old seeker on a squiggle chase, but neither would she willingly let go of him—while hope remained that his search could carry her to the stars.

"As long as you are on Imhotep," she said, "that's the place to start, and I do know my way around Imhotep as well as anybody. Now for openers, can you explain what you're after and why you think you might find a clue here?"

She drained her stein and signalled for more. Hassan brought a bucket to recharge Axor's mug as well. Meanwhile the Wodenite, serene again, was telling her:

"As for the Foredwellers, their traces are more than an archaeological puzzle. Incredibly ancient as they are, those artifacts may give us knowledge of the Incarnation.

"For see you, young person, some three thousand standard years have passed since Our Lord Jesus Christ walked upon Terra and brought the offer of salvation to fallen man. Subsequently, upstart humankind has gone forth into the light-years; and with Technic civilization has traveled faith, to race after race after race.

"About such independently spacefaring beings as the Ymirites, one dares say nothing. They are too alien. It may be that they are not fallen and thus have no need of the Word. But painfully plain it is that every oxygen-breathing species ever encountered is in no state of grace, but prone to sin, error, and death.

"Now our Lord was born once upon Terra, and charged those who came after with carrying the gospel over the planet. But what of other planets? Were they to wait for human missionaries? Or have some of them, at least, been granted the glory of their own Incarnations? It is not a matter on which most churches have ventured to dogmatize. Not only are the lives, the souls, so different from world to world, but here and there one nevertheless does find religions which look strangely familiar. Coincidence? Parallel development? Or a deeper mystery?"

He paused. Diana frowned, trying to understand. Questions like this were not the sort she was wont to ask. "Does it matter? I mean, can't you be as good a person regardless?"

"Knowledge of God always matters," said Axor gravely. "This is not necessary to individual salvation, no. But think what a difference in the teaching of the Word it would make, to know the truth—whatever the truth may be. If science can show that the gospel account of Christ is not myth but biography; and if it then finds that his ministry was, in empirical fact, universal—would not you, for example, my dear, would not you decide it was only reasonable to accept him as your Saviour?"

Uncomfortable, Diana tried to shift the subject. "So you think you may get a hint from the Foredweller works?"

"I cherish hopes, as did those scholars who conceived the thought before me. Consider the immense timeline, millions of years. Consider that the Builders must have been too widespread and numerous, too learned and powerful—yes, too wise, after their long, long history—to be destroyed by anything material. No, surely they abandoned their achievements, as we, growing up, put away childish things, and went on to a higher plane of existence.

Yet surely, too, they nourished a benign desire to ease the path for those who came after. They would leave inscriptions, messages—time-blurred now, nearly gone; but perhaps the writers did not foresee how many ages would pass before travel began again between the stars. Still, what better could they bequeath us than their heritage of Ultimate Meaning?"

Diana had her large doubts. Likewise, obviously, did others, or Axor wouldn't have had to bum his unpaid way across the Empire. She didn't have the heart to say that. "What have you actually found?" she asked.

"Not I alone, by no means I alone. For the most part, I have merely studied archaeological reports, and gone to see for myself. In a few instances, however—" The Wodenite drew breath. "I must not boast. What I deal with are the enigmatic remains of occasional records. Diagrams etched into a wall or a slab, worn away until virtually blank. Codings imprinted in molecules and crystals, evocable electronically but equally blurred and broken. Some, nobody can comprehend at all. Some do seem to be astronomical symbols—such as signs for pulsars, with signs for hydrogen atoms and for numbers to give periods and spatial relationships. One can estimate how those pulsars have slowed down and moved elsewhere, and thus try to identify them, and thence the sun toward which a record conceivably points. . . .

"On a barren globe five parsecs from here, amidst the tailings of a former mining operation, I found clues of this kind. They appeared to me to whisper of the sun Patricius."

Axor broke off, crossed himself, stared into remoteness.

After a while Diana made bold to speak again. "Well, your .... your reverence, you needn't despair yet. What say we establish ourselves in town for a few days? You can rest up while I arrange conferences and transportation and so forth. You see, nothin' has turned up in the mountains; but Tigeries do tell about islands with what may be natural formations but might also be ruined walls, except that Imhotep never had any native sophonts. If that doesn't work out, I can inquire among spacefolk, get us passage offplanet, whatever you want. And it shouldn't cost you very heavily."

Axor smiled. The crocodilian expanse of his mouth drew a shriek from a joygirl. "A godsend indeed!" he roared.

"Oh, I'm no saint," Diana answered. He couldn't be so naive as to suppose she had immediately fallen in love with his cause—though it looked like being fun. "Why do I offer to do this? It's among the ways I scratch out my livin'. We got to agree on my daily wage; and I'll be collectin' my cumshaws on the side, that you don't have to know about. Mainly, I expect to enjoy myself." To mention her further dreams would be premature.

Axor put spectacles on nose to regard her the better. "You are a remarkable young being, donna Crowfeather," he said, a surprisingly courtly turn of phrase. "If I may ask, how does it happen you are this familiar with the planet?"

"I grew up here." Impulsively, perhaps because she was excited or perhaps because the beer had started to buzz faintly in her head, she added: "And my father was responsible for most of what you'll see."

"Really? I would be delighted to hear."

It was generally easy to confide in a chance-met xeno, as it was not with a fellow human. Furthermore, Axor's manner was reassuring; and no secrets were involved. The whole quarter knew her story, as did Tigeries across reaches of several thousand kilometers.

"Oh, my father's Dominic Flandry. You may have heard of him. He's become an Admiral of the Fleet, but forty-odd years ago he was a fresh-caught ensign assigned to the planet Starkad, in this same sector. Trouble with the Merseians was pilin' up and—Anyway, he discovered the planet was doomed. There were two sophont races on it, the land-dwellin' Tigeries and the underwater Seafolk; and there were five years to evacuate as many as possible before the sun went crazy. This was the only known planet that was enough like Starkad. It helped that Imhotep already had a scientific base and a few support industries, and that Daedalus was colonized and becomin' an important Naval outpost. Just the same, the resettlement's always been a wild scramble, always underfunded and undermanned, touch and go."

"The Terran Empire has many demands on its resources, starting with defense," said Axor.

"Although one must deplore violence, I cannot but admire the gallantry with which Admiral Magnusson cast back the Merseian attack last year."

"The Imperial court and bureaucracy are pretty expensive too, I hear," Diana snapped. "Well, never mind. *I* don't pay taxes."

"I have, yes, I have encountered tales of Admiral Flandry's exploits," said Axor in haste. "But he cannot have spent much time on Imhotep, surely."

"Oh, no. He looked in once in a while, when he happened to be in the region. A natural curiosity. My mother and he—Well, I keep tellin' myself I shouldn't blame him. She never did."

Once Maria Crowfeather had admitted to her daughter that she got Dominic Flandry's child in hopes that that would lead to something permanent. It had not. After he found out on his next visit, he bade a charming, rueful goodbye. Maria got on with her own life.

"Your mother worked in the resettlement project?" Axor inquired tactfully.

Diana nodded. "A xenologist. She died in an accident, a sudden tidal bore on a strange coast, three standard years ago."

Maria Crowfeather had been born on the planet Atheia, in the autonomous community Dakotia. It had been among the many founded during the Breakup, when group after ethnic group left a Commonwealth that they felt was drowning them in sameness. The Dakota people had already been trying to revive a sense of identity in North America. Diana, though, kept only bits of memory, fugitive and wistful, about ancestral traditions. She had passed her life among Tigeries and Seafolk.

"Leaving you essentially orphaned," said Axor. "Why did nobody take care of you?"

"I ran away," Diana replied.

The man who had been living with Maria at the time of her death did not afterward reveal himself to be a bad sort. He turned out to be officious, which was worse. He had wanted to marry the girl's mother legally, and now he wanted to put the girl in the Navy brat school on Daedalus, and eventually see to it that she wed some nice officer. Meanwhile Tigeries were hunting through hills where wind soughed in waves across forests, and surf burst under three moons upon virgin islands.

"Did not the authorities object?" Axor wondered.

"They couldn't find me at first. Later they forgot."

Axor uttered a splintering noise that might be his equivalent of a laugh. "Very well, little sprite of all the world, let us see how you guide a poor bumbler. Make the arrangements, and leave me to my data and breviary until we are ready for departure. But can you give me an idea of what to expect?"

"I'll try, but I don't make any promises," Diana said. "Especially these days. You didn't arrive at the best time, sir."

Scales stirred above the brow ridges. "What do you mean, pray?"

Grimness laid grip on her. She had ignored

the news as much as possible. What could she do about it? Well, she had mentally listed various refuges, according to where she would be when the trouble exploded, if it was going to. But here she was committing herself to an expedition which could take her anyplace, and—"That ruckus with the Merseians last year was just a thing off in space," she said. "Since, I've kept hearin' rumors—ask your God to make them only rumors, will you?—Sir, we may be on the edge of a real war."

Chapter 2

On Daedalus, the world without a horizon, a Tigery was still an uncommon sight, apt to draw everybody's attention. Targovi had made an exception of himself. The capital Aurea, its hinterland, communities the length of the Highroad River as far as the Phosphoric Ocean, no few of the settlements scattered elsewhere, had grown used to him. He would put his battered *Moonjumper* down at the spaceport, exchange japes with guards and officials, try to sell them something, then load his wares into an equally disreputable-looking van and be off. His stock in trade was Imhotepan, a jackdaw museum of the infinite diversity that is every planet's. Artifacts of his people he had, cutlery, tapestries, perfumes; things strange and delicate, made underwater by the Seafolk; exotic products of nature, skins, mineral gems, land pearls, flavorful wild foods—for the irony was that huge Imhotep had begotten life which Terrans, like Starkadians, could safely take nourishment from, whereas Terra-sized Daedalus had not.

For a number of years he had thus ranged, dickering, swapping, amusing himself and most whom he encountered, a generally amiable being whom—certain individuals discovered too late—it was exceedingly dangerous to affront. Even when tensions between Merseia and Terra snapped asunder, sporadic combats erupted throughout the marches, and at last Sector Admiral Magnusson took his forces to meet an oncoming armada of the Roidhunate, even then had Targovi plied his trade unhindered.

Thus he registered shock when he landed in routine fashion a twelvemonth later, and the junior port officer who gave him his admission certificate warned: "You had better stay in touch with us. Interplanetary traffic may be suddenly curtailed. You could find yourself unable to get off Daedalus for an indefinite time."

"Eyada shkor!" ripped from Targovi. His tendrils grew stiff. A hand dropped to the knife at his side. "What is this?"

"Possible emergency," said the human. "Understand, I am trying to be friendly. There ought to be a short grace period. If you then return here immediately, I can probably get you clearance to go home. Otherwise you could be stranded and unable to earn your keep, once your goods were sold and the proceeds spent."

"I . . . think . . . I would survive," Targovi murmured.

The officer peered across his desk. "You may be right," he said. "But *we* may not like the ways you would find. I would be sorry to see you jailed, or gunned down."

The Tigery looked predatory enough to arouse qualms. His resemblance to a man was merely in the roughest outlines. He stood as tall as an average one, but on disproportionately long and powerful legs whose feet were broad and clawed. Behind, a stubby tail twitched. The torso was thick, the arms and their four-fingered hands cabled with muscle. The round head bore a countenance flat and narrow-chinned, a single breathing slit in the nose, carnivore teeth agleam in the wide mouth. Beneath the fronded chemosensor tendrils, eyes were slanted and scarlet-hued. The large, movable ears were scalloped around the edges as if to suggest bat wings. Fur clothed him in silkiness that had now begun to bristle, black-striped orange except for a white triangle at the throat. His voice purred, hissed, sometimes growled or screeched, making its fluent Anglic an outlandish dialect.

He wore nothing at present but a breechclout, pocketed belt, knife, and amulet hung from his neck—these, and an oxygill. Its pleated pearly ruff lifted from his shoulders at the back of the head, framing the latter. Strange it might seem, to observe such a molecularly-convoluted intricacy upon such a creature, and to recollect what chemical subtleties went on within, oxygen captured and led into the bloodstream through capillary-fine tubes surgically installed. Yet it gave him the freedom to be barbaric, where he would else have been encumbered with a helmet and pump, or have perished. His kind had evolved under an air pressure more than nine times the Terran.

"I think your efforts might fail," he said low. Easing: "However, surely naught untoward will happen. You are kind to advise me, Dosabhai Patel. You wife may find some pleasant trinket in her mail. But what is this extremity you await?"

"I did not say we are bound to have one," replied the officer quickly.

"What could it be, does it come on us?"

"Too many wild rumors are flying about. Both naval and civil personnel are under orders not to add to them."

Targovi's chair had been designed for a human, but he was sufficiently supple to flow down into it. His eyelids drooped; he bridged his fingertips. "Ah, good friend, you realize I am bound to hear those rumors. Were it not best to arm me with truths whereby I may slay them? I am, of course, a simple, wandering trader, who knows no secrets. Yet I should have had some inkling if, say, a new Merseian attack seemed likely."

"Not that! Admiral Magnusson gave them a lesson they will remember for a while." Patel cleared his throat. "Understand, what happened was not a war."

Targovi did not overtly resent the patronizing lecture that followed, meant for a half-civilized xeno: "Bloody incidents are all too common. It is inevitable, when two great powers, bitter rivals, share an ill-defined and thinly peopled buffer zone which is, actually, an arena for them. This latest set of clashes began when negotiations over certain spheres of influence broke down and commanders in various locations grew, ah, trigger-happy. True, the Roidhunate did dispatch a task force to 'restore order.' Had it succeeded, the Merseians would undoubtedly have occupied the Patrician System, thereby making this entire sector almost indefensible and driving a salient deep into the Empire. We would have had to settle with them on highly disadvantageous terms. As you know, Admiral Magnusson beat them back, and diplomats on both sides are trying to mend things. . . . No, we are in no immediate danger from outside."

"From inside, then?" Targovi drawled. "Even we poor, uprooted vaz-Toborko—aye, even the vaz-Siravo beneath their seas—have learned a little about your great Empire. Rebellions and attempted rebellions have grown, regrettably, not infrequent, during the past half century. The present dynasty itself, did it not come to power by—?—"

"The glorious revolution was necessary," Patel declared. "Emperor Hans restored order and purged corruption."

"Ah, but his sons—"

Patel's fist struck the desktop. "Very well, you insolent barbarian! Daedalus, this whole system, the Empire itself were in grave peril last year. Admiral Magnusson rectified the situation, but it should never have arisen. The Imperial forces in these parts should have been far stronger. As matters stood, under a less brilliant commander, they would almost certainly have been smashed." He moistened his lips. "No question of disloyalty. No *lèse majesté.* But there is a widespread feeling on Daedalus, especially among Navy personnel, that Emperor Gerhart and his Policy Board have . . . not been well advised . . . that some of the counsel they heeded may actually have been treasonable in intent . . . that drastic reform has again become overdue. The Admiral has sent carefully reasoned recommendations to Terra. Meanwhile, dissatisfaction leads to restlessness. He may have to impose martial law, or—Enough. These matters are not for subjects like you and me to decide." Nonetheless eagerness lighted his features and shrilled in his voice. "You have had your warning, Targovi. Be off, but stay in touch; attend to your business and nothing else; and you will probably be all right."

The trader rose, spoke his courteous farewell, departed. In Terran-like gravity he rippled along, his padded feet silent across the floor.

Well-nigh the whole of Aurea was new, built to accommodate the burgeoning sector defense command that had been established on the planet, together with the civil bureaucracy and private enterprises that it drew. Architecture soared boldly in towers, sprawled in ponderous industrial plants. Vehicles beswarmed streets, elways, skies. Around the clock, the throb of traffic never ceased.

Hardly anything remained of the original town, demolished and engulfed. It had been small anyhow, for colonization was far-flung, enclaves in wilderness that could not be tamed but only, slowly, destroyed. Still, a bit from early days clung yet to a steep slope beneath the plateau. Targovi went there, to an inn he knew.

He mingled readily with the crowds. He might be the sole member of his race on Daedalus, but plenty of other xenosophonts were present. The vague borders of the Terran Empire held an estimated four million suns, of which perhaps a hundred thousand had some degree of contact with it. Out of that many, no few were bound to have learned from Technic civilization—if they had learned nothing else—the requirements for traveling between the stars. They included spacehands, Naval personnel, Imperial officials, besides those engaged on affairs of their own. Then too, colonization of Daedalus had not been exclusively human by any means. It made for a variegated scene, which Targovi enjoyed. His inmost wish was to get beyond this single planetary system, out into the freedom of the galaxy.

Descending, he followed a lane along a cliff. On his left were walls time-gnawed, unpretentious, reminiscent of those in the Old Town of Olga's Landing. On his right were a guard rail, empty air, and a tremendous view. The river glimmered silver, grandly curved, through hundreds of kilometers of its valley, sunset bound. That land lay in shades of dark, metallic green, save where softer tones showed that farmsteads or plantations had been wrested out of it. The northern mountains and the ice fields beyond them, the southward sweep of plains, faded out of sight, lost in sheer distance.

Closer by, the headwaters of the river rushed

downward in cataracts. The mountainside was covered with native growth. Although air was cool at this altitude, Targovi caught a harsh pungency. Raindrops that were cars flitted to and fro through heaven. A spaceship lifted, her gravs driving her in silence, but the hull carving out muted thunder.

Ju Shao's inn perched ramshackle on the brink. Targovi entered the taproom. The owner bounded to greet him: a Cynthian by species, small, white-furred, bushy-tailed. "Welcome back!" she piped. "A sweet sight, you, after the klongs who've been infesting this place lately. What will you have?"

"Dinner, and a room for the night," Targovi answered. "Also—" His eyes flickered about. Besides himself, the customers thus far were just four humans in Navy uniform, seated around a table, talking over their liquor. "What mean you by 'klongs'?" he asked. "I thought you got folk here as well-behaved as is reasonable. Those who're not, the rest always cast out."

"Too many are akindle nowadays," Ju Shao grumbled. "Young, from Navy or Marine Corps. They yell about how the Imperium's abandoned us and how we need strong leadership—that sort of spew. They get drunk and noisy and start throwing things around. Then the patrol arrives, and I have to waste an hour recording a statement before I can clean up the mess." She reached high to pat his hand. "You're the right sort. You stay quiet till you need to kill, which you do without fuss. We can cook you a nice roast, real cowbeef. And

I've gotten a packet of that stuff they grow on Imhotep—*ryushka*, is that the name?—if you'd like some."

"I thank you, but the Winged Smoke is only for when I can take my ease, out of any danger," Targovi said. "Bring me a bowl of tea while I talk with my . . . friends yonder. Afterward, aye, rare cowbeef will be good to taste again, the more so if you add your crinkletongue sauce, O mother of wonders."

He strolled to the occupied table. "Health and strength to you, Janice Combarelles," he said, translating the Toborko formality into Anglic.

The blond woman with the ringed planet of a lieutenant commander on her blue tunic looked up. "Why, Targovi!" she exclaimed. "Sit down! I didn't expect you back this soon, you scoundrel. You can't have escaped hearing how uneasy things have gotten, and that must be bad for a business like yours."

He accepted the invitation. "Well, but a merchant must needs keep aware of what is in the wind. I had hopes of finding you here," he said, truthfully if incompletely.

"Introductions first," Combarelles said to her companions. "This is Targovi. You may have noticed him before, roving about with his trade goods. We met when I was on a tour of duty in the Imhotep garrison. He helped vastly to relieve the dullness." Her corps was Intelligence, for which the big planet had slight demand. Starkadians of either species were not about to turn on the Empire that had saved them from extinction.

She named the others, men of her age. "We're out on the town, relaxing while we can," she explained. "Leaves may soon be hard to get."

Targovi lapped from the container that Ju Shao had brought him. "Forgive a foreigner," he requested. "The subtleties of politics lie far beyond his feeble grasp. What is it that you tauten yourselves against? Surely not the Merseians again."

"Yes and no," Combarelles replied. "They'll pounce on any weakness they think they see in us—"

"Same as we should do to them," muttered a man who had been drinking hard. "But the Empire's gone soft, bloated, ready to pay anything for one more lifetime's worth of peace, and to hell with the children and grandchildren. When are we going to get another Argolid dynasty?"

"Sh!" Combarelles cautioned. To Targovi: "He's right, though, after a fashion. His Majesty's badly served. We, out on the frontier, we've been made sacrificial goats to incompetence. If it weren't for Admiral Magnusson, we'd be dead. He's trying to set matters right, but—No, I shouldn't say more." She ignited a cigarette and smoked raggedly. "At that, the Merseians aren't infallible. I've found a terrible bitterness among them too."

"How could you do that?" Targovi asked innocently. "Merseia is far and far away."

Combarelles laughed. "Not all the Merseians are. Well, you see, actually I've been talking to prisoners. We took a few in the battle, and exchange hasn't yet been negotiated. My section has responsibility for them, and—No. I'd better not say any more except that we had a lot of luck, though that wouldn't have helped much if the admiral hadn't taken advantage of it. Tell us how things are on Imhotep. At least there we humans have been accomplishing something decent."

Targovi spun out anecdotes. They led in the direction of smuggling operations. "Oh, yes," Combarelles laughed, "we have the same problems."

"How could you, milady?" Targovi wondered. "I know no way to land unbeknownst, as guarded as this globe is, and they always inspect my humble cargoes."

"The trick is to set down openly, but in a port where inspectors don't go. Like Zacharia."

"Za—It seems I have heard the name, but—" In point of fact, he was quite familiar with it. He also knew things about the running of contraband which the authorities would have been glad to learn. Feigned ignorance was a way of leading conversation onward.

"A large island out in the Phosphoric Ocean. Autonomous since pioneer days. Secretive. If I were Admiral Magnusson, I'd set the treaty aside. He has the power to do it if he sees fit, and *I* would see fit." Combarelles shrugged. "Not that it matters if untaxed merchandise arrives once in a while and goes discreetly upriver. But . . . I've retrieved reports filed with Naval Traffic Control. I can't really believe that some of the vessels cleared to land on Zacharia were what they claimed to be, or else were simple smugglers. They looked too sleek for that."

"The admiral knows what he's doing," asserted a man stoutly.

"Y-yes. And what he's not doing. Those could be ships of his—No more! Say on, Targovi."

Targovi did. He told tales of his farings to the vaz-Siravo in their seas. On Starkad, his race and theirs had often been mortal enemies. Feelings lingered, not to mention abysses of difference. They tried to get along together these days, because they must, and usually they succeeded, more or less, but it could be difficult. This led to chat about the care and feeding of Merseians. . . .

Prisoners were not maltreated, if only because the opposition could retaliate. In particular, officers were housed as well as feasible. *Fodaich* Eidhafor the Bold, Vach Dathyr, highest among those plucked from ruined ships of the Roidhunate, got an entire house and staff of servants to himself, lent by a prosperous businessman who anticipated governmental favor for his civic-mindedness. It was guarded by electronics and a couple of live sentries. Lesser captives were held almost as lightly. Where could they flee to, on a planet where they would starve in the wilds and every soul in every settlement would instantly know them for what they were? The house was in a fashionable residential district a hundred kilometers north of Aurea. It stood alone on a knoll amidst flowerbeds, hedges, and bowers.

True night never fell on Daedalus. The city

was distance-dwindled to a miniature mosaic of lights, sparse because it had no need to illuminate streets. Sunlight was a red-gold ring, broadest and most nearly bright to the west, where Patricius had lately set, fading and thinning toward the east, but at this hour complete. Otherwise the sky was a gray-blue in which nearly every star was lost.

Eidhafor awoke when a hand gently shook him by the shoulder. He sat up in bed. Windows filled the room with dusk. Beside him stood a form shadowy but not human, not Merseian—"Hssh!" it hissed. "Stay quiet." Fingers increased their pressure, not painfully, but enough to suggest what strength lay behind them. "I mean you no harm. Rather, I wish you well. If you do not cry out, then we shall talk, only talk."

"Who are you?" Eidhafor rasped, likewise in Anglic. "What are you? How did you get in?"

The stranger chuckled. Teeth flashed briefly white below the ember gleam of eyes. "As to that last, *fodaich*, it was not difficult, the more so when unawaited. A car that landed well away from here, a hunter who used his tricks of stalking to get close, a pair of small devices—surely the *fodaich* can imagine."

Eidhafor regained equilibrium. If murder had been intended, it would have happened while he slept. "Under my oath to the Roidhun and my honor within my Vach, I cannot talk freely to an unknown," he said.

"Understood," the stranger purred. "I will ask no secrets of you: nothing but frankness, such as I suspect you have already indulged in, and doubtless will again when you return home. It could well prove in the interest of your cause."

"And what is your own interest?" Eidhafor flung.

"Softly, I beg you, softly. You will presently agree how unwise it would be to rouse the household." The stranger let go his grip and curled down to sit on the end of the bed. "No matter my name. We shall concern ourselves with you for a while. Afterward I will depart by the way I came, and you may go back to sleep."

Eidhafor squinted through the gloom. He had felt fur. And those ears and tendrils—He had seen pictures in his briefings before the fleet took off. "You are a Starkadian from Imhotep," he declared flatly.

"Mayhap." The eyes held steady. Could they see better in the dark than human or Merseian eyes?

If so, they beheld a being roughly the size and shape of a big man. Standing, Eidhafor would lean forward on tyrannosaurian legs, counterbalanced by a heavy tail; but his hands and his visage were humanoid, if you ignored countless details. External ears were lacking. The skin was hairless, pale green, meshed by fine scales. He was warm-blooded, male, wedded to a female who had borne their young alive. His species and the human had biochemistries so closely similar that they desired the same kinds of worlds; and it might well be that the mind-sets were not so different, either.

"What could a Starkadian want of a Merseian?" he asked.

"It is true, there is a grievance," whispered back. "Had the Roidhunate had its way, all life on Starkad would long since be ashes. The Terrans rescued some of us. But that was a generation or more ago. Times change; gratitude is mortal; likewise is enmity, though apt to be longer-lived. If I am a Starkadian, then imagine that certain among us are reconsidering where our own best interests lie. Furthermore, Merseia almost took control of this system, thus of Imhotep. The next round may have another outcome. It would be well for us to gain understanding of you. If I am a Starkadian, then I have taken this opportunity to try for a little insight."

"A-a-ahhh," Eidhafor breathed.

Captain Jerrold Ronan was in charge of Naval Intelligence for the Patrician System. That was a more important and demanding job than it appeared to be or than his rank suggested. Subordinates had reason to believe that he stood high in the confidence of his superiors, including Admiral Magnusson.

Hence it would grossly have blown cover for Targovi, obscure itinerant chapman, to see him in person. Instead, the Tigery called from his van, away off in the outback. The message went through sealed circuits and an array of encoding programs.

At contact, by appointment: "Well?" snapped Ronan. "Be quick. Matters are close to the breaking point. I can't spare time for every hint-collector who imagines he's come across a sensational piece of revelation." He sighed. "Why did I ever give you direct access to me?"

The least of ripples went across Targovi's pelt, and underneath. His tone held smooth. "The noble captain is indeed overburdened, if he forgets the honor that his dignity requires he grant those who operate in his service. Let me remind him that he himself felt, years agone, an individual like this one could prove uniquely able to gather special kinds of clucs."

The man's thin, freckled countenance drew into a scowl. "You and your damned pride! Close to insubordination—" He calmed. "All right. I'm harassed, and it probably has made me rude. You did pick up some useful leads in the past."

They had been leads to nothing enormous; nevertheless, they had been useful. Like humans, Merseians employed various agents not of their own species. A racial and cultural patchwork such as Daedalus, remote from the Imperial center, was vulnerable to subversion—and not just from Merseia; the Empire seethed with criminality, dissension, unbounded ambitions. To hold the sector, the Navy must be the police force of their main-base planet. Colonists tended to feel less constrained in the presence of an affable nonhuman trader than with somebody more readily imaginable as working undercover.

"I think this time I have truly significant news," Targovi said.

The screen image ran fingers through its red hair. "You've been on Daedalus a while?"

"Yes, sir. Going to and fro on my usual rounds, and some not so usual. Looking, listening, talking, snooping. Scarce need I tell the captain how much discontent is afoot, sense of betrayal, demands for amendment—especially in the Navy—although it may be that many persons spoke more freely before me than they would have before others. Sir, I cannot but feel that this sentiment is very largely being fomented. To a natural aggravation, which should but cause grumbling, come unfounded allegations, repeated until everyone takes their truth for given; inflammatory slogans; hostile japes—"

"That's merely your impression," Ronan interrupted. "And, no offense, you are not human. You are not even properly acquainted with Technic civilization. I hope you have something more definite to tell."

"I do, sir. First, scant doubt remains that spacecraft have been calling at Zacharia island, suspiciously often, for more than a year. I have garnered accounts of sightings by dwellers on the mainland and sailors who were at sea. They thought little about it. Yet when I compared data from the main traffic control bank, a most curious pattern emerged. Activity has been going on yonder, sir, and I misdoubt it is not harmless smuggling. Could it be Merseian?"

"No. Have a care. Remember, the Navy conducts secret operations. You will speak no more about this, not to anybody. Do you understand?"

Targovi glided past the question. "Sir, there

is another eldritch thing, directly concerning the Merseians. I have word from green lips."

Ronan started. "What? How? Who with? How dared you?"

Targovi imitated a human smile. It made his teeth sheen sharp. "The captain must permit me my own small secrets. Did we not agree that any value I might have lies in my ability to work irregularly? Rest assured, no harm was done. Again, I have simply wormed out confidences which would not otherwise be forthcoming—although bits of memory and feeling that the Merseians let drop before their guards should have been heeded more closely than they were."

Ronan swallowed hard. "Say on."

"Those officers who know what actually happened are bewildered. Several are embittered. It is like the impression here that Daedalus was left neglected to face danger alone; but this impression has more reason behind it. Sir, the Merseian fleet was led with unprecedented stupidity. Its advance squadrons flew straight into the trap that Admiral Magnusson had set at Black Hole 1571—although the hazard should have been plain to any commander who knew aught of astrophysics or naval history. Then, instead of re-forming to mount a rescue operation, *Cyntath* Merwyn split his main strength north and south, creating two pincers which Terra's rear echelons broke one by one. It should never have happened."

"Aren't you glad it did?" Ronan asked dryly. "I daresay harsh things have been done to high-ranking people, back in the Ridhunate. It doesn't publicize its failures."

"Sir, this was a failure too grotesque. An experienced, senior officer admitted as much to me. His rage came nigh to making him vomit." Targovi paused. "And yet, captain, and yet . . . our fleet could have pursued the advantage gained further than it did. It could have inflicted far worse damage. Instead, it was content to let the bulk of the enemy armada retreat."

Ronan flushed. "Who are you to talk strategy? What do you know that Admiral Magnusson did not? Has it occurred to you that his first duty was not to risk our forces, but to save them?"

"Captain, I simply suggest—"

"You have said quite enough," Ronan bit off. "Do you care to submit a detailed report? No, don't answer that. It would be worthless. Or worse than worthless, in the present explosive situation." His image stiffened. "Agent Targovi, you will drop this line of inquiry. That is an order. Return to Imhotep. Do not, repeat not attempt any additional amateurish investigation of matters which do not concern you. If we should have an assignment for you later, you will be informed."

The Tigery was quiet for a space.

"May I ask why the captain is displeased?" he ventured.

"No. Official secrets."

"Aye, sir. If I have transgressed, I am . . . sorry."

Ronan relented a trifle. "I'll accept that you didn't know any better."

"Very good, sir. But—Well, about my *Moon-*

jumper, sir. Of course, everybody thinks I bought her, and my piloting instruction, out of my gains from storming a pirate stronghold on Imhotep. I can return now, with half my cargo unsold, claiming a family crisis. But would it not arouse wonder, should I fail to come back soon to Daedalus?"

"Are you that well known?" The man considered. "As you will. You do have a living to make." Part-time clandestines received a pittance for their efforts, though retirement benefits, when they could plausibly claim to be living off their savings, were fairly good. "But watch your actions. If you step over the bounds, you're dead."

"Understood, sir. Aught else? No, sir? Out." Targovi switched off.

By himself, he sank into thought. Rather, he went racing away on a dozen different trails of thought, the hunter's thrill along his nerves. Certain suspicions were strengthening.

He needed help, and was unsure where to seek it. Well, since he must go home anyway, he could begin there. If he probed deeper, he might die. Quite possibly. But if not—if he did a deed that they would notice on Terra itself—

Chapter 3

At the Olga's Landing spaceport, he took his van from the hold of his ship. It was equally plebeian in appearance, a long and lumpy metal box, scratched and dented, meant for hauling stuff, with a control cab and a couple of passenger benches forward. Retractable wheels and pontoons seemed to be as much in case the gravs failed as for surface use.

Unlike the ship, the van had more capabilities than it showed. When Naval Intelligence had recruited and sketchily trained young Targovi, it provided him such equipment as he might conceivably need sometime. That was not usual for an agent whose anticipated job was simply to keep alert and report anything dubious he noticed in the course of his ordinary rounds. However, Targovi was a son of Dragoika, and she was chief among the Sisterhood that led the Tigeries of the Toborkozan region. Moreover, she was an old friend of Dominic Flandry. Though he had not visited the Patrician System for a decade and a half, he and she still exchanged occasional communications; and he had risen to Fleet Admiral, and gained the ear of the Emperor.

One gave little extras to the restless son of Dragoika.

Targovi took off in a soft whirr. The mountains reared grandly around. Most were white-capped; glaciers shimmered blue-green under the shrunken sun. Pioneers had melted the snow off Mt. Horn and emplaced thermonuclear fires underground to keep rock and air liveably warm. Now the ice bulls and the frost-loving plants they had grazed were gone. Woods fringed the city. Agriculture occupied lower reaches, as far down as sea level. But humans dared not breathe there, unless through a reduction helmet. At those pressures, the gases their lungs required became poisons.

It was otherwise for Targovi. After he had left the range behind and was humming east above its foothills, he pulled his oxygill out of its tiny sockets. Already it had been forcing him to inhale shallowly. He stowed it in its case with care, although the fabric was hard to damage, and proceeded to a wholly comfortable altitude. That was no lengthy descent, as steep as the density gradient is under Imhotepan gravity.

The continent rolled away beneath him, a single forest, infinite shadings of green and gold, silvered with rivers and lakes, mysterious as the Land of Trees Beyond where some aged people believed the spirits of the dead went. Overhead, the sky was deeply blue, fleeced with clouds, the great half-disc of the moon Zoser ghostly above the sea that presently hove in sight. A splendid world, he thought. Not Starkad, nothing could be, but why mourn for that which was forever lost? His generation had come to life here, not there. As yet they were few, often baffled or slain by a nature alien to them; but in time they would win to understanding, thence to mastery, and their descedants would dwell throughout the planet.

It was not sufficient for Targovi.

He located the Crystal River and followed its course till it emptied into Dawnside Bay. There, where a harbor could lie sheltered from tidal turbulence, the Kursovikians had built their new town. Other societies had settled elsewhere, seeking to carry on their particular ways, but the Kursoviki folk were largely seafarers.

They were also those who had always been in closest contact with the Terrans, whose mission headquarters stood on a ridge to the west. Low and softly tinted, the building looked subordinate to the gray stone mass on a hilltop that was the Castle of the Sisterhood. Targovi knew how much of an illusion that was.

Nonetheless, Toborkozan had struck roots and grown; it could survive without further help if need be. Houses—timber, often bearing carven totems on the roofs—were spread widely along cobbled streets. The waterships in port were nearly all wooden too, archaic windjammers because those had been what the wrights knew how to make; but most had gotten auxiliary engines, and some were hovercraft of fairly modern design. A ferrocrete field on the northern headland offered landing to aircars, as well as the gliders and propeller-driven wingboats which various Tigeries had constructed for themselves.

Targovi, privileged, set his vehicle down in the courtyard of the Castle and got out. Guards raised traditional halberds in salute. They carried firearms as well, for emigration had not extinguished every feud or kept fresh ones from arising, not to mention lawlessness, and it was better to watch over your own, yourself, than depend on the Terrans. Targovi learned that his mother was in her apartment and hastened thither.

Dragoika lived high in the Gaarnokh Tower. Gaarnokhs had not been among the species which could be introduced on Imhotep, but memory lingered of their horned mightiness. She was standing in a room floored with slate and walled with granite. Tapestries gentled it a trifle. Books and a single seashell goblet were from Starkad. The rest—bronze candelabrum, things of silver and glass, massive table, couches whose lines resembled a ship's—were crafted here. Carrying capacity between suns had been so limited; much worse decisions had had to be made than to abandon the works of an entire history. She was looking out an open ogive window, into the salt breeze and onward to surf on the reefs beyond the bay.

"Greeting, mother and chieftain," said Targovi.

Dragoika turned, purred, and came to take his hands in hers. Though the female mane that rippled down her back was grizzled, she moved lithely. The sumptuous female curves had become lean, but her breasts jutted proud. True, they weren't ornamental adipose tissue like human dugs, they were organs muscular and vascular, from which her infants had sucked not milk but blood. Targovi had seen Terran speculations that the need to maintain a high blood supply made her sex the more vigorous one, and that this accounted for its dominance in most Tigery cultures. His doubts about that did not in any important way diminish his respect for her.

"Welcome home, youngest son," she said. "How fared you?"

"Into a wind that stank of evil," he replied. "How fare the folk?"

"Well enough . . . thus far. But you are back sooner than is wont. It would not be for aye, this time?"

"It would not. It cannot. I tell you, death was in the wind I snuffed upon Daedalus. I must return."

Her tendrils drooped. "Ever will you go forth—someday, if you live, beyond any ken of mine. Overbold are you, my son."

"No more than you, mother, when you skippered a ship on the Zletovar Sea and the vaz-Siravo rose beweaponed from beneath."

"But you are male." Dragoika sighed. "The Terran example? Are you driven to do everything a female can do, as I've heard their females were once driven to match the males? I hoped for grandchildren from you."

"Why, you shall have them. Just find me a wife who's content if I'm often away."

"Or always away, like him who begot your friend Diana?" Dragoika's mood lightened. She did send a parting shot: "Long will it be ere many vaz-Toborko besides yourself are found on Daedalus, let alone worlds among the stars. How like you your celibacy?"

"Not much. It measures my feelings for you, mother, that I came here before seeking the waterfront minxes. However, if this is the price to pay—There is naught a fellow can get so far behind on, nor so quickly catch up on."

She whistled in merriment. "Well, then, scapegrace, come have a smoke and we'll talk." She surveyed him closely. "It was not filial piety brought you first to me. You've somewhat to ask."

"I do that," he admitted. Excitement pulsed within him. Dragoika got word from around this globe. If anyone could aid him onward, it was she.

The wind blew slow but powerful. It filled the upper square sails, lower fore-and-aft canvas, and jibs that drove *Firefish* southeast. Seas rushed, boomed, flung bitter spindrift off their crests; they shimmered green on their backs, dark purple in their troughs. Following the wake soared a flock of flying snakes.

Abruptly the lookout shouted. Sailors swarmed to the rail or into the rigging to see. Captain Latazhanda stayed more calm. She had received word on the ship's radio, and given directions.

The van lumbered down, extended pontoons, sought to lay alongside. Though Targovi maneuvered cautiously, he nearly suffered a capsizing. Waves under this gravity moved with real speed and force. His second pass succeeded. Leaning out an opened door, he made fast a towline tossed him and let his vehicle drop aft. He flew across on a gravity impeller.

Besides the crew, their passengers were on deck to meet him. He thrust aside awe at his first in-the-flesh sight of a Wodenite, and turned toward Diana Crowfeather. She sprang over the planks and into his arms.

"Targovi, you rascal, how wonderful!" she warbled. "What're you doin' here?" Anxiety smote. She stepped back, her hands still on his shoulders, and stared at him through the vitryl that snugged around her head. Aside from it and its pump, she was briefly clad. No matter the broad orbit, Imhotep's atmosphere has a greenhouse effect felt even at sea. "Is somethin' wrong?"

"Yea and nay," Targovi replied in his language, which she understood and the Wodenite presumably did not. "I would fain speak with you alone, little friend." He purred. "Fear not. I, the trader, have in mind to give you, in swap for this adventure of yours, a bigger and wilder one."

"Oh, but I've promised Axor—"

"He will be included. I count on you to persuade him. But let me be about my devoirs."

Saluting Latazhanda, he explained that he carried an urgent message. She and her crew were a rough lot, but had the manners not to inquire what it was. "I daresay you know whither we're bound," she remarked. "The Starboard and Larboard Islands, where this mad pair want to look at what may be ruins left by fay-folk of old." She rumbled a chuckle. "They're paying aplenty for the charter."

"Need is that I must take them from you. But I'll make your loss good, my lady. A fourth of the fare." Targovi winced as he spoke. The price would come out of his purse, and it was uncertain whether the Corps would ever honor that expense account.

"A fourth!" yowled Latazhanda. "Are you madder than they? I declined a lucrative cargo to make this trip. Three-fourths at least."

"Ah, but so enticing a puss as you cannot fail to attract the offers of ardent agents." Much consignment, brokerage, and other shoreside business was in male hands. "How I envy them. Your charms cause me to reward you with a third of the passage money you're forgoing."

Latazhanda gave him a long look. "I've heard of you, the chapman who goes beyond the sky. If you've time to take hospitality, your stories should be worth my accepting a mere two-thirds."

They haggled amicably and flirtatiously until they reached an agreement which included his spending the night in her cabin. She enjoyed variety, and he did not mind that part of the bargain at all.

What with additional introductions, and leisured preliminaries of acquaintanceship with F. X. Axor, the hour was near sunset when Targovi and Diana could be by themselves.

That was in the crow's nest on the mainmast. He balanced against the surging and swaying as easily as any of his race, and it delighted her so much that she took a while to calm down and pay heed.

Wind swirled in shrouds, bore iodine odors. The ship creaked and whooshed. A low sun threw a bridge over the waters. Forsaking this quest for another would not be quite easy.

"My mother Dragoika told me about you and your comrade, of course," Targovi began. "You had called on her and she helped you arrange this transportation. My thanks to the gods, for you two must be their very sending."

"What do you want of us?" she asked.

'How would you like to go to Daedalus and roam about?"

"Oh, marvelous! I've only seen Aurea and its neighborhood—" Diana checked herself. "But I did promise Axor I'd be his guide, interpreter, assistant."

"Axor will come along. In fact, that is the whole idea."

"But don't you understand? He isn't travelin' for pleasure, nor for science, really. To him, this is a . . . a pilgrimage. We can't go 'til he's looked over the stones on those islands."

"They've lasted thousands of years—millions, if he is right. They can wait a bit longer. Tell him, what's true, this is a chance he had better seize. Soon none but Navy ships may be going between Patrician planets."

"What? Why?"

"And Javak the Fireplayer alone knows when the spacelanes will be open again. If Axor must be stranded, better on Daedalus than Imhotep. That air helmet of his seems to pain him."

"Yes, I think it does, though he never complains. It had to be made special for him. He's comfortable in Olga's Landin'."

"But what would there be for him to do? Whereas Daedalus may well be the world that has what he's seeking. Likelier, I should think. Have any such things ever been found on globes the size of Imhotep? Chances are, he's wasting his efforts. You, small person, are not, because you are having a glorious time simply traveling. However, you can have the same on Daedalus, and more. No need for a helmet. Plenty of handsome young men."

Diana sniffed and tossed her head as much as she could under these conditions. "I can take care of myself, thank you. Do you know of anything yonder that might be Foredweller remains?"

"In my traffickings I have seen curious sights, and heard tell of others. Once we're there, I will ask more widely and more closely, until I have a goal or three for you."

She gave him a hard stare. "Why do you want this?"

"Well, as a trader who smells trouble uptime, I need better information—"

She laughed. "Let's not play pretty games. Nobody can overhear us. You're no more a simple packman than I am. I've known for years. What you really are, it wouldn't've been polite to ask . . . 'til now."

He joined an acrid mirth to hers. "Hai, little friend of the universe, you are your father's daughter! . . . I suspected that you suspected. Certain remarks you made, looks you pierced me with, already ere your limbs lengthened—not what a child shows the son of her mother's associate when he's come back from an adventure and put her on his lap to tell her about it. . . . Aye, trusting you to keep silence, I admit to turning an honest credit now and then by keeping my senses open on behalf of your father's corps. Is that terrible?"

"Contrariwise," she replied enthusiastically. "The Navy staked you, didn't it? I never really believed what you said about the pirates."

"Well," he growled, miffed, "we can talk further another time. What matters this evening is that devils are loose. They know me too well on Daedalus. But who would be wary of an innocent old priest and his young girl companion, wandering about on a purely religious expedition?"

Diana tensed. "What'd we really be doin'?"

"Essentially, distracting attention from me. I have business I want to pursue, best not discussed here. You two will be conspicuous without posing a threat to anybody."

She scowled. "I can't just *use* him."

"You'll not." Targovi spread his hands. "Who dares say there are no Ancient relics along the Highroad River and—on islands beyond? Already millions of years ago, that must have been a good place to settle. I'll help you gather information about it."

She bit her lip. "You tempt me. But it isn't right."

"Think why I do this," he urged.

"Why?"

"Because everything I have seen, heard, discovered on Daedalus shouts a single thing. Admiral Magnusson plans to rebel. His forces will hail him Emperor, and he will lead them in an assault on Gerhart's."

Silence fell, save for wind, sea, and ship. Diana clutched the rail of the crow's nest, which was pitching violently, and stared horizonward. Finally she said low: "No big surprise. Olga's Landin', too, has been abuzz with rumors. People are mainly afraid of an Imperial counterattack. I've lined up several hidey-holes for myself. But prob'ly that's foolish. Why should anybody strike Imhotep? We'll simply wait the whole thing out."

"You care not about revolt and civil war?"

Diana shrugged. "What can I do about it? 'Twouldn't be the first time it's ever happened. From what I've heard, Olaf Magnusson would make a fine Emperor. He's strong, he's smart, and he can deal better with the Merseians."

"What makes you believe so?" Targovi asked slowly.

"Well, he . . . he's had to, for years, in this borderspace, hasn't he? When things finally blew up, it wasn't his fault. He met them and gave them a drubbin'. They respect strength. I've heard him blamed for not followin' up the victory and annihilatin' their fleet, but I think he was right. The Roidhun might not have been free to forgive that. Didn't you often advise me, always leave an enemy a line of retreat unless you fully intend to kill him?

As is, we're back at peace, and the diplomats are workin' on a treaty."

"Ah, you are young. Myself, I have lost faith in the likelihood of water spontaneously running uphill, teakettles boiling if set on a cake of ice, and governments being wise or benevolent. Tell me, what do you know about Admiral Magnusson?"

"Why, why, what everybody knows."

"What is that? Spell it out for me. I am only a xeno."

Diana flushed. "Don't get sarcastic." Calming: "Well, if you insist. He was born on Kraken . . . m-m . . . forty-some Terra-years ago. It's a hard, harsh planet for humans. They grow tough, or they die. An independent lot; their spacefolk trade outside the Empire as well as inside, clear to Betelgeuse or Merseia itself. But they give us more'n their share of military recruits. Magnusson enlisted young, in the Marines. He distinguished himself in several nasty situations. Durin' the dust-up with Merseia at Syrax, he took command of the crippled ship he was aboard, after the officers were killed, and got her to safety. That made his superiors transfer him to the Navy proper and send him to the Foundry—the officer school in Sector Aldebaran. It has a fierce reputation."

"What did he do during the last succession crisis?"

"Which one? You mean the three-cornered fight for the throne that Hans Molitor won? Why, he—m-m, his age then—he must've been at the academy yet. But the accounts I've seen tell how he did well when a couple of later rebellions needed squelchin', plus in negotiatin' with the Merseians, so you can't say he hasn't been loyal. In fact, he's seldom visited Terra and never played office politics, they say, but he's risen fast regardless."

"It did no harm that he married a Nyanzan heiress."

"Oh, foof! You've got to have money to go far in the service, civil or military. I know that much. It doesn't mean he doesn't love her."

"That is the official biography. What have you learned about him as a person?"

"Oh, just the usual sort of thing you see on the news. No, I've also talked with some of the boys who serve under him. What they tell sounds all right to me. He does seem pretty humorless and strict, but he's always fair. The lowliest ranker who deserves a hearin' will get it. And he may be curt in everyday life, but when he unrolls his tongue—" Diana shivered. "I caught his speech last year, of course, after he'd saved us from the Merseians. I still get cold prickles, rememberin'."

"A hero, then," said Targovi down in his throat.

Diana's gaze sharpened. "What's wrong?"

"Best I say no more at this stage," he demurred. "I could be mistaken in my fears. But ask yourself what elements—criminal, mayhap—could be conspiring to take advantage of chaos. Ask yourself what harm I can work on any innocent party by helping uncover the truth, whatever the truth may prove to be."

"Um-m-m." She stared out beyond the sunset. "Persuadin' Axor—because I will not fool him, Targovi, though I could maybe shade the facts a trifle—m-m-m. . . . Yes, if I said Daedalus is a better huntin' ground for him, and we'd be wise to get there while we're sure we can, and you'll take us because you're sort of interested yourself—I think that would satisfy him. You see, he really does believe in goodness."

"Which you and I are not certain of. But we are certain of evil," said Targovi. His tone had gone steely. "You might also, Diana Crowfeather, consider the cost of a civil war launched by your hero. Destruction, death, maiming, pain, grief, billionfold. You are more compassionate than I am."

Chapter 4

The home of Admiral Sir Olaf Magnusson lay in the desirable tract a hundred kilometers north of Aurea. It was small, and the interior austere, for a man of wealth and power. But such was his desire, and any decisions he made, he enforced. The only luxuries, if they could be called that, were a gymnasium where he worked out for at least forty minutes in every fifteen hours, and an observation deck where he meditated when he felt the need. Naturally, his use of these was restricted to times when he was there, which had not been many of late.

He stood on the deck and let his gaze range afar—a tall man, thickly muscular, with wide, craggy features, heavy blond brows over sapphire-blue eyes, thinning sandy hair. The face was tanned and deeply lined; its left cheek bore the seam of a battle scar which he had never troubled to have removed and which had become a virtual trademark. What he saw was a vast sweep of land and sky. Close by, the land had been terraformed, planted in grass, roses, hollyhocks, Buddha's cup, livewell, oaks, maples, braidwoods, and more, the gardens of an empire brought together around human houses. Beyond was primeval Daedalus, trees and brush, leaves a somber, gleaming green, never a flower. Those were not birds that passed above, though their wings shone in the evening light as the wings of eagles would have. The sun, sinking west, had begun to lose its disc shape. Haze dimmed and reddened it enough for vision to perceive that, because the rays came through ever more air as it dropped below what should have been the horizon. Golden clouds floated above.

Olaf Magnusson did not really see this, unless with a half-aware fraction of his mind. Nor was he rapt in the contemplation of the All that his Neosufic religion enjoined. He had striven to be, but his thoughts kept drifting elsewhere, until at last he accepted their object as the aspect of the Divine which was set before him tonight.

Strength. Strength unafraid, unhesitant, serving a will which was neither cruel nor kind but which cleanly trod the road to its destiny. . . . He could not hold the vision before him for very long at a time. It was too superb for mankind. Into his awareness there kept jabbing mere facts, practicalities, things he must do, questions of how to do them—yes, crusades have logistic requirements too—

A footfall, a breath reached his hearing. He swung about, his big frame as sure-footed as a fencer's or a mountaineer's, both of which he was. His wife had come out. She halted, a meter away. "What's this?" he demanded. "Emergency?"

"No." He could barely hear her voice through the cold, whittering breeze, as soft as it was. "I'm sorry. I wouldn't have interrupted you, except that it's getting late and the children are hungry. I wondered if you would be having dinner with us."

His basso rasped. "For something like that, you break in on my devotions?"

"I'm sorry," she repeated. Yet she did not cringe, she stood before him in her own pride. And her sadness. "Ordinarily I wouldn't. But since you are going away for a long while at best, and God knows if you will ever come back—"

"What gives you that idea?"

Vida Lonwe-Magnusson smiled a bit. "You'd never have married an idiot, Olaf, no matter how much money she brought with her. Allow that I've gotten to know you over the years, in part, and I follow the news closely, and have studied history. What date have you set for the troops to spontaneously proclaim you Emperor? Tomorrow?"

Surprised despite himself, he gave her a long look. Unflinchingly, the brown eyes in the black face returned it. The slender body in the simple gown stood straight. They were excellent stock on Nyanza, their ancestors as ruthlessly selected by a hostile nature as his had been, although the oceanic planet had prospered afterward more than cold and heavy Kraken ever could. Among his thoughts when he was courting her had been that a crossbreeding should produce remarkable offpsping.

Warmth touched him from within. "I wanted

to spare you anxiety, Vida. Maybe what I actually did was cause you needlessly much. I never doubted your loyalty. But the fewer who knew, the better the odds. Premature disclosure would have been disastrous, as you can surely understand. Now everything is ready."

"And you are really going through with it?"

"You will be Empress, dear, Empress of the stars we never see on Daedalus."

She sighed. "I'd rather have you. . . . No, self-pity is the most despicable of all emotions. Let me only ask you, Olaf, here at the last moment, why you are doing this."

"To save the Empire."

"Truly? You've always had the name of a man stern but honorable. You gave your oath."

"It was the Imperium that broke faith, not we who fought and died while noblemen on Terra sipped their wine and profiteers practiced their corruptions."

"Is war the single way to reform? What will it do to the Empire? What of us, your people—your family—if you draw away our defenses? You kept this sector for Terra. Now you'll invite the Merseians to come back and take it."

Magnusson smiled, stepped forward, laid hands on her waist. "That you needn't worry about, Vida. You and the children will be perfectly safe. I'll explain in my proclamation, and details will go into the public data banks. But you need just think. This sector is my power base. Until we've occupied and organized significant real estate elsewhere, this is where our resources and reserves are. And the

Patrician System is the keystone of it. Nearly every other set of planets in the vicinity is backward, impoverished, or totally useless to oxygen breathers. That's why the base *is* here, and the industries that support it. Gerhart's first thought will be to strike at Daedalus, cut me off from my wellspring. So of course I must leave enough strength behind to make that impossible, as well as to back my campaign. The Merseians will know better than to butt against it. I promise!"

"Well—" She shivered, stiffened, and challenged: "What else do you promise? Why should anybody go over to your cause, besides your devoted squadrons? Oh, I'm not saying you would be a bad ruler. But who can possibly be good enough to justify the price?"

"You have heard me talk, both at home and in public," he said. "I don't claim to be a superman or anything like that. Conceivably, a better candidate exists. But where? Who else will make the Imperium strong and virtuous again?"

His voice dropped, became vibrant: "And Vida, I will make up for lives lost, by orders of magnitude. For I will hammer out an end to this senseless, centuries-old conflict with the Roidhunate. The Merseians aren't monsters. They're aggressive, yes, but so were we humans in our heyday. They'll listen to men who are strong, as I've shown them I am, and who are reasonable, as I will show them I am. It has already happened, on a smaller scale. The galaxy has ample room for both our races.

"Will not a dream like that appeal to worlds gone weary?"

There was a stillness that lengthened. The sun began to spread itself out in a red-golden arc.

Vida laid her head against her man's breast. He closed his arms about her. "So be it," she whispered. "I'll hold the fort as best I can. You see, I often think it's foolish, but the fact won't go away that I love you, nor do I want it to."

"Good girl," he said into the fragrance of her hair. "Sure, let's enjoy a family dinner."

That would be a chance to re-inspire his sons.

Chapter 5

Moonjumper toiled out of Imhotep's gravity well, but once in clear space her gravs had the force to boost her across to Daedalus in less than fifty hours, at the present configuration of the planets. Within the potbellied hull, Targovi considerately maintained both weight and pressure at Terran standard, and wore his oxygill. Having put the ship on full automatic, he joined his passengers in the saloon. That was an elegant word for a dingy cabin into which Axor must coil himself while Diana perched on the table.

They had dimmed the lights and were looking in wonder at a viewscreen. It showed the receding globe, luminous white and blue-green; three ashy-silver moons; crystalline blackness aswarm with fire-gems that were stars; the radiant road of the Milky Way. "God will always be the supreme artist," rumbled the Wodenite, and crossed himself.

Targovi, who was a pagan if he was anything, fingered the charm suspended at his throat. It was a small turquoise hexagon with a gold inlay of an interlinked circle and triangle. "Supreme at surprises, too," he said. The longing surged in him. If this miserable tub of his had a hyperdrive, if he could outpace light and seek the infinite marvels yonder!

Yet a planet could keep presenting a person astonishments throughout his lifetime. The trick was to avoid any that were lethal. "It were wise to make sure you twain know what to expect when we arrive," he declared. "Daedalus has its uniquenesses. Diana, I would have to crawl over our friend to reach the cooler. Will you open it and serve us? You'll find meat, beer, cold tea, bread for yourself and for the Reverend if he wishes."

"*I* wish you'd remembered to stow some fruit," she complained mildly. "I do love frostberries, and promised F. X. a taste."

"There may be some in Aurea, imported." Targovi bounded to the table and curled up near the girl. He could do things like that in a low gee-field, and was so used to the gill that it was no nuisance. But he did need to keep active, lest his flesh go slack. He braced himself against what was going to hurt. "Let me not forget to supply you with money, unless Axor has more left him than I believe. You'll be buying all your food, as well as most other things. Food can get expensive on Daedalus, and you may be faring for many a day."

"Ah . . . I have heard, yes, I have heard that the native life is inedible by us," Axor said.

Diana, busy improvising a sandwich, nodded. "None is known that's poisonous, nor any disease we can catch," she told him, "but the flip side of this is that we get nothin' out of whatever we eat. Plant and animal kingdoms evolved there too, but not like yours or mine or Targovi's. Proteins with d-amino acids, for instance. Here." She handed him the sandwich. It was hefty, but vanished in his maw as a drop of water vanishes on a red-hot skillet. She whistled and set herself to carve him a piece of the roast—about half.

"Thus it was necessary to introduce Terran and similar plants, later animals?" he inquired.

"Aye," Targovi said, "the which wasn't easy. Plants need their microbes, their worms, a whole ecology ere they can flourish. And the native life wants not to be displaced. And it is adapted to the environment. Every patch of soil to be cultivated must first be sterilized down to bedrock—radiation or chemicals—and then the new organisms patiently nurtured. And meanwhile the old ones keep trying to reconquer it. Aquaculture is harder still."

"Why did the settlers make the effort?"

"It was cheaper than depending on synthetics. Also safer, in the long run. Industries can be shattered more readily than farms."

"You misapprehend, my son. I meant that I cannot see why humans chose to invade a planet like that in the first place."

"Oh, my, you are unworldly, aren't you, sweetheart?" Diana said while she fed him. "But you Wodenites never have been hell-bent to colonize like us. Is that because you don't breed so crazily? Anyhow, planets where humans can live without a lot of fancy gear aren't that common. Artificial miniworlds are fine . . . if you don't mind scanty elbow room, strict laws, dependency on outside resources, and vulnerability to attack. Else you take what you can get. By the time David Jones discovered Daedalus, the best places in known space were already claimed, and goin' into unknown space meant such a long haul that settlers would be cut off from their civilizations."

" 'Civilizations,' plural," Targovi pointed out. "It wasn't only humans who arrived. Members of several races with more or less the same requirements came too. Some wanted simply to homestead, or to make a living by serving the homesteaders. But some had their special interests. Weird is the patchwork you'll find on Daedalus."

"Fascinating," said Axor. "I daresay that, as a political necessity, these communities enjoy basic local autonomy."

"Aye. Most won it in early days, negotiating with a weak planetary authority. Certain regions on Daedalus did have much potential. Islands especially; those were easiest to defend against the encroachments of native life. This happened in the Commonwealth era, you realize, when government was loose everywhere. After the Empire took over, the greatest of the baronies were rich enough to buy an Imperial pledge that they would be left alone as long as they paid their tribute and caused no trouble."

Diana passed out beverages and slathered mustard on bread for herself. "The Empire's always been fairly tolerant, hasn't it?" she remarked.

"It is becoming less so, I fear," the Tigery

mumbled. "And as for what a 'new broom' might sweep away from us—"

"Then in spite of what you've said about Admiral Magnusson," the girl tossed back, "wouldn't he be off his orbit to try for the throne? I mean, he's got to operate out of Daedalus to start with, but if the dwellers don't like the idea and begin undercuttin' him—"

"They will meekly do whatever they are told, aside from black marketing and the like," Targovi said. "Likewise the fighting men. I'm sure many will be less than glad at being taken from home, back to war, this soon. But what will they dare do save shout hurrah with everybody else? Yours is a magnificent species in its fashion, little friend, but like every species it bears its special weaknesses."

He stroked his chin. His tendrils lay back flat, and a fang gleamed into view. "Furthermore," he murmured, "Magnusson, who is no simpleton, will have made his alliances with powerful factions on Daedalus. They will help keep order at his back, until he has overrun enough space elsewhere that Daedalus no longer matters. There are Paz de la Frontera . . . Lulach . . . Ghundrung . . . Zacharia—Zacharia—Aye, surely he has his understandings with persons in these and other places."

Axor looked distressed. "This conversation is taking a horrid turn," he said. "What can we do about it but tend our private affairs and pray to God for mercy upon helpless beings throughout the galaxy?"

"Well, we can get to Daedalus ere Javak

looses his flames and we are forbidden to travel," Targovi said, not for the first time.

"Yes, yes, I understand, and you are very kind, aiding me on my quest." Axor gusted a sigh that nearly knocked Diana's beer bottle over. "We were speaking of happier matters. You were, *kh-h-h*, briefing me on Daedalus—the planet itself, pure from the hand of the Creator, before sinful sophonts arrived. I seem to recall mention of its being extraordinary in numerous ways."

"Well," said the human around a mouthful of sandwich, "it doesn't have a horizon."

Axor elevated his snaky neck. "I beg your pardon?"

"The parameters—pressure and temperature gradients, mainly—they're just right for light to get refracted around the curve of the globe. Theoretically, if you looked straight through a telescope, you'd see your own backside. Of course, in practice mountains and haze and so forth prevent. But the cycle of day and night—about a fifteen and a half hour rotation period, by the way, which is short for an inner planet anywhere—that's quite an experience."

"Dear me. Amazing."

"I have read of the same thing elsewhere," Targovi said, "but those worlds chance not to be habitable."

"In fact," Diana added, "I've heard how Terra itself'd be like that, if it kept the same air but was a few kilometers less in radius. How much less? Thirteen, is that the figure? Nothin' to speak of as far as gravity and such are concerned. Daedalus happens to fit those specs."

"Or else God made it thus, for some purpose that perhaps the Foredwellers came to know, and we ourselves may someday," Axor crooned. "Oh, wonderful!"

The word came as *Moonjumper* was in approach curve. The planet filled vision ahead. Its huge polar caps were blinding white. Between them the tropics, seventy degrees wide, and the subtropics shone azure on the seas, dun and deep green on land, beneath clouds which the rotation twisted into tight spirals. The single moon, Icarus, stood pockmarked behind.

Suddenly the outercom picked up a message on the official band and blared it forth. Against his will, after his vital recommendations for military and political reform had been ignored, Admiral Sir Olaf Magnusson had bowed to the unanimous appeal of his valiant legionaries, that he take leadership of the Terran Empire before it crumbled in chaos and fell victim to every consequent evil. He had imposed martial law. Civil space traffic was suspended, unless by special permit. Sensible persons would instantly see why: an average-sized vessel moving at interplanetary speeds carried the energy of a small- to medium-yield nuclear warhead.

As far as possible, citizens should carry on in their usual occupations, obedient to the authorities. Infractions would be severely punished. But there was nothing to fear, rather there was everything to await, a dawn of hope. In six hours the new Emperor would broadcast, explaining, reassuring, arousing his people. "Stand by. The Divine, in whatever form It manifests Itself to you, the Divine is with us."

"Eyada shkor!" Targovi breathed. "Once I read of an ancient tombstone on Terra. Upon it stood, 'I expected this, but not so soon.' "

"What'll we do?" Diana asked, webbed into a seat beside him in the cramped control cabin. "Turn back?"

"No. We are locked into Ground Control's pattern. Doubtless I could arrange release, but—it is natural for me to continue as programmed. The whole object of this game has been to get our feet on yon ball." Targovi brooded. Abruptly:

"See here. Were you not the child of Maria Crowfeather and Dominic Flandry, I might feel guilt at casting you adrift. As it is, I must work with what tools I have, and thank the gods that the steel is true. I meant to tell you more than I have done, as soon as we were at large, but now that must wait. Already have I told you too much for your safety, mayhap. However, it has been little more than my suspicions of what was about to strike, together with fears of what use certain folk might make of the uproar. Surely these thoughts have occurred to others. If you know naught further, you have naught further to conceal, and I do not think they will interrogate you too fiercely, the more so when Axor is clearly uninvolved in these matters. Stay calm, hold fast to your wits, make your own way, as you have ever done."

She half reached for him, withdrew her hand, and said only a little unsteadily, "What do you mean?"

"Why, I have reason to think it could be unhealthy for me to linger after we land," he replied. "Therefore I will not. Imagine that they suspect me of gunrunning, or allegiance to the Molitor dynasty, or intransigent mopery, or whatever. Aye, it's a shock that your companion has been in deep waters. You knew only that I offered you a ride to Daedalus in order that you and Axor might be my blind, for purposes you had no reason to suppose were fell. Do you hear me?"

Then they did clasp hands.

Daedalus had no weather control. A rainstorm was upon Aurea when *Moonjumper* descended. That would be helpful to Targovi, though he could surely have managed without.

A squad of Imperial marines waited to arrest the persons aboard. At the last minute, Targovi cut Ground Control off and, manually, set down on a vacant spot across the field. He went straight out the airlock and disappeared in the downpour. Efforts at chemotracking were soon nullified by the manifold smells in the old quarter. Known associates of his, such as the innkeeper Ju Shao, denied knowledge of his whereabouts. Too much else was going on for Security to pursue the matter in detail. A Tigery outlaw would be practically helpless and hopelessly conspicuous on Daedalus anyway, would he not?

Meanwhile the squad had surrounded his passengers and taken them off to detention. At first the marines were nervous, weapons ready. But they got no resistance. The pretty girl actually smiled at them, and the dragon gave them his blessing.

Chapter 6

"The hour is upon us."

Tachwyr the Dark, Hand of the Vach Dathyr, stood silent for thirty pulsebeats after he had spoken, as if to let his words alloy themselves with the minds of his listeners. They were the members of the Grand Council over which he presided—the captains, under the Roidhun, of Merseia and its far-flung dominions.

Their faces filled the multiple screens of the communication set before him. He had had it brought out onto a towertop of his castle. At this tremendous moment he wanted to stand overlooking the lands of his Vach, while its ancient battle banners snapped above him in the wind. The sun Korych cast brilliance on forested mountainside, broad fields and clustered dwellings in the valley beneath, snowpeaks beyond. A fangryf winged on high, hunting. On a terrace below, his sons stood at attention, in ancestral armor, honoring their forebears and their posterity, the wholeness of the Race.

"That which we have worked for in secret has come to pass amidst trumpet calls," Tachwyr said. "Our patience reaps its reward.

The word has reached me. Magnusson has risen. Already his ships are on their way to combat."

A hiss of joy went from every countenance. Gazes became full of an admiration that approached worship. He, Tachwyr the Dark, himself a commander of space squadrons until he succeeded to the Handship of the Dathyrs and ultimately got the lordship of Merseia—he, this gaunt and aging male in a plain black robe, had brought them to triumph.

He knew what the thought was, and raised a cautionary arm. "Not yet dare we exult," he said. "We have scarcely begun. Victory could elude us, as it eluded generation after generation before us. The great Brechdan Ironrede fashioned a scheme that would have ruined the Terrans utterly, and saw it crumble in his grasp. In his name, after the name of the Roidhun, shall we go forward."

"What precisely is the news?" asked Odhar the Curt.

"Scarcely more than I have said," Tachwyr answered. "The dispatch will enter your private databases, of course, and you can study it at leisure; but do not expect much detail across a gulf that is many parsecs wide and deep."

For an instant the wish twinged in him, for some interstellar equivalent of radio, instantaneous, rather than courier vessels and message torpedoes which might at the very best cover slightly over half a light-year per hour. If the pulsations of warped space that made them detectable across twice that distance could be modulated—And indeed they could, but only within detection range. The same quantum uncertainties that made it possible to evade the speed limitations of the relativistic state made it infeasible to establish relay stations. . . . Well, everybody labored under the same handicap. Much of Tachwyr's plan depended on using it against the enemy.

"Have instructions gone to our embassy on Terra?" inquired Alwis Longtail.

"Not yet," Tachwyr said. "First I want this group to consider my draft of the letter. You may well have suggestions, and in any event you should know just what the contents are."

"Is there any reason why those should be specific?"

"No, nothing has changed in that respect. We must trust Chwioch to fit his actions to whatever the situation happens to be." That faith was not misplaced. Chwioch might bear the sobriquet "the Dandy" from his youth, but even then he had been bailiff of Dhangodhan, and at present he could better be called "the Shrewd"—except that he preferred the Terrans underestimate him. He would find—no, create—a pretext for breaking off the negotiations toward a nonaggression pact which he had so skillfully been prolonging. That would send waves of dismay over nobles, rich commoners, and intellectuals throughout the Empire, which in turn would bring an outcry for a "new politics" pointed in a more comforting direction.

Meanwhile Chwioch would explain, on every occasion he could find or make, that in the absence of such a pact, incidents leading to armed clashes were inevitable. When a single capital ship carried weapons sufficient to devastate an entire planet, and when the Empire could not keep its own house in order, Merseia was obliged to secure the debatable regions. This might sometimes require hot pursuit, into space claimed by the Empire. Obviously the Riodhunate regretted every occurrence, and stood ready to renew efforts to establish a lasting peace as soon as the Terran government was able to join in.

But the Terran government was going to be preoccupied for a period that might run into years. . . .

"When shall we put the Navy on full alert?" asked Gwynafon of Brightwater.

"Perhaps never," Tachwyr said. "Definitely not soon, barring the unforeseeable contingency. After all, the Terran embassy here will be reporting what it observes. The commanders of chosen units are already prepared for action. Best we not be too impulsive as regards them, either. Let events develop a while."

The question had been ridiculous, especially since the entire strategy had been under repeated, intensive discussion. However, Gwynafon was new on the Council—and not very intelligent—and a nephew of the Roidhun—You used what materials the God put at your disposal.

Brief pain slashed through Tachwyr. Had Aycharaych been alive—The original plan was his, and he had taken a direct part in the early preparations. But Aycharaych died when the Dennitzans bombarded his planet. At least, he vanished; you could never be altogether sure of anything about the Chereionite. With him had passed away the central machinery of Merseia's Intelligence Service. The Roidhunate had been half blinded, hideously vulnerable, impotent to take any initiative, for a decade or worse, while a new structure was being forged. If Terra had struck meanwhile—

But that wasn't in the nature of an Empire old, sated, and corrupt. Instead, its politicians wondered aloud why their realm and the Roidhunate kept failing to reach agreement. Was there not an entire galaxy to share?

As if any responsible Merseian leader could turn his attention elsewhere, when such a power lurked at his back! Once upon a time humankind had borne the same universe-spanning ambitions that the Race did now. It might well come to cherish them again—if not on Terra, then on the daughter worlds. Or a different but allied species might, the Cynthians or the Scothani for example. Even in its decadence, the Empire had the means to pose a mortal threat. It must be nullified before the Race could be fully free to seek that destiny the God had set.

We shall, ghost of Aycharaych, we shall. During those selfsame years of our misery, your scheme was coming to fruition. This is the day when victory begins.

Chapter 7

After the warships had glided from orbit, starward bound, the effective ruler of the Patrician System was Lieutenant General Cesare Gatto, Imperial Marine Corps. The civil governor and bureaucrats carried their routines on as best they were able, but this had never amounted to much. Since Daedalus became sector headquarters, the Navy had taken over most functions, from planetary police to mediator between communities. Gatto reigned as Magnusson's deputy, almost his viceroy.

It was thus somewhat of a surprise, as overworked as Gatto was, when he had the prisoner Diana Crowfeather brought to his office. Or perhaps not. A husband and father, he had never lost his taste for femininity. Besides, this was an unusual case, more so than he let on to his subordinates.

"Please be seated," he said as the door closed behind her. She took a chair and regarded him across the desk. He was a small, well-knit man with a high forehead above a furrowed, hooknosed face and pale blue eyes. His uniform tunic had the collar open and was devoid of the many decorations he had earned. A cigarette smoldered between his fingers.

His look in return was appreciative, baggy though the coverall was that had been issued her. "I'm afraid this past pair of weeks has been wearisome for you," he went on. "I hope the physical conditions, at least, were acceptable."

"It wasn't bad," she answered. "Except for the questionin' and, worse, the worry about my friends. Nobody would tell me a damn thing." Her tone defied more than it complained.

"Separate interrogations are standard procedure, donna. Rest assured, the Wodenite has suffered no harm. I hear he's spent most of his time screening books from the public database. Scholarly works and slushy novels."

"But what about Targovi?"

"The Imhotepan—I wish I knew. He's dropped from sight. Have you anything to add to your claim, and the Wodenite's, that you two cannot tell why he fled? Has some new thought occurred to you?"

"No, sir." Her chin jutted. "It might help if we had a better idea of why we were seized in the first place."

Gatto stared at his cigarette, puffed, raised his glance to hers, and said: "Very well, I'll be frank. You see, you and your companion have received clean bills of health. You yourself are known on Imhotep, of course, and a check by Security agents there verified the Wodenite's story of being on a religious tour, eccentric but harmless. Nobody can imagine how either of you could be conspirators, nor did interrogation indicate it. At worst, you persist in trying to find excuses for the Tigery. You could both have been released earlier, if the urgencies of preparing for Emperor Olaf's departure hadn't caused everything else to be postponed."

Diana bounced to her feet, radiant. "We can go? Terrific!"

"Sit back down," he said. "We're not quite done yet. Listen. I would probably never have known of your existence—I do have things to keep me busy—if it weren't for the special circumstances. Captain Jerrold Ronan is our head of Naval Intelligence. He personally ordered that the datafile of this, ah, Targovi be flagged. Therefore, when Targovi came back to Daedalus, the order to hold him for investigation was automatic. Ordinarily Captain Ronan's office would have disposed of the case as he saw fit. However, he has left with the Emperor, to handle similar duties during the campaign. Since the 'hold' order originated on such a high level, it was among those referred to me for review when I took charge here. Otherwise you'd doubtless have been released much sooner. As it was, nobody knew just what to do about you, and word took time to percolate up through channels, as frantic as the situation has been. I was struck by the report and decided to inquire further, personally. Something odd has been going on."

Diana's exuberance faded. "What? I'm as puzzled as you are. Oh, Targovi did drop hints about big game afoot, but nothin' definite."

"I know."

She flushed angrily. A narcoquiz was an undignified procedure, though they had had the decency to detail a couple of women officers to carry it out on her. "Be glad you turned out to know no more," Gatto said. "That would have called for a hypnoprobing, to extract everything. After all, we don't have the drugs or the equipment to process a Wodenite."

Diana gulped, mastered rage and anguish, became able to say: "Then you realize I'm aware Targovi was—*is* an undercover agent for Intelligence. Axor hasn't heard that, by the way. He'd only be sad about the, uh, duplicity. But why the flamin' hell did Targovi's own chief, uh, Ronan, want him checked out?"

"That is not in the database," Gatto replied. "Still, it seems obvious. Not everybody supports Emperor Olaf. Captain Ronan must have had reasons to suppose Targovi favored the Gerhart regime and was somehow in a position to make trouble. The fact that he eluded arrest and fled fairly well bears this idea out." He narrowed his eyes. "Your interrogation revealed that his action was not a complete surprise to you."

"Well, no Tigery ever took kindly to bein' caged. And I sympathize!"

"What is your attitude toward the succession crisis?"

Diana picked her words with care. "The quizzin' must've brought that up. But prob'ly not very clearly, because it's not very clear to me. Maybe Magnusson would do better by the Empire. I'm just a woods colt; I don't savvy politics." Her head and her voice lifted. "I *am* horrified at the prospect of civil war, and I'll be damned if I'll stand in a crowd shoutin' hooraw for anybody!"

Gatto smiled. "I like your outspokeness. Better curb it in public. . . . Well, you and Axor will be free to go as soon as I've issued the order. I'll also give you two a requisition on the first available passage back to Imhotep, though you may have to wait a while for that. Keep in touch with the provost's office, and you'll be notified."

She shook her head. "Thanks. But we came here to look for Foredweller remains, and I don't want to let Axor down."

"Ha, I suspect mainly you want an adventure. Have a care. Air traffic is strictly limited and controlled. Ground transportation is apt to be slow and precarious." His tone harshened. "If you are hoping to make contact with the renegade, out of some mistaken sense of loyalty to him, forget it. If it should happen, call the patrol immediately. Anything else will be treason, and punished accordingly."

Diana sighed. "I don't see how poor Targovi could manage that."

"No, the chances are that he is already dead. Else he would have been seen by now. I'm sorry, donna Crowfeather. I realize you were fond of him. Bear in mind how he hoodwinked and used you."

She made a faint noise and started to rise. "Well, I'll be on my way."

"No, wait. I feel a certain responsibility. You're a young and attractive lady, unused to cosmopolitan environments. And much of Daedalus is becoming unruly. With most Navy personnel off to fight for his Majesty, the patrols are stretched thin. We have to concentrate on guarding vital areas. You propose to take off for the yonderlands. I think that would be most unwise."

Diana settled back. "Why? Don't the folk support your glorious leader?"

Gatto frowned. "I'm thinking about ordinary civil disorder and crime. Any counterrevolutionary activity will be smashed, promptly and totally."

"You really have given him your heart, haven't you?" she asked low.

He reddened and ignited a fresh cigarette. "Donna, I am an officer of the Imperial Navy. As such, I follow the orders of my superiors. But my allegiance is to the Empire itself, to the civilization that is ours. I do sincerely believe Sir Olaf will provide the kind of government we've been sorely in need of."

"Whether it's worth the price, you aren't sayin'."

"It is not my business to express political opinions." Gatto made a chopping gesture. "Enough." He smiled. "What I want to talk about a few minutes longer is you. I am concerned. Targovi's ship and planetside vehicle are impounded. You and Axor will only be allowed to reclaim money and personal possessions from them. The inventory says that the cash isn't much. It can support the two of you for a while, but the Wodenite's food requirements are large, and any travel you undertake will soon exhaust the purse. Do give up your folly. I'll see to it that you both get safe, pleasant housing till you can return to Imhotep. And you might enjoy sightseeing with a, ah, a native guide, when I have some spare time."

"Thank you, sir. I've promises to keep, though. Don't worry about my safety, when I'm with Axor. Actually, he wouldn't swat a buzzbug, but people needn't know that, hm?"

Despite impatience to be off, she invested half an hour in being charming to the general.

Chapter 8

The faces of war are two.

First there is its face of technology, organization, strategy, tactics, and, yes, philosophy. This confronted Admiral Sir Olaf Magnusson, the man who would be Emperor, and the higher officers serving him.

His fleet was not all gathered at Patricius. While he had summoned more of it there than was usual, more yet was perforce based throughout the sector—working out of much smaller stations than Daedalus and Icarus held—or on sentry-go through its spacelanes. Some commanders of these units, he knew, would rally to him when they got the news. Others, left to their own devices, would not. He must make sure of as many as possible.

Hence his primary force moved ahead of any dispatches to them, in a complex path which took it within communication distance of most squadrons. Arriving, he would make his proclamation and issue his orders to join him. Since in each instance he had overwhelming firepower at his beck, and since he *was* the sector commandant, he met no resistance. A number of the captains he summarily replaced, for over the years he had taken care to gather dossiers; but these he merely sent to cool their heels, in no disgrace. After thinking matters over, quite likely a fair percentage of them would give him their pledges.

Inevitably, couriers and message torps slipped by, bringing their accounts before he did. About half the units receiving these stayed where they were, waiting for him, if only because their leaders were unsure what else to do. The rest started off to join Gerhart. Not every ship got that far. Some underwent mutinies and turned back to Magnusson. Many men, women, and nonhumans adulated him.

The second face of war is different for every individual. Consider Ensign Helen Kittredge. We pick her name at random out of personnel data. These say little more about her than that she was twenty Terran years of age, born and raised amidst the starknesses of the planet Vixen, winning appointment to the Foundry, doing well as a cadet, newly commissioned and assigned to energy weapons control aboard the light battleship *Zeta Sagitarii*. That ship was in the detachment of Captain Fatima bint Suleiman, operating out of an asteroid belt in the lifeless system of a nameless sun. Bint Suleiman was among those who voluntarily sought out Magnusson. We may assume that Kittredge was of high heart and cheered the move. Besides idealism, she must have remembered that promotions were bound to become rapid.

Except for Patricius and a few other key stars, Magnusson made no effort to leave his sector defended. Instead he took the initiative, spearing straight on into the inner Empire. One might suppose that this invited the opposition to cut his lines of supply and communication. Actually, interstellar space is too incomprehensibly vast. Traffic need just move by slightly circuitous routes, varied from trip to trip, to be safe from detection and interception by any except the wildest unlikelihood.

Nor did Magnusson keep his fleet together for long. Grown large, it was still smaller by a seemingly appalling factor than the might which the Imperium could have massed against him. Nevertheless he divided it in five. Four, under trusted admirals, swung north and south and clockwise and counterclockwise, essentially running interference for him. The main part, himself in charge, drove directly toward Sector Aldebaran. *Zeta Sagittarii* was along, trailing his flagship, the superdreadnaught *N. Aquilae*.

This likewise represented sound thinking. The fact was that the Imperium could not bring more than a fraction of its forces to bear. The rest must keep stations whatever happened, lest barbarians, bandits, and separate insurrections wreak such havoc that nothing would remain to rule over. There was also dread of what the Merseians might do. Furthermore, it is virtually impossible to compel battle in space. He who does not want to fight can run away. Beyond a light-year's distance, his hyperdrive vibrations are undetectable.

Hence Magnusson could apply great strength wherever he chose, at least in the outer sectors of the Empire. The regions around Sol, more populous and heavily guarded, he must avoid until he had organized sufficient power to invade them. He set about doing this.

It might appear he was overextending himself, and that if nothing else, the Gerhart faction could destroy him by attrition. He had reasons to expect that his advance would be too swift and decisive for that. However, he did go through the initial stages of his campaign in a straightforward manner.

Superficially, the procedure was simple. The five insurgent fleets went to planetary systems which were important because of location, population, industries, resources, or whatever the consideration might be. Each fleet swept aside any garrison vessels, which it always outnumbered and outgunned. Thereupon a world lay under threat of nuclear bombardment from on high. Even it it had ground defenses, the cost of using them looked prohibitive. Besides . . . well, did it matter that much who was Emperor? What had Gerhart done that beings, cities, continents should die for him? The martial law which Magnusson's people imposed scarcely touched civilians in their daily lives. They themselves promised glory and better times. Oftener than not, they were born on the planet in question, quietly recruited in advance.

Discipline was strict among the Olafists. Incorrect behavior brought punishment quick, condign, and public. This helped ingratiate them with local inhabitants. Moreover, they were apt to be young, friendly, eager, with stories to tell that put sparkle into dull provincial existences.

We can imagine Ensign Helen Kittredge on leave—let us say, on Ansa, which is like an idyll of Terra. Moonlight in a warm night shimmers across a lake; music sounds from a pavilion, but she and a young man of the planet have left its dance floor and wandered out along the water, under trees which breathe fragrance into the air. Earlier she lectured him earnestly on the new day that Emperor Olaf will bring, but now she has been swaying laughterful in his arms, and they sit down on soft turf, and perhaps she says yes, when the war is over she will take a long liberty here, but that time may be far off and meanwhile the night is theirs. . . .

Leaves were brief, because a fleet must go on to the next sun and the next. One may ask why the Gerhartists did not come in as soon as their foes had left and reclaim every conquest. The answer is multiplex. Such attempts would have been expensive, both to the Navy and to the worlds: for the Olafist detachments occupying them, though small, were busily enhancing defenses, and sure to fight while hope remained. Then too, the Imperium was in disarray, taken by surprise, its high command striving to make sense out of reports that came in late and garbled. Also, the idea was quite sensible that recapturing a few globes would be of scant use while Magnusson's wolf packs were on the prowl. Better to kill those first. Then the rebels left behind would have no choice but to surrender, especially if amnesty was offered their rank and file.

Therefore, slowly, often chaotically, the regular Navy marshalled what forces it could spare and went in search of combat.

The first major engagement occurred near a dim red dwarf star which had, then, merely a catalogue number, but which afterward was known to spacefarers as Battle Sun. Scoutcraft on both sides had been casting about, probing, peering, feeding into computers whatever scraps of data they could glean, dashing back to report. Gradually the pictures emerged, and the masters came to their decisions. They would fight.

Rear Admiral Richard Blenkiron, director of operations for Sector Aldebaran, personally led his armada. He was no coward. Terran-born, he was, besides, a man of considerable wit and charm. Unfortunately, he was not well suited to his position, being a political appointee serving out this assignment in preparation for something less martial and more lucrative. Nobody had foreseen war would reach these parts, as far inward as they lay.

Magnusson had anticipated that, and bypassed several occasions of combat. In two-dimensional terms, it can be said that he made an end run. If he could scatter the Aldebaranian fleet, hostiles at his back would hardly matter. They could be taken care of piecemeal. Meanwhile terror on Terra would be his ally. Therefore he too went looking for battle.

"Now hear this," intones the intercom system of *Zeta Sagitarii*. A recording of Sir Olaf's message to his crews follows. He expects that all will do their duty, and win a victory never to be forgotten. Surely Ensign Kittredge joins in the customary cheers. Thereafter, coolly above a hammering heart, she takes her station.

Since both leaders wanted to meet, they advertised themselves on the way, traveling in dispersed formation to maximize the sphere of detectability. Upon making contact, they deployed according to their respective plans. The gap closed rapidly.

Interstellar war bears no more resemblance to interplanetary than the latter does to planetside combat. Shuttling in and out of quantum multi-space at thousands or even millions of times a second, a ship under hyperdrive is essentially untouchable by an ordinary weapon. A concentrated energy beam or material barrage just might happen to intercept often enough to do significant damage, but the odds against that are huge, and in any event a warcraft has her protections, armor plate, absorbers, computer-controlled negafields to repel incoming matter. Only when the drives of two vessels are in phase do they become solid, vulnerable, to each other.

It is not extraordinarily difficult to match phase. There is a limited range of jump frequencies that are feasible to use, for any given type of ship; and they are not infinitely divisible, but quantized. Of course, a standard evasive tactic is to keep shifting the frequency. This requires the enemy to predict the next one. In that, high-speed stochastic analysis is valuable though not infallible.

Since the object is to harm the adversary, phase-change evasion is merely one maneuver among many. Indeed, not uncommonly, by eerie tacit consent, ships turn off their hyperdrives and slug it out in the relativistic mode, at speeds far below that of light.

When near enough, Blenkiron used quasi-instantaneous modulated hyperwaves to call Magnusson and demand surrender. The reply he got was polite and cold. The exchange had been a formality thoughout.

The fleets interpenetrated and began to fight. Rays and missiles flew. Nuclear detonations flowered in ghastly brief beauty. Where they connected, metal and flesh became incandescent gas. It whiffed away into space. Billions of years hence, some of it may minutely take part in the formation of new stars.

The old stars enclose everything in radiance. The Milky Way glows phantom-bright. Nebulae and sister galaxies glimmer mysterious. Glimpses go by, ships hurtling, graceful as dancers. None of this does Ensign Kittredge see. Her universe has shrunk to steel, meters, readouts, manual controls, brief commands from unseen lips. A reek of ozone is in the air. Once or twice the hull shudders to a distant burst.

N. Aquilae moved majestic at the center of Magnusson's command. Her planetoidal size, and the hundreds of live crewfolk as well as thousands of machines that this required, these were not basically for offensive purposes—although she did have the capability of laying waste a world. They were to provide such a host of defensive missiles, projectiles, rays, such a density of shielding fields, that the admiral and his staff would remain alive to make their assessments and give their orders.

Zeta Sagittarri was much less protected. She existed for the purpose of directly killing enemies.

The saying is ancient, that the first casualty of any battle is your own battle plan. Magnusson knew this and allowed for it. He had a general idea of what he hoped to do, but was flexible about it and permitted his captains broad discretion.

Blenkiron, on the other hand, could think of nothing but to hold his armada in standard configuration, as nearly as possible. That did maximize the mutual defense of his ships. When they had reduced the foe sufficiently, the formation was to open up, englobe the survivors, and deal death on them from every quarter. Such was the theory.

Magnusson had lured him to this exact place, and prepared it beforehand. Ships of his lay in orbit about Battle Sun, in normal state, dark, powerplants throttled down to life-support minimum—virtually undetectable. The fleet that flaunted itself looked inferior. Blenkiron's should have checked for hidden reserves, but found itself too busy; also, Battle Sun is surrounded by dust and gas, residue of a stillborn planetary system, which complicates surveyance. When Magnusson judged the moment ripe, he ordered the summons.

Abruptly his extra force went into hyperdrive—risky, that close to a stellar mass, but their engines were especially well tuned, so losses were light—and entered the fray. They did so from all directions, admittedly sparse but nonetheless pouring fire inward while Magnusson's main body drove straight through the opposed formation, loosing every demonic energy in its weapons.

Zeta Sagitarii has been part of this thrust. She takes a hit astern. It is, actually, a near miss, which does not vaporize her; but it wrecks the engine section and sends radiation and red-hot chunks of metal sleeting everywhere else. Or so we postulate. What we know is simply that she was lost.

Blenkiron panicked. He did not fall into gibbering idiocy, but he saw his fleet shattered and knew not what to do. The captain of the flagship, one Tetsuo Ogawa, became a hero by calmly "advising" him. By fits and starts, the Terrans broke off the engagement. For the most part they withdrew in good order. The majority escaped.

They were, however, in no condition to continue the fight. Magnusson had become free to lay his hand on all of Sector Aldebaran.

Zeta Sagitarii drifts off, sublight, a cold and twisted lump. In some intact compartments, capacitors maintain temperature and air renewal. It is not enough. Rescue craft, searching through the flotsam of battle, will not come within detection range of this hulk—as enormous as the least of reaches is between the stars—before their squadrons must proceed onward. Surviving crew will die of thirst, those who do not go in blood and vomit, of acute radiation poisoning.

We would like to imagine Ensign Kittredge is spared that. Suppose her turret split open under the blast. Exposed to the vacuum of space, she would lose consciousness within thirty seconds. A piece of metal shearing through her heart or her skull would be quicker still.

Admiral Sir Olaf Magnusson's victory became classic in the annals of warfare.

Chapter 9

Diana's visitor surprised her. She had met Cynthians before, as ubiquitous as their species was, but not often, and never this person. For a moment she and he exchanged appraising looks. It was a male, she saw. If he had been wearing much more than a pouch and his silky white fur, she could not have been sure; the secondary sexual characteristics were few. Bipedal, though with arms nearly as long as his legs, he stood about ninety centimeters tall. Toes and the six fingers on either hand were almost equally prehensile. A bushy tail lifted up behind the round head and its pointed ears. Blunt-muzzled and long-whiskered, the face sported a natural blue-gray mask around luminous emerald-hued eyes. His voice was high-pitched, its Anglic clear though apt to come trilling and hissing through the pointed teeth.

"You are milady Crowfeather?" he said. "Permit self-introduction. I hight Shan U of Lulach. Is your Wodenite companion present?"

"No," she replied. "I don't know when he'll be back. What can I do for you?"

"Perhaps it is I who can do you a favor,

milady. I have heard your partnership is in search of Ancient relics."

Diana decided this was understandable. She was merely one more human, but Axor inevitably generated gossip. "Well, yes. So far we've drawn blank. The public database screened nothin' for us that looked the least bit promisin'. He went off today to talk with the local priest of his church, in case the padre had heard of anything. I gather the parish takes in a big territory." She smiled wryly. "No doubt the two of them'll go on to every sort of theological shop talk."

"You cannot expect to find much information recorded about a planet when most of its land is wilderness that does not sustain colonists," declared Shan U. "Prospectors, timber cruisers, and other nonscientific explorers have scant incentive to go to the trouble of preparing scientific reports. The geographical separation of communities hinders the dissemination of locally available information." He arched his tail. "Ah, but it may be that I can put you in the way of some clues."

The heart sprang in Diana's breast. "You can? What? How?"

"Peace, I pray you. I am not, myself, qualified to be your guide. I am the captain of a riverboat. It will shortly be departing for Lulach. Now plying the great stream, year after year, one is bound to hear many a tale, and I recollect mentions, now and then, of impressive ruins glimpsed. Rumors about you and, especially, your companion having trickled as far as the waterfront, I thought I should come urge you to seek farther for informants."

"Oh? Where?"

"Why, along the river itself. Lulach alone holds many a merchant who has traveled widely over this planet, many a searcher for natural wealth who has adventured deep into the wildernesses. And beyond Lulach—Well, at any rate, I can convey you that far, and back again afterward if you discover zero there and decide not to range more widely. Would you like to inspect my vessel?"

"Where is it?"

"In the valley, at Paz de la Frontera, the head of navigation."

Diana's consideration was brief. If nothing else, she was sick of the cheap hotel where she and Axor had taken lodgings. At first she had enjoyed wandering around Aurea, seeing what there was to see and, as opportunity offered, asking about inexplicable structures. Now she had used those activities up, and had been sitting boredly in her room watching a teleplay. The latter end of this past couple of weeks had become wearisome.

In fact, she had begun regretting her refusal of Gatto's offer. Her immediate reason for that had been the fact that here she and Axor were on Daedalus; once they left it, they would probably not be able to return for a long time, if ever. Why not stay and investigate as originally planned? She was confident that the commandant would still be willing to arrange berths, if Daedalus turned out to be a blind alley—though while she waited for a ship, she might have trouble fending him off. The past several days had almost brought her to the point of thus swallowing her pride and making her appeal. What a waste of time, when there was that unfinished expedition on Imhotep to start all over again!

Her second reason for staying had, as Gatto guessed, been the desire, against every reasonable hope, to learn what had become of Targovi. As the initial exuberance of freedom damped down, she had more and more felt anger and grief on his behalf gnaw at her. Here was a chance to forget them for a while, and maybe even accomplish something.

"Sure," she caroled. "Just a minute."

Having recorded a message for Axor, she skinned out of her clothes and into brief shorts and skimpy blouse. The lowlands were hot in summer. To her belt she attached purse and knife. She kicked her bare feet into sandals. "Let's go, Joe."

Air traffic was under pettifogging emergency restrictions, but a train system, built in pioneer days, still ran, and a station lay near the hotel. As the car they had boarded whirred up off the ground and started downhill above the guide cable, Diana and Shan U settled into a seat. She took the window side and kept her gaze outward, upon the landscape. Unoffended, he stuffed a pipe with dried leaves that smelled like warm saddle leather when he lit them, and conversed.

"The Highroad River has always been a main artery of travel," he said in answer to a remark of hers. "It should become still more so in the present situation. Roads between the settlements along it range from wretched to nonexistent, and as for flight, why, now the very omnibuses are subject to endless, arbitrary inspections, delays, and other such nuisances. Boats remain free of this. Should you find that you do wish to go to Lulach, my *Waterblossom* is no speedster, I grant you, but the fare is modest, accommodations are comfortable, food is good, and the leisured pace will enable you to learn much about our planet en route—which is highly advisable if you would strike into its outback. You will also find yourselves in entertaining company. This trip it includes a live, traveling show."

"What?" asked Diana absently. She was watching the mountains fall away in ridges and steeps that became jungled hills. Clouds loomed ahead, brooding rain; lightning flickered in their depths. The wind of its speed shrilled faintly into the ancient car.

"Another Cynthian, albeit from Catawrayannis rather than the mother world. She brought her tricks, together with a performing beast, to earn her keep while she toured Daedalus, as she had been doing elsewhere. Such restless individuals are frequent in my race."

Wistfulness tugged at Diana. Maybe she could work up an act of her own and take it to the stars?

"Then, abruptly, space traffic, which had been well-nigh unrestricted, was well-nigh banned in and out of Daedalus," Shan U continued. "Poor Wo Lia found herself marooned in Aurea, while events held folk cemented to the newscasts, who might otherwise have come to see her performance. For a while she tried, but was near despair when I chanced to enter Ju Shao's inn, where she was staying."

Diana's attention revived. Ju Shao—hadn't she heard that name before? From Targovi? Memory was vague. "What's that?"

"*O-ai*, a place in the slum quarter, with a miscellaneous clientele, since it is both cheap and tolerant. I suggested to Wo Lia that she invest what remained of her funds in passage with me. People at our ports of call will doubtless be glad to see her show, and in Lulach, amidst her own species, she can find work of some kind to tide her over."

Diana hoped the skipper was not merely a glib salesbeing. Well, she'd inquire among his crew, and if the word was good—a riverboat trip should be all kinds of fun.

The train terminated at Central Station in Paz de la Frontera. That was some distance from the river. Diana started walking, under the guidance of Shan U, who skipped along with the gait of an arboreal. Meanwhile she looked around in wonderment.

The air was a steam bath, full of odors rank, smoky, sweet, indescribable. An overcast hung low, but as yet the rain was only an occasional heavy, spattering drop. For a space she threaded through a crowd between drab walls, but then suddenly she was out in the open. Bushes and thorny trees grew well apart across dusty ground. At a distance she spied farmland, food animals grazing on Terran grasses, grainfields a-ripple under a sullen wind. Closer at hand, on every side, were the clusters of habitation. Each group of houses, shops, public buildings had its distinctive style—here façades square and featureless, surrounding hidden courtyards; there domes and spires; yonder broad expanses of vitryl in metal frames; and on and on. None amounted to more than a few score units, most were less. Spaces between them varied from a roadway to some two hundred meters, but were always clearly that: boundaries, buffers. Traffic was sparse, mainly closed-up groundcars whose riders gave pedestrians wary glances. Children romped outside the settlements, always in distinct clutches. A band of men, in everyday subtropical garb but distinguished by scarlet brassards, tramped around a wooden stockade. Though they bore no firearms, simply knives and staves, they were plainly a kind of militia.

"Events, the upheaval, the uncertainty of everything, have made Paz tense," Shan U observed. "Riots have happened. I will be glad to depart."

Diana nodded. She knew the history of the area, in outline. It had been founded in early Imperial times as a colony of veterans who wished to stay on Daedalus with their families after discharge. Each household received help in establishing itself, especially in converting its grant of land to agricultural usefulness. The practice had continued to this day.

The trouble was, and worsened decade by decade, that the Empire recruited its defenders from an ever more motley set of human societies on Terra's daughter and granddaughter planets. Like tended to settle down with like, and not to get along very well with unlike. The situation might have been happier, given more openings to the outside; but Daedalus, afar in a frontier region, was relatively isolated. Rivalries festered. Nonhumans had long since abandoned any thought of living in Paz.

She remembered her mother quoting a quip of her father's: "The Terran Empire is a huge melting pot. However, what appears to be melting is the pot."

After passing through a couple of hamlets where life seemed to go on about as usual, the road entered one whose walls were mortared stone underneath tile roofs. Nobody else was in sight. Doors stood barred, windows curtained or shuttered. Silence closed in, save for muttering thunder and the *spat* of raindrops on pavement. Shan U glanced around uneasily. "Best we make haste," he counselled. "This section has suffered an outbreak of lawlessness, and peaceable people have withdrawn till the Navy can send a patrol."

Four men came out of a lane and deployed across the way. They were dirty, unkempt, sour-smelling; beard stubble showed that two had not used any inhibitor for some time. One kept a pistol tucked under his belt, one flourished a club, one carried a knife, while a bola danced in the hands of the fourth.

"Well, well," said the first. "Well, well, *well*. Just stop where you are, if you please."

Shan U crouched, mewed, bottled his tail.

Chill crawled along Diana's spine. "What do you want?" she demanded.

"Oh, nothing bad, nothing bad." They slouched and sidled forward. "Welcome to our fair com-mu-nity, little lady. How'd you like a good time?"

"Kindly let us by."

"Now, now, don't be in such a rush." The pistoleer stroked the butt of his weapon. His free thumb he jerked at the bola man, who grinned and sent a ball whistling through the air. "Easy, take it easy. Just a friendly warning. You make a rush to get away, and Chelo here, why, Chelo hasn't had any live target to practice on for days. That thing could break your ankle, lady. All we want to do is show you a real good time, and maybe have a little fun with the monkey-cat. Come along, now."

Diana lunged. Her knife flew forth. It was Tigery steel, the back heavy and rasp-surfaced, the edge sharp enough to cut a floating hair. Suddenly the shirtfront of the pistoleer gushed red. He howled. She pushed him against the clubber. They fell together. She stepped on the Adam's apple of the clubber, and heard it crack, in the course of attacking the knifeman. He slashed at her not unskillfully, but she parried, gave him the rasp across his face, and opened his fighting arm on the inside from elbow to wrist, after which he lost interest in anything but trying to stanch the blood. At this range the bola artist could not exercise his craft well. She severed the cord of a ball that snapped toward her, swayed back out of the way of the rest, and chased him several meters before letting him escape.

"C'mon," she said through the ululations at her feet, "let's get out of here 'fore the cops arrive."

"Hee-yao!" gasped Shan U as they made off. "I thought I knew about handling trouble, but you—"

"Oh, I don't go lookin' for fights," Diana said. "In fact, I hate them. I'd've tried to talk or bluff us past those klongs peacefully. But they weren't listenin'. Well, I grew up amongst Tigeries on Imhotep, and when they see danger clear before them, they don't shilly-shally."

Targovi, I learned from you. Pain smote her. *What has your fate been, dear brotherlin'?*

"Do you think the, the casualties will live?"

"I didn't try to do anything fatal, but there wasn't time for finickin', was there? Does it matter?"

Beneath the coolness she felt a dull but strengthening shock. She hadn't done anything like this before—not really—though Targovi had put her through lots of practice; and she had been around when a couple of Tigery brawls got bloody; and she had, herself, perforce been physically pretty emphatic three or four times when human males got the wrong idea and couldn't be persuaded out of it otherwise. *I'll prob'ly have the shakes for a while, once the adrenalin wears off. But not for long, I hope. I mustn't let what I've been through, what I've seen, prey on my mind. Nothin' was done here except justice. The war, now, the war is different, people killin' people they've got no grudge against and have never even met. Though some wars in history have been the lesser evil, haven't they?*

I don't know, she thought in rising weariness. *I simply don't know. How good it'll be, floatin' quietly down the river with Axor, if that works out.*

She lost track of time and was a bit startled when they came to the waterfront. Warehouses bulked behind wharfs where a medley of craft lay tied and a hodgepodge of persons, human and nonhuman, bustled about. Machines scurried among them. Beyond, the stream flowed broad and brown. The opposite shore was dimmed by a thickening rain. Shan U registered a feline dislike of the wet, but Diana welcomed its warm sluicing. She felt cleansed.

They reached *Waterblossom*. The riverboat was easily a hundred meters long, though so wide that that was not immediately evident. Four loading towers and a couple of three-tiered deckhouses did not much clutter her. The low freeboard was garishly painted in stripes of red and gold; the topworks were white, brass-trimmed. Her captain had said she was made of Terran and Cynthian woods, which Daedalan organisms did not attack, and driven by an electric engine. Should he be unable to recharge its capacitors otherwise, he carried a steam generator which could burn nearly anything.

Half a dozen Cynthians and two humans were on deck, cheerily helping wheel a cage toward shelter from the rain. "*Ay-ah,* behold

Wo Lia, the performer." Shan U pointed. "Come aboard and meet her. We can all have a nice cup of alefruit cider."

Diana frowned. She hated the idea of confining any creature. Still, yon beast didn't seem mistreated. More or less mansize, it hunkered on four limbs, black-furred, its head obscured by a heavy mane. She spied a short tail, and the forepaws had an odd, doubled-up look about them. Well, who could possibly know all the life forms, all the wonders of every kind, that filled the Imperial planets, let alone the galaxy and the universe? To fare forth—!

Shan U led her over the gangplank. She passed near the cage.

"Hs-s-s, little friend," went a whisper. Coming from low in the lungs, it sounded like an animal noise to anybody who did not know the Toborko language. "Stay calm. We will talk later. Make sure you and your camarado take passage on this boat."

Barely, Diana reined herself in. The humans doubtless noticed how she tensed before relaxing, but could put that down to the exotic surroundings. The Cynthians doubtless paid no heed to her shifts in stance or expression.

She forced herself to look afar, out again across the river. Underneath tangled strands of mane, the face in the cage was Targovi's.

Chapter 10

Waterblossom set forth after the thunderstorm that had been brewing reached explosion point and then spent itself. Sweeping the length of the valley with that swiftness and violence which the rapid rotation of the planet engendered, it turned the air altogether clear. From her place in the bows, Diana looked westward across a thousand kilometers or more.

This was the first tranquil moment she had had in hours. The time had been frantic during which she made her way back to Aurea, located Axor, persuaded him—not easily, because her arguments were thin at best, and her excitement didn't reinforce them—to come along, got their baggage packed, returned through lightning-vivid cataracts of rain, settled into her tiny stateroom and improvised accommodations for the Wodenite down in the hold with the freight. Dinner had been served while the weather slacked off. Now the crew had cast loose and the boat was on her way.

Diana couldn't hear the engine, but its purr went as a subliminal quiver through her bare feet, and she did catch a faint gurgle from aft, the turbo drive at work. Speed was low, as ponderous and heavily laden as the hull was. At first traffic teemed, everything from rowboats to hydrofoils, but as Paz fell behind, the river rolled open, a brown stretch two kilometers wide from bank to forested bank, rippling around snags and sandbars, only a couple of barges and a timber raft under tow in the distance ahead. Quiet descended, and a measure of coolness. Flying creatures darted and skimmed, light amber on their wings.

Never before had Diana seen so far over the horizonless world. Ahead of her, the river and its valley went *on*. As that view grew ever more remote, they dwindled, shrank together, became at last a shining thread between burnished green darknesses; yet still she could see them. Whenever an opening appeared in the woods brooding on either side of her, she likewise looked across immensity. Left, the green lightened as forest gave way to prairie that eventually blurred off in haziness. Right, beyond foothills, she glimpsed toylike snowpeaks, the mountain range that warded off the glaciers of the Daedalan ice age.

The sinking sun kindled a sudden gleam far and far ahead. Why, that must be the ocean! Diana's pulse quickened. Vapors made the disc golden-red, softened its glare till she could gaze directly. It spread itself out until it was a great step pyramid—and out and out, stretching to become arcs of luminance curving north and south around what would have been worldedge on another planet.

There was no real night. Day slowly turned into a glimmering dusk, shadowless, starless apart from brilliant Imhotep and a few scattered points high overhead. She could easily have read by the light, though the range of vision contracted until everything beyond three or four kilometers—except Paz and Aurea behind her, a couple of villages before her, aglow—faded vaguely into dimness. Gradually sunshine became a complete ring. It was broadest and brightest in the direction of Patricius, a little wider than the disc by day. There it shone orange in hue, with a muted fierceness of white underneath. It narrowed and reddened as it swept away, until when it had closed itself opposite—some while after it had begun to form—it was a fiery streak. The sky near the ring went from pale blue sunside to purple darkside, shading toward violet at the zenith; below, the ring enclosed a darkness which was the planetary bulk.

Presently the moon Icarus rose in a confusion of silver which coalesced to a half shield as it climbed.

The forests ashore were full of shadow, but the river sheened like mercury on its murmurous course.

Diana did not reckon up how long she stood rapt, watching the hours unfold. When the deck shivered beneath hoofs, and a bone-deep basso rumbled forth, she came back to herself with a shock like falling off a cliff.

"Ah, a beautiful, incredible sight indeed," said Axor. "What an artist the Creator is. This experience might almost justify our making the journey we are on."

Misgiving pierced Diana. "Almost?"

"Why, I fear ours is a bootless expedition. I have been in the saloon, speaking with person after person, crew and passengers, including the two humans. None can attest to any objects that might be Foredweller remains. One did bespeak large ruins under the northern mountains, but another, who had actually been there, said they are remnants of a Terran mining operation, abandoned centuries ago when the ore gave out." A sigh boomed. "We should have stayed on Imhotep and completed our investigation as planned. Now we are confined on Daedalus for an indefinite time and . . . I am no longer young."

Guilt took her, however lightly, by the throat. "I'm sorry."

Axor lifted a hand. "Oh, no, no, dear friend. I do not blame you in the least. You urged upon me what seemed best to you in your—your impetuosity. Nor do I pity myself. That is the most despicable of emotions. I should not have let you rush me into taking this passage. My mistake, not yours. And we are seeing wonders along the way."

Diana braced herself. "We may even find what you're after," she said, as stoutly as possible. "These are just regular river travelers aboard with us, and, uh, one outworlder. In Lulach we'll find people who get around more on this planet." She hesitated. "A Zacharian, maybe. That island is mysterious. You've talked to me about how the Ancient relics on

Aeneas have influenced the whole culture of the settlers. Could something like that be on Zacharia?"

"Well, we may hope." A bit of cheer lifted in Axor's tones. " 'And now abideth faith, hope, and charity, these three; but the greatest of these is charity,' " he quoted. "Yet hope is no mean member of the triad."

Again she hated what she was doing to him, and wondered whether the need could ever justify it. She knew so little thus far. She had in fact, she realized, acted on faith—faith in Targovi—with hope for adventure and accomplishment, but damn small charity.

She squared her shoulders. Maybe some Daedalan place really did hold something for her old pilgrim.

Axor stretched luxuriously, an alarming sight if you didn't know him. "I thinking, before going to bed, I would like a swim," he said. "Do you care to come along? I can easily catch up with the boat when we are finished, and carry you with me."

For a moment Diana was tempted. To frolic in yonder mightily sliding current—But she had no bathing suit, and didn't want to risk the men aboard seeing her nude. They appeared decent enough, in a rough-hewn fashion. However, after the incident in Paz, she'd rather not give anybody the wrong impression.

More important, she suddenly and sharply realized, here was her chance to talk to Targovi. "No, thanks," she said in a haste that drew a quizzical glance. "I'm tired and, uh, I want to watch this spectacle more. Go ahead. Have fun."

The Wodenite undulated over the rail. It was astonishing how gracefully he could move when he chose. He entered the water with scarcely a splash. Suffused light shimmered off his scales and spinal sierra. His tail drove him cleanly away.

Diana glanced aft. A Cynthian lookout perched atop the bridge, within which the pilot was occupied. Neither was paying her any attention, nor would they overhear low-voiced conversation. Everybody else had gone below; most of them were used to the magical ring, as she was not. She pattered over the planks.

Behind the after deckhouse, an awning had been stretched to shelter the cage which held Wo Lia's performing beast. It cast a degree of darkness over Targovi. She saw him as a shadowy figure rhythmically astir—exercises, to keep in condition while imprisoned. She hunkered down.

His catlike eyes knew her instantly. "Aaah, s-s-s, at last," he breathed, and crouched to face her. "How goes it, sprite?"

"Oh, I'm all right, but awful puzzled, and poor Axor's terribly discouraged," she blurted. "What's goin' on, anyway?"

He changed his language to Toborko, in a monotone which lost many nuances of that most musical tongue, but which would seem to a casual passerby as if the animal were crooning some weird song while the human, curious, listened.

"Well deserve you what explanation I can

give, O valiant child, the more so when I shall belike call upon you to render services and take hazards such as neither of us can foresee. Vast are the stakes in this game, but the rules poorly known and capriciously changeable.

"You understand I have not been entirely a huckster but also an agent covert of Imperial Intelligence. My part was mainly to pass on to my superiors whatever I came across that seemed of possible interest, on this world near the Merseian marches and visited by beings of countless kinds. Yet did I help uncover one espionage undertaking, and found leads to others.

"Nevertheless, when I scented something truly enormous upon the wind, not only did my warnings go unheeded, I was forbidden to utter them or to continue in my search. More of that later, when we can talk freely and at length. Enough tonight that I have cause to believe Magnusson's revolt is not simply another uprising of angry men against bad masters. And from Zacharia the forbidden come breaths of still more strangeness than erstwhile.

"Aye, in Axor I saw a movable blind for myself. Attention will be upon him, but unlikely ever a suspicion. He can go in his harmlessness where most folk are banned, and I, I can perchance skulk behind. You, Diana Crowfeather, walk betwixt and between. What part you may play is, as yet, hidden in dawn-mists. I think you will play it well. You know my Tigery nature—sorry would I be to lose you, but sorry am I not for putting you at risk. Nor do I suppose you are ireful. You stand to win glory, with all that that may bring in its train. However this may be, clear was that only through you could I recruit unwitting Axor.

"Ill was our luck, that the rebellion erupted just as we were approaching Daedalus. Else we could have landed and gone our ways, disappearing into the hinterlands by virtue of nobody thinking to keep watch over us. As was, knowing what standard procedures are, I foresaw that my reappearance at the time of crisis would automatically provoke precautionary detention if naught else. Whereupon the gigantic plot I have smelled would roll unhindered onward.

"Accordingly, I escaped. It seemed likely that you and Axor would be released after interrogation, for you did in fact know nothing. The question was how to keep myself free when the hue and cry was out for me, and how to rejoin you afterward.

"Therefore did I hide until after I felt sure the patrol would have visited Ju Shao's inn in Lowtown, and then sought it. She and I are friends of old, and I have in the past done her some favors when, hm, the Imperial authorities grew overly officious. You understand that an Intelligence agent has need of such connections. She tucked me away, kept me fed, and meanwhile conducted discreet inquiries.

"These soon turned up Wo Lia. She is actually an adventurer among the stars—aye, from Catawrayannis, albeit a return to her birthworld would be inadvisable—mainly a gambler, but not above occasional racketeering.

The ship whereon she arrived had departed again; the interdict on civilian space travel left her stranded; uproar, and preoccupation with public events, gave her scant opportunity in Aurea. Hence she proved quite willing to take the role of intinerant showperson. In Lulach she can establish herself, one way or another, until the Empire calms down, one way or another. Ju Shao helped me disguise myself, and Wo Lia persuaded our good captain that, if he sought you out, he could belike sell a couple of tickets.

"Thus are we bound off. Needs must I remain in confinement till we reach Lulach. There will I slip free, and folk will feel sympathy for Wo Lia, whose performer escaped and may well starve to death in an inedible jungle. As for me, I have . . . business in Lulach."

"Can you trust her?" Diana whispered. "She might turn you in for the reward. I s'pose there is one."

"She, like Ju Shao, expects reward far more substantial, should our cause triumph. Why not? Funds ought to be abundantly available then, together with openings to the stars."

"But what *is* our cause? If you're on the side of Emperor Gerhart—why? To head off a civil war? But you can't; it's already begun. Mightn't Olaf Magnusson be the better man anyway? And what can we possibly do, stuck here on Daedalus, that'd make the slightest difference?"

She had, unthinkingly, used Anglic. "S-s-s-s!" Targovi warned. "Abide your time. Later we will talk." He settled back into a beast posture, as if falling asleep.

Diana sensed another presence. Turning her head, she saw that a human male had come on deck and was approaching. "Ah, hi," he called. "I thought I'd find you enjoying the view and the fresh air. But what's so interesting about the livestock?"

She rose and walked out from beneath the awning. "Oh, it's a kind new to me," she answered. "I don't know what planet it's from. Do you?"

"No. Wo Lia was evasive when I asked. Maybe export of that kind is illegal." The man beamed. He was young and rather good-looking. "Uh, care for a stroll around the deck? Such a lovely night. I'm still wide awake."

"Well, I am too, sort of." Diana joined him.

They paced. "We should get better acquainted," he said. "We'll be on this boat for a fairish while. I can show you around our ports of call, if you want, and Lulach when we get there. My pleasure."

She smiled. "Why, thank you." A flirtation should be fun, if she took care to keep it within limits. Besides, she might learn something useful.

Chapter 11

A dozen light-years off, the twin blue giant suns that were Alpha Crucis dominated heaven. Even as images in a viewscreen they left burning after-images, and it would have been dangerous to let an unprotected eye dwell upon them.

The immediate danger, though, was closer at hand, where the Merseian task force clashed with a Terran flotilla that had been unfortunate enough to intercept it. *Cyntath* Gadrol of the Vach Ynvory, called Cannonshield, commanding from the dreadnaught *Ardwyr*, had sprung his trap and set to work inflicting maximum destruction before the outnumbered Imperials should break off and flee. Where missiles burst, new stars bloomed in dreadful brief beauty. Where a rosy cloud swelled from one of them, rapidly fading away into blackness, a ship and her crew had died. The battle raged through a volume trillions of kilometers across.

Yet it was principally a holding action, cover for the squadron that slipped free and made for the real destination at utmost pseudovelocity. *Qanryf* Bryadan Arrowswift, Vach Hallen, watched a yellow light-point swell hour by hour, until at the end of five it outshone Alpha Crucis and magnification revealed its disc. Despite his nickname, well-earned at home, Bryadan could stay quiet like that for a span like that: for he was on a hunt. Faint but marrow-thrilling, the energies driving the cruiser *Tryntaf* pulsed through him. Air from the ventilators, cold because his home was on an arctic shore of the Wilwidh Ocean, bore a likewise half-sensed exhilaration in reeks of ozone and oil. Telltales flashed, meters quivered, displays danced through his cave of control machines. Their operators poised alert, speaking only when needful but then softly singing the words, as if in dreams of the triumph to come.

When his ship and her companions pierced the comet cloud, Bryadan tapped an intercom button. The face that sprang into the small screen was youthful, handsome, the green of the complexion slightly yellow because of partial Lafdiguan ancestry. It was also startled. "Foreseer!" exclaimed *Afal* Uroch of the Vach Rueth. He slapped hand to breast and tail to boots in salute. "At the captain's orders."

"In the name of his Supremacy the Roidhun," Bryadan responded with equal formality. "Are you prepared?"

"Yes, foreseer. The crew are ready and eager. Does the *qanryf* have some new word for us?"

"Yea and nay." Bryadan leaned forward. "I want to lay stress upon certain details in your orders. Yours will be the most precarious part of this entire operation. If you carry it off well, it will be the very heartspring."

Uroch dared grin. "*Khraich*, they don't call me 'the Lucky' for nothing."

"With due heed to your honor," said Bryadan carefully, "I remind you that young, ambitious officers are apt to confuse courage and rashness. Your record of exploits has caused you to be chosen for your present assignment. Yet those same deeds required more dash than wisdom. Not that your judgment was ever unsound—in the particular circumstances you encountered. These will be different. We are to wield the surgeon's knife rather than the sword. In your case, it is especially important to uphold the distinction. Exactly what will happen, only the God knows. You may find yourself taken by surprise, in desperate straits, and tempted to unleash your entire firepower—since you are responsible for your crews, and thus for their wives and children. Or else you may see the enemy wide open to total destruction. In either instance, *afal*, you will resist the lure. Die if you must, together with those who have trusted you; or retreat unsuccessful if you must, taking years to live down the scorn of brother officers to whom you are forbidden to explain; but confine yourself to the precise goal given you."

A slight change of color and posture, a barely visible twitch of lips away from teeth, were all that Uroch revealed. "Yes, foreseer."

Bryadan made the gesture of affection, rare from a senior to a junior, and softened his tone. "I repeat, *afal*, my regard for your honor is of the highest. And so is my regard for your intelligence. Would I otherwise have approved you for this task? The God willing, and I believe He is, you will return with glory upon you. True, we cannot proclaim it in the universe—not yet—but your peers will know, and perhaps even your Roidhun."

Hurt in the face turned to stiffly controlled joy.

"I have this to add, and it is my real reason for addressing you now," Bryadan went on. "Before we lost contact with the main force, *Cyntath* Gadrol issued an announcement. Scoutships have reported Terran reinforcements approaching, but at such low strength that he can hold them, too, in play. We will have days, if necessary, to complete our task here, before the opposition can bring up sufficient power that we must withdraw. Therefore, *afal*, take your time. Explore the options before you choose. Remember that, useful though it be, our undertaking is only a fractional part of the great unrevealed plan by which our superiors direct us. The destiny of the Race reaches ahead through millionfold years. Good hunting, *afal*."

"And to you, foreseer," Uroch answered. As the screen blanked, exultation blazed from him.

The Merseians ran on hyperdrive as deeply into the gravity well of the Gorrazani sun as they dared. When they reverted to relativistic state, they assumed intrinsic velocities carefully arranged beforehand, aimed at the habitable planet of the system. They crossed the gap in less than three hours, under decelerations that would have made molecular films of living tissue if interior forcefields had not compensated.

The Gorrazanian home fleet got no chance to muster. Such units as were in orbit near the planet deployed and put up a gallant defense. Bryadan's command smashed it. Squadrons began to arrive from farther away. He broke them in detail. Meanwhile his broadcasters trampled local transmissions underfoot as they blared in the principal languages of the region:

"All folk heed, we wish you no harm. We are here expressly at the request of your rightful chieftains, the Liberation Council which wills an end to centuries of oppression. His Supremacy the Roidhun recognizes the Liberation Council as the legitimate government of the Gorrazanian Realm. Even so, we of Merseia have no desire to intervene in your affairs. Consider simply how remote our dominions are. It is the sheerest altruism for us to cross such stretches of space, under peril of attack by the aggressors of Imperial Terra, in answer to an appeal—not to give military aid, no, not for any warlike purpose, but to convey hospital supplies to the valiant armies of your Liberation Council. If we come armed, it is for self-defense. If we fight, it is because we were set upon, without the least provocation on our part. Note that we do not pursue the fleeing units of the lawless and discredited Folkmoot regime—"

Uroch wasn't listening. It was enough for him that the leaders of the Race had, in their wisdom, decreed certain actions be carried out here, and that a certain amount of blat must accompany the doing. Besides, he was busy.

As *Tryntaf* whipped in hyperbola close by the globe, his escadrille shot from her launch ports. It numbered a score, Fangryf-type gunboats, about midway between the Terran Comet and Conqueror classes—six-male craft, lean and deadly, equally at home in atmosphere and interplanetary space. They hit air at speeds that sent shudders through their hulls, made red flames around them, and left thunders trailing behind that rolled from horizon to horizon.

Braking, at the pilot console of his own vessel, Uroch saw land and sea sweep away beneath him: wrinkled mountains, multitudinously verdant plains, shining waters. Such buildings as he spied in magnifying screens were mostly low, rounded, widespread; few towers speared aloft, as they pridefully did on Merseia or Terra. It was in the nature of this species to expand underground—"in the bosom of the Mother," they often said. Despite scanty landmarks, he knew where he was going. He had been through exhaustive briefings.

What he did not know was what he would encounter along the way—Haa, yes, he did now! Warcraft flocked over the curve of the world to meet him.

"Evasive action," he said coolly into the

outercom. "Close formation. Do not fire on them until ordered. Concentrate on defending yourselves." Underneath, his heart thuttered.

The Merseian group screamed about and headed northwest, at a mere kilometer of altitude. The Gorrazanians took a while to straighten out their formations and give chase. Bullets, missiles, energy beams raked ahead of them. The Merseian gunners, superbly computer-guided, shot down most of the material projectiles. Those that got through, and the rays, generally missed; those that struck, forcefields and armor generally absorbed. A member of the escadrille, flying rear guard, did fall—flash of light, tail of smoke, shattering burst on the ground. Uroch raised hand in homage. They would be remembered, yon brave males, if their comrades lived.

The sun dropped behind him. He flew through night, under stars and a small, hurtling moon. Occasional flickers aloft told of the battle in space. Metal throbbed around him. He heard the shrilling of cloven air. Information from orbit registered on his data displays: another opposition force was bound his way from the east.

But ahead, sheer, its heights coldly agleam with snow and glaciers, loomed a mountain range. Its contours were engraved on Uroch's brain well-nigh as fully as they were in his computer programs. This was why he had studied the planet unmercifully hard, the long way from Merseia: so that he could develop his contingency plans. The move that he found himself making was altogether in his style;

and he had hand-picked his follower pilots and made them learn nearly as much as he knew.

In a wild swoop, he lifted. Crags clawed after the belly of his craft. Ahead was a pass between two peaks, and on the far side an immense, many-branched canyon. Flesh could never have steered through, at the speeds wherewith he and his traveled. Robots could, barely. His living brain told them to do it.

Cliffs reared out of abyssal darknesses. Sonic shocks broke snowfields apart and sent them away in avalanches; clouds and plumes rose off them to glisten beneath the moon. Their rumbling drummed through the howl of outraged air.

No few of the Gorrazanian flyers were taken by such surprise that they crashed before they could pull clear. Shards and skulls went skittering down the heights. The rest of the defenders buzzed about in dismay. They had lost contact with the enemy.

As he emerged above a wintry lowland, Uroch fought temptation. He could bring his escadrille quickly around and take the pursuit from behind, catch them in their bewilderment, shatter and scatter a force that outnumbered his three or four to one. What a deed! They'd sing about it in ships and halls throughout the Roidhunate, for centuries to come.

He remembered his captain's words, set his jaw, and flew straight onward. The directive had been clear from the beginning. *"Except for the objective, you will inflict minimal damage.*

Wherever consonant with that objective and with maximum survival in your force, you will choose evasion over confrontation. If it appears that a major action is necessary to accomplishment of the purpose, you will withdraw as expeditiously as possible to your mother vessel, or to whatever other transport is most suitable."

Never had he been under orders more difficult to follow. He began to realize what it meant to be in the high command. Perhaps, flickered through him, that was another reason he had been chosen for this undertaking. Could they have him in mind for greater things? . . . *Dismiss that. Carry on your hunt.*

Inevitably, he had broad discretion. After a quick review of the data, he made his next decision and issued his instructions. The Merseians lifted spaceward.

He saw the planet in sapphire and silver splendor, the sun rising in dawn-hues over its brow; but his attention was aimed along a radius vector ahead, where two warships maneuvered about and lobbed lightnings at each other. However tenuous, the ionized gas that lingered for seconds after a nuclear detonation sufficed to hide his group from detection, when they orbited free-fall as he told them to. Thus he shook off the second ground-based flotilla that had been trying to intercept him.

The orbit soon bent his flyers back into atmosphere. With judicious nudges of thrust, they sought a hurricane which was traversing a southern ocean, and hid themselves in its violence. That required daring as well as skill;

but people had reason to call Uroch "the Lucky."

As that luck would have it, the storm lumbered to the very shore he wanted. Otherwise he would have tried something else, maybe for several days. In the event, he could shout, "Haa-aa and away!" His warriors burst from the clouds and winds. They went like shooting stars above sere hills and a broad, green, canal-veined valley.

It was not well defended. The Gorrazanians had relied mainly on their space fleet. What planetary units they had were dispersed around the globe; a substantial portion was still at the antipodes, trying to find Uroch's raiders. Missiles and aircraft lifted in low numbers. The Merseians swatted them and came to rest, a-hover on their grav drives, above the target.

Aside from communication and detector masts, and a tower for local weather control, it revealed nothing special to the eye. Some domes snuggled into a landscape ruddy with ripening grain. Three sleepy villages clustered within a few kilometers: archaic earthen buildings, for the Gorrazanians are a conservative breed, no matter how many mercenary soldiers they export. A large modern structure, squarish and garish as their tastes called for, might have been a school or a museum or something of that kind.

Uroch didn't know. He had not even heard, officially, what it was that he was supposed to destroy. In the course of his studies en route he had deduced that it was probably a key command center—police, military, however you wanted to designate a corps trying to suppress revolutionary guerrillas. Without it, the Folkmoot would not be disastrously handicapped against the Liberation Council, but counterinsurgency operations would be set back.

It seemed a trivial reason for dispatching warships across hundreds of light-years and getting into a fight with the Terrans themselves. Uroch had schooled himself to refrain from wondering. The great lords of state had their plan. His duty was to execute his part thereof.

And . . . by the God, by all the pagan gods of the forefathers—he was about to!

"Goal attained," he said flatly into the outercom, while joy sang in his blood. "Fire by the numbers."

His flyer threw the first missile. It flashed in the sun, it smote, it blossomed as blue-white as Alpha Crucis. Dust, smoke, vapor rose in a column that swelled as it grew, reached the bottom of the stratosphere, smeared itself across heaven. Megaton after megaton followed. In the end there lay a monstrous crater, incandescent until its sides cooled to glass. The canals ran dark and poisoned. Everywhere around, the crops were afire.

"*Arrach*, let's go!" Uroch shouted.

How he and his males fought their way through vengeful metal swarms; how they won back to *Tryntaf*; how *Tryntaf* and her sisters returned to Gadrol's victorious fleet; how the Merseians, who had taken few losses, eluded Terran search and returned home without further combat—this is the stuff of epic. Yet behind it lay always a cool intelligence, whose painfully garnered knowledge and carefully crafted schemes made the heroism possible.

For Uroch, sufficient was that he came back to his wife, his sole wife thus far, and to the first son she had hitherto borne him, with a tale that would ring the lad on to achievements of his own, in those unbounded years that reached before the Race.

After the raid, night fell. A full moon rose above that which had been the villages. Light rippled bleak, shadows moved, under the hastening white shield. Wind rustled. It was cold, harsh with ash; the lethalness was not perceptible.

Big and shaggy, a Gorrazanian female sat beneath the remnant of a wall. In her four arms she rocked her dead child. In her rough voice she sang it a lullaby that it had always liked.

Chapter 12

Miriam Abrams Flandry started home barely in time. Although news of civil war was recent, and nothing untoward had yet happened in the lanes between Sol and Niku, already apprehension pervaded the entire Empire. Word came in that, here and there, malcontents of many different sorts were proclaiming themselves adherents of would-be Emperor Olaf and making trouble or outright disaster for local authorities. Insurance rates had begun to skyrocket, which caused shipping firms to abandon route after route. It was natural to cancel service to the planet Ramnu, Niku IV, early on. There was no economic incentive to continue, after the quick announcement that the climate modification project was suspended for the duration of the emergency.

The woman had been on the surface, in the field, isolated among primitive autochthons. She just managed to catch the last liftoff for Maia. Of course, had she been stranded, Fleet Admiral Sir Dominic Flandry would have taken steps to get his wife back. He might well have unlimbered his speedster *Hooligan* and gone after her himself. But her survival meanwhile, on the grim world she loved, would have been doubtful.

As was, Maia III—Hermes—continued important enough that she could book passage from there directly to Terra. The vessel being a luxury liner which numbered noblefolk among her passengers, she had armed escort all the way, never mind how useful those ships might have been on the battlefront.

The xenologist kept to herself during the voyage, taking no part in its entertainments and intrigues. At meals she was minimally civil to her tablemates. It wasn't only that they and their games bored her. (Attractive and alone, she could have had a succession of bed partners; and after weeks among nonhumans, the physical sensation would have been welcome; but she would have had to *talk* with them, even *listen* to them. She'd rather wait for Dominic. The fact that he had probably not been waiting for her, in that sense, made no difference.) It was that she was full of grief and fear.

Grief for her dear Ramnuans, who had given her the name "Banner" that she still bore. She had come to see how the project was progressing, that would put an end to the planet's repeated civilizations-destroying glaciations, and how it was affecting the cultures she had studied for so long before her retirement. Shortly after she arrived, the order to shut down came in. Considering how bureaucracy operated, if Magnusson's insurrection were crushed immediately, which it obviously could not be, months must pass until work resumed. Ramnuans would perish by the additional thousands, or worse.

Fear for the Empire, Technic society and, yes, those other societies the Empire enclosed. Old and rotten it might be, its outworks crumbling less because strength had failed than because the will to be strong had. Nevertheless it was all that guarded the heritage of humanity and humanity's allies. Sometimes Flandry let his personal defenses drop in her presence and spoke of the Long Night that lay beyond the fall of the Empire.

And she had her kinfolk on Dayan to think about, and her natives on Ramnu, and friends strewn about among the stars, and—she and Dominic were not yet too old for a child or two. Not quite, he approaching seventy and she approaching fifty, given antisenescence plus the kind of DNA repair they could pay for. Besides, she had years ago deposited some ova in a biobank.

They had always been too busy, though, she and he; and now this wretched affair had begun.

He met her at debarkation, attired in a uniform that got them waved straight through inspection, and hurried her to the apartment they kept in Archopolis. There the champagne and caviar and such had to wait a while longer.

When they had feasted, the darkness would no longer be denied. She asked what the truth was—not the news, but the truth. Reluctantly, he told her.

"The latest dispatches we've received make unpleasant reading. In just these weeks, Magnusson's driven a salient in nearly as far as Aldebaran. Of course, he isn't sitting on everything from there back to his Patrician base. And his blitzkrieg is bound to slow down while he consolidates those gains. But he needn't do much toward that end, you realize. He dominates the whole volume of space already. He can snap up any significant traffic that doesn't flow the way he wants, and lay waste any planet that won't give him whatever support he demands. None will refuse. Who can blame them?

"His forces have won every battle to date, except for a couple of draws. Most engagements have been fairly small; but seeing what harm a single capital ship can do, each victory has been a lopsidedly big addition to his score. He is a brilliant tactician, and his overall strategy is basically the same as what carried Hans Molitor to the throne." Flandry narrowed his gray eyes and stroked his mustache. "Or is it, entirely?" he murmured.

Banner regarded him across the table and spread her hands in an immemorial gesture. She was a lean, strong-featured woman, her own eyes luminous green, silver-streaked brown hair falling to her shoulders. "Do you suppose he can win?" she asked.

"He might." Flandry ignited a cigarette and inhaled deeply. "In view of the latest developments, his chances are starting to look pretty good. When I saw our darling Emperor Gerhart a week ago, he was in an absolute hissy fit."

One reason the apartment was costly to rent was that it included state-of-the-art antibugging devices. Technicians personally loyal to Flandry made periodic inspections to be sure the system was still working.

Banner sighed. "Rhetorical question—or is it? Would it really be so awful if Magnusson took over? How did the present dynasty come to power, anyway, and how much is Gerhart really worth?"

"I keep telling you, darling scientist, you should take more interest in human history and politics," Flandry said. "Not but what it's understandable you don't. A filthy subject. I often wish I'd been born into some era like the Second Sugimoto, when everybody could cultivate his vine and fig tree, or his private arts or vices, without having to worry who'd come climbing over the wall next." He reached above the glasses and plates to stroke her cheek. "To be sure, then I'd never have met you."

Abruptly he got to his feet. The bathrobe flapped around his ankles as he strode to the transparency and stood raggedly smoking. Through a light rain and an early dusk, the city flashed hectic, as far as vision could fare. Within this room, the odor of roses and the lilt of a Mozart concerto receded toward infinity.

"I'm against revolutions," he said low. "No matter the alleged justification, it's never worth the short-range cost—lives and treasure beyond counting—or the long-range—ripping the fragile fabric of society. You know how in my younger days I did what I could to help put down a couple such attempts. If afterward I signed up with old Hans, why, the Wang dynasty had collapsed utterly, and he was the least bad of the contending war lords. At that, he turned out to be a tolerable Emperor, didn't he? Neither a figurehead nor a monster. What more dare we expect? And we may owe something to the memory of Edwin Cairncross, inasmuch as his try at usurpation was what got us reacquainted with each other, but surely you'll agree he was an undesirable sort."

She secured the sash of her kimono and went to join him. He laid an arm around her waist. His straight-lined countenance writhed into a smile. "Sorry about the oratory," he murmured. "I'll try to keep it properly caged henceforward."

She leaned close. "I never mind. It's nice to see you relax from your perpetual clowning." Her innate seriousness rose afresh. "But you haven't answered me. All right, the Empire was bumbling along fairly peacefully, and Magnusson's revolt is a disaster. Don't I know it myself? However—my parents always told me to look at every side of a question—would his success be a catastrophe? I mean, I've heard you say often enough that we no longer have any such thing as legitimate government. Maybe Magnusson would be better than Gerhart, who is rather a swine, isn't he?"

"Well, yes, he is," Flandry admitted, "although a shrewd swine. For a moderately important instance, you know he doesn't like me, but he's given to taking my advice, because he sees it's practical. And . . . Crown Prince Karl does have a high opinion of me, and is a thoroughly decent boy." He snickered. "If I'm still alive when he inherits the throne, I'll have to set about curing him of the latter."

She stared outward and upward. Stars were lost in the haze of light from the towers everywhere around, but—"Does it make that much difference who is Emperor? What can he, what can any person, any planet, do to change things?"

"Usually very little," Flandry agreed. This was by no means the first time they had been over the same ground. They were both aware and concerned, she less cynically than he. But some open wounds do not allow themselves to be left alone; and tonight they were feeling a freshly inflicted one. "The Policy Board, the provincial nobles, the bureaucrats and officers, the inertia of sheer size—Still, even a slight shift in course will touch billions of lives, and perhaps grind them out. And occasionally a pivotal event does happen. More and more, I wonder whether we may not be about to have that experience again."

"What do you mean?"

Flandry ran fingers through his sleek gray hair. "I'm not sure. Possibly nothing. Yet every intuition, every twitchy nerve I've developed in decades I misspent as an Intelligence agent when I might have gone fishing—my hunch screams to me that something peculiar is afoot." He pitched his cigarette expertly away, into an ashtaker, and swung about to face her, hands on her shoulders. "Listen,

Banner. You've been in the yonderlands, you haven't followed the input as you would've with me if you'd stayed home. The Merseians have now hit us."

She gave him a stark smile. "Is that a surprise? Haven't they always taken what advantage they could, when the Empire's been in disarray? Nibbles here and there, no *casus belli* that might unite us against them—obviously, not in this case either, if the story hasn't been released."

"This case is oddly different," Flandry said. "There've been the predictable skirmishes in the marches, yes. No major thrust. But . . . they sent a task force, which passed straight through Imperial space—they sent a strike force to Gorrazan, on the far side of us."

"What?" She stiffened. "Why? It doesn't make sense."

"Oh, it does, it does, when you contemplate it from the proper, skewed angle." He spoke softly, as was his wont when discussing terrible things. "Yes, the Realm of Gorrazan is the pathetic souvenir of a botched attempt at empire, a few colonies and clients on a few second-rate worlds near the home sun. Yes, its government has been plagued by insurrectionists who proclaim a bright new ideology—God, how long has the universe endured the same old bright new ideologies?—and the rebels are known, to everybody except our journalists and academics, to have Merseian inspiration and help. Trouble at our backs. Certainly I'd instigate the identical thing behind Merseia if I could.

"But now—" He drew breath. "Word came in the other day. The Merseians sent a 'mercy mission'. They declare the need was so urgent they had to traverse our space, hoping we wouldn't notice, and we were wicked to pounce on them as they were in Sector Alpha Crucis approaching their destination. It was a shame that we compelled them to trounce what forces we could bring to bear. The diplomats will be discussing who's to blame, and who's to pay what reparations to whom, and the rest of that garbage, for years to come. Oh, yes, business as usual.

"But the fact is, the Merseians *could* have passed through unknown to us, if they'd wanted. They made their presence blatant when they neared our Alpha Crucis frontier. Our units had no choice but to attack and take losses. Meanwhile a Merseian detachment punched through to Gorrazan itself. It made rags of the home defense fleet. It could have blown up every governmental installation. The rebels could have taken over entirely. We'd either have intervened to prevent, and found ourselves bogged down in a nasty, lasting little war; or, likelier, we'd have done nothing, and in due course had a pro-Merseian power at our backs, small and weak but an almighty nuisance.

"Instead, the raiders contented themselves with taking out the Folkmoot's main command center. The government's badly hurt, but it can still fight. The Gorrazanian civil strife proceeds."

"What does that imply?" She guessed his answer.

"Why, when the news breaks, as it inevitably will, the powers that be in the Empire will fall into a rupturing controversy. Some will want to tie down strength in watchfulness, diametrically opposite to Magnusson's campaign, lest the situation explode in our rear end. Others will claim there's no danger in those parts, whether because the Liberation Council hasn't yet won or because the Liberation Council represents progress and this past incident proves how wrong we are to keep provoking the Roidhunate. The waste of energy, the confusion of purpose among us would be unbelievable if it didn't have so many precedents." Flandry shrugged. "Oh, the Merseians have studied us. They understand us better than we understand them. And . . . Magnusson has the kudos of having beaten them in battle, but he also promises that when he becomes Emperor, he'll negotiate a permanent peace with them."

"How do you read the sign?" she whispered.

"The entrails, do you mean?" His laugh turned into a groan. "I don't try. I know better. I only see that a most useful piece of psychological warfare has just been waged on Magnusson's account. Coincidence? Or an attempt to further the cause of sincerely desired peace? I can only nurse my suspicions. What can I, here on Terra, find out for sure? How can I?"

Again he laughed, but cheerfully, and hauled her to him. "So never mind, sweetheart! Let's enjoy ourselves while we may."

Chapter 13

Being a mostly Cynthian town, Lulach looked smaller than it was. Buildings snuggled under trees, their roofs often decked with planted sod and their walls with flowering vines. Many houses were in the branches above—vegetation introduced from the mother world frequently grew enormous—where foliage hid them behind the play of sun and shadow. Streets were turf-covered, narrow and twisting, not many vehicles upon them and those compact. Wherever they could, dwellers went arboreally rather than on the ground.

A few large structures rose along the waterfront, among them a rambling timber inn. Diana and Axor established themselves there and set about exploring the area. Wo Lia took a room in the same place and got her performing animal put in its stable; local folk made considerable use of beasts for riding and hauling, though the farms to the north were mechanized.

Toward dawn, when fog off the river dusked the light night of Daedalus, she went out there, explaining to a sleepy kitchen helper whom she passed that she must see to the creature's well-being. The helper paid no particular attention to the cloth-wrapped bundle Wo Lia carried—for cleaning the cage, no doubt.

The stable was warm, murky, its air sweetened by a smell of horses and sharpened by a smell of changtus. Wo Lia groped her way to the cage and undid the catch on its door. Targovi bounded forth. *"Har-rugh!"* he growled. "You took your time."

"I had to wait till you could get away unseen, didn't I?" she replied. "That cursed sun-ring makes life hard for entrepreneurs."

Targovi stretched and yawned mightily. "Ah, but this feels wonderful! Pray to your little gods that you never have to be locked up."

By his count, a pair of Terran weeks had passed since *Waterblossom* left Paz. He could scarcely have endured this confinement, had Wo Lia not let him out on a chain at every stop along the way, to dance and do tricks while she played a flute and collected coins. "What news have you heard?" he asked.

"Fresh word has lately come from the war front, borne by a courier boat to Aurea. Great excitement. Admiral Magnusson has offered to negotiate with Emperor Gerhart. He has his nerve, no?"

"Ai, he needn't fear immediate peace. It sounds good and helps smooth the way for his next onslaught. If ever the Imperium is ready to bargain in earnest, it will be too late for the Imperium, save that Magnusson might let Gerhart and his councillors retire to some obscure set of palaces and carouse themselves to death." Targovi crouched to unfold the bundle and examine its contents. "Any tale of the Merseians?"

"Of course. How could anybody on Daedalus not want the latest gossip about the neighbors? It's vague, though, except that a Navy spokesman insisted we have nothing to fear from them. A later commentary by several learned academics pointed out that, since the Merseians want a lasting peace as badly as all right-thinking Terrans do, they would probably rather see Magnusson on our throne, even though he did defeat them more than once in the past. So they will refrain from any actions that would look as if they were taking advantage of an opportunity he had created for them."

"Assuredly that is what learned academics would say." Targovi opened his purse and counted the money within. "This sum isn't quite what I remember."

"I had expenses," said Wo Lia blandly.

"Well, you weren't too generous to yourself, I see. The funds were bound to be lean regardless—and likewise, I fear, are those of my companions, by now." Much more important, anyway, was his combat knife. Targovi rose. "Best I be off. Fail not in the part that remains for you to play, for if you do, you will come to harm that may well prove fatal. On the other hand, success should bring excellent baksheesh."

"I know. If *you* fail, I will kindle a light for your ghost. *Wan jin rao.*"

Targovi slipped forth and vanished into the fog. Wo Lia waited a while before scurrying back and screaming for the landlady. Her priceless trained animal, the mainstay of her livelihood, was gone! She had cast about unavailingly, finding no trace. Had it escaped because the stablehands were careless? Had it been stolen? She demanded help in searching, the entire staff, the patrol, a posse of citizens. If the magnificent, irreplaceable creature was not found, she would have compensation. She would demand justice, she would file suit, she would not cease until she had her rightful due!

On the riverbank beyond the docks, screened by brush as well as murk, Targovi thankfully removed the mane from his head. Besides being messy and itchy, it had interfered with the oxygill it covered, making him chronically short of breath. A quick chemical rinse out of a bottle Wo Lia had provided, followed by a dip in the stream, got the black dye off his fur. He toweled himself fairly dry and put on the clothes his accomplice had brought him. Besides his breechcloth and belt, this included a loose robe with cowl that she had purchased in Aurea according to his specifications. While he was making no further attempt at disguise for the nonce, a full garment might come in handy at some later time.

The sun was again a disc, low above the river. Mist was breaking into thin white streamers, as warmth seeped into the valley. Though hunger gnawed in Targovi's guts, he decided he had better establish himself before seeking a foodstall. He padded back into town and through twilight still blue under the trees. Passersby gave him looks but sounded no alarm.

He had counted on that—bet his life on it, in fact. The public cry for him had not most likely been confined to the Aurea vicinity. Nobody would have imagined he'd be able to get this far undetected through habitation; and had he tried to make his way through the backwoods, he would have perished. Planet-wide bulletins would merely add to an already enormous perturbation.

Here in Lulach he continued just the trader from Imhotep whom folk had long known. He could have arrived on any of the numerous boats that came and went, day and night. Cynthians are inquisitive by nature, perhaps even more than humans; however, this was essentially a community of small businesses, therefore one which did not intrude on privacy.

Targovi knew he was yet on the "Wanted" list at patrol stations everywhere. Such interchange of information was automatic. Anybody who thought to inquire of the data bank at local headquarters would get a full description of him and his misdeeds, including the reward offered. He had spent a considerable while in his cage figuring out what to do about that.

The station house was a frame building in a grove of ocherous-glowing fruit trees. (A shame that no colonist could enjoy more than the sight. The flesh was not poisonous, but its flavor was almost nil and, eaten, it would make an inert mass in the stomach.) Since the founding of a major base on Daedalus, the Navy had taken over most police functions, except in areas such as Zacharia that retained autonomy. Few places required much in the way of law enforcement. A detail was apt to consist largely of personnel recruited in the district, who had served elsewhere but were now approaching retirement age. At need, they could summon swift help from outside.

Entering, Targovi found a Cynthian who sported a lieutenant's comets on a collar that was her principal outfit, chatting with a couple of elderly enlisted ratings. "Why, hail," she said in surprise. "What brings you here?"

"Something that calls for a confidential meeting, Rihu An," he replied.

She chirred her kind of laugh. "Do you have smuggled goods for sale, you rogue? The market has gotten brisk, too much so for my poor monies."

"No, this is more interesting."

She led him to the outer office, closed its door, and crouched expectant. "I lay on you a secret you must keep," he said. "Only in seeming am I a footloose peddler. The truth is that for long I have been a secret agent for Intelligence."

Her tail bottled. "What say you?"

He made a deprecating gesture. "Oh, I am no Flandry. I am among many who go about, alert, reporting whatever they learn, and sometimes helping in some or other petty operation. You know of us. You did not know I am of the fellowship. Urgency requires I reveal it to you."

Albeit relatively unsophisticated, Rihu An was capable. "Prove it."

"Certainly." He glided to the computer terminal. "*Ng-ng-r-r*, to avoid possible sleight-of-hand, would you care to take this yourself?" She sprang to the desktop. "Key for Central Database, please. Now key for Restricted—I'll turn my back while you put in your identification and certify you have a need to know. . . . Are you done? Very well, next comes this." He recited a string of numbers and letters.

Inwardly, his battle readiness heightened. He did not tense; that would have been dangerously self-limiting. Rather, he relaxed his body utterly, opening every sense to the fullest, until he caught the least whiffs of dust and smoke in the air, the least early-morning traffic murmurs from the town. This was his crucial moment.

The entire code for agents could have been changed. He was guessing that nobody had gone through that cumbersome process at an unscheduled time in the midst of crisis.

The announcement that he was a fugitive from arrest identified him simply as Targovi the merchant. One never blew a cover needlessly; in this case, it would have started people wondering whether other lowly individuals were agents too. Targovi was guessing that the warrant for him had only been entered in patrol databases, not in those of his service. The latter would be an inconvenient reminder to the corps of how divided against itself the Navy was; and it would probably not be of any help in laying him by the heels.

A wiser decision might well have been to go ahead and make the cross-correlation. Targovi was guessing that wisdom was in short supply these days. Magnusson's uprising must inevitably have generated limitless confusion. Moreover, it surely appalled many persons in the armed forces. On Daedalus they dared not protest; but they would drag their feet in carrying out orders, especially if those orders were less specific than might have been the case under normal circumstances.

If his assumptions proved wrong, Targovi would break out. If possible, he would avoid doing serious harm to Rihu An or her underlings, whom he knew and liked. He had friends hereabouts who would give him shelter while he hatched a new scheme.

As was, she turned wide eyes on him and breathed, "You, scruffy wanderer and tavern brawler, are in the guardians too? . . . Well, what do you require?"

Relief flooded through him. "I may say but little, other than that I keep my pelt as clean and well-groomed as yours. These are evil days."

"True," she said unhappily.

"We, you and I and all our kind, we cannot take sides against either of the rival Emperors, can we? What we serve is the Empire itself. What we obey is the orders we get from our superior officers."

"True," she said again. Her reluctance was plain to hear. Knowing her as he did, he had counted on it. She would not rebel against the rebellion—that would have been pointlessly self-destructive—but she would not be zealous either. Had the station commandant, Lieutenant Commander Miguel Gomez, been on duty, Targovi would have waited till he went off. Gomez was an honorable sort, but rather lavish in his admiration for Sir Olaf Magnusson. Luckily, commandants don't generally take night watches.

"Well, then," Targovi said, "my assistant concerns possible subversives and spies. Never mind whether they may be working for his Majesty Gerhart, or the Merseians, or whomever. I have my suspicions, of one Wo Lia, who arrived lately on Shan U's *Waterblossom* from Paz. She is a scoundrelly character. Tracking her, I have gotten reason to think she may be more than that. Ere she can carry out whatever purpose has brought her—if it be something other than turning a few dishonest credits—I must follow her back trail, insofar as that is on record."

Rihu An waved at the terminal. "Serve yourself."

"M-m-m, this involves more than straightforward data retrieval. Consider how complex and unstable matters were at the time of Sir Olaf's proclamation, which seems to be about when she landed on Daedalus. May I use your prime machines?"

Once more he prepared himself for trouble. The request was irregular. Rihu An might well insist on referring it to Gomez, who might well ask embarrassing questions. However, Targovi's confidence in chaos paid off afresh.

She readily assented, took him to the inner office, and left him alone.

Ho-ho, ho-ho, he thought in Terran fashion, as he settled down at the keyboard. His life had fairly well convinced him that every strength has its inherent weakness. Arrangements here were illustrative. If important data are available to anyone who has obtained the retrieval code, they are available from practically any terminal. The resolution of that difficulty is to make them accessible only through particular units, which can then be physically guarded—an extra layer of defense. Now he had wormed his way through. He could not only read out, he could write in.

Part of his clandestine training had, naturally, been in computer technics. He had studied further on his own. And, piloting a poorly automated spacecraft between planets, for years, he had gotten a great deal of practice at improvisation.

His short, powerful fingers danced across the board. Caution was necessary. An attempt to do too much would set off alarms, and he couldn't be sure what "too much" was. The information he fed into the database was strictly local and only slightly false. It admitted that he, Targovi, had been detained when he last landed at Aurea from Imhotep. That was understandable, with everything in uproar and most loyalties a matter of conjecture. Investigation had cleared him and his passengers. They were all harmless, if eccentric.

In his capacity of secret agent, he fed in his "finding" that Wo Lia was not up to any mischief that mattered politically—just in case somebody, as it might be Rihu An herself, took a peek. The fact of his being such an agent was to remain restricted information.

None of this cookery went to Central Database in Aurea. Programs there could too readily detect an intrusion. Targovi was satisfied to modify the records at Lulach and add a "Correction: Override" command. Why should a minor outpost like this maintain elaborate precautions in its system?

Whoever happened to inquire directly of Aurea would get quite a different story. If he thereupon compared what the terminals here had to tell, the well-known fat would be in the proverbial fire.

Targovi didn't expect that. In Aurea, if officialdom gave him any further thought whatsoever, he was presumed dead. In Lulach he had roused no dubiety. A civilian wanting to check up on him would almost certainly do so by retrieving the public record in this town. That would declare him to be just a merchant from Imhotep. If the civilian had access to patrol records—which, in the case against which Targovi was making provision, he might well have—they too would show nothing significantly different . . . in Lulach. It was most unlikely that such a person would call Aurea instead, or in addition. Why should he? Public hullabaloo about a Tigery outlaw would have died out and been to all intents and purposes forgotten. It was nearly impossible that the inquirer would go through the rigmarole involved in getting access to Intelligence data.

Granted, the possibility did exist that the person would prove to be that ultra-cautious. The probability of it was small but finite. If it came to pass, the remainder of Targovi's existence would doubtless be short and unpleasant. That didn't worry him. The risk gave an extra tang to his faring.

On his way out, he stooped low to whisper in Rihu An's ear: "I was wrong. We needn't concern ourselves with Wo Lia. She'll belike steal several of your citizens blind, but not in ways that will make them complain to you. I do, though, have others to trace. Remember, I am nobody but the trader whom everybody knows. It would be as well if you gave the station personnel the idea that all I wanted to do was make you a business proposition, which you very properly declined."

"That shall be," she answered as quietly. While he was engaged in the inner office, she had stayed alone in the outer, as if still conferring with him. In Intelligence work, the less you let people observe, the better.

"Abide in peace and repletion." Targovi departed. He had a second call to pay, but first he wanted breakfast.

Chapter 14

From their island the Zacharians exported a variety of foods and high-quality manufactured goods to the rest of Daedalus. Keeping the business entirely in their own hands, they maintained dealership in every important community. The local one occupied a building near the waterfront. Its artificial material, curved contours, and metallic hues marked it arrogantly out. Targovi must stand at a scanner and request admission before the door opened.

The woman who appeared was handsome in his sight, comely in that of most humans. Medium tall, full-hipped but slender and somewhat small-bosomed, she moved as lithely as he did. A brief white gown set off glowingly olive, flawless skin. The hair on her round head was light-brown, lustrous, falling springily to the wide shoulders. Her face was high of cheekbones, straight of nose, firm of chin, lips delicately sculptured, brows arched above gold-brown eyes whose largeness was not diminished by the epicanthic folds.

"Greeting, Minerva Zachary," he said.

She smiled. "Minerva has served her turn

here and gone home." The voice was a musical contralto. "I am Pele. Who are you that knows her?"

"I beg your pardon, donna."

"Well, when members of our species often fail to tell us apart, I can hardly blame you." Zacharians were always as polite as occasion demanded—in their judgment.

Looking closer, Targovi began to see the differences. Fine lines in the countenance showed that Pele was distinctly older than Minerva; their kind aged slowly but were not immortal. She spoke with a faint accent suggesting that Anglic had not been the principal language in her home when she was a child; the islanders purposely kept several tongues in daily use. She didn't walk precisely like her predecessor; the islanders also made a point of practicing a variety of sports.

"Your name, please," she demanded rather than asked.

"Targovi—of Imhotep, as is obvious. I am a trader who has shuttled between my planet and this for years. On Daedalus I often proceed along the Highroad. They know me right well here."

Pele studied him. He could not have come to order any of her expensive wares. "I have no desire for trinkets."

"Could we speak in private? I am sure milady will be interested."

"Well—" She shrugged and led the way inside. The front of the building was the office; the rear, shut off, was the residence. Persons whom factors had entertained said those rooms— such of them as guests saw—were rather severely outfitted and decorated, though everything was of the best and, in its fashion, beautiful. The chamber which Targovi entered held conventional furniture, adjustable for comfort. Its commercial equipment was unobtrusive but first class allowing a single individual to handle everything. The few pictures had been changed; Pele evidently preferred landscapes from alien planets to the more familiar scenes that Minerva chose. The musical background was now complex, atonal, impossible for the Tigery to appreciate. Did the esthetic tastes of a Zacharian alter as he or she passed through life?

"Be seated," Pele said. They took facing chairs on a richly textured blue carpet. "What is your errand?"

He knew little of her breed. His acquaintance with Minerva had been slight, instigated by her because she grew curious about him and not pursued for long. Otherwise he had only glimpsed Zacharians by chance, mostly in Aurea. They never seemed to leave their island in substantial numbers, unless they made interstellar trips out of their spaceport. Theirs was a society closed to outsiders. It made no production of secretiveness, exercised no censorship or anything like that. It simply didn't communicate much, nor admit any but a few selected visitors. None of those were journalists. People who returned talked freely enough of the uniqueness they had encountered; two or three of them had written books about the place. But nothing of its inwardness ever came through. It was as if each Zacharian face were a smiling mask.

Nevertheless Targovi could see that Pele wanted him to come to the point. "I approach you, donna, more on behalf of two friends than myself," he began. "Now I shall not insult you by claiming I have no personal concern in the matter. My situation is precarious. I landed at Aurea just as Sir Olaf Magnusson made his . . . declaration. Civilian space traffic is banned saved by special permission, which has not been forthcoming for me thus far. Conveying passengers—the two I bespoke—rather than trade goods, I have naught to barter for the necessities of life, and scant money lingers in my purse."

The woman frowned. "This is no charitable organization, and it has no job openings."

Targovi imitated a human smile, keeping his lips closed because his carnivore's teeth could give the wrong signal. "I ask no favors, donna," he said ingratiatingly. "Already I am in your debt." He touched the oxygill that rose out of his robe. "Was not this, that keeps me breathing, produced on Zacharia?"

The flattery was wasted. "You paid for it, or somebody did. I have heard your species is physically strong. Try for a position as a dockhand, day laborer, or the like. Most backwoods communities lack adequate machinery."

"No, hear me out, I pray you. Those whom I carried from Imhotep are unusual. I think they have something to offer which your people will find worthwhile. At least, the Wodenite does."

That caught her attention. "The Wodenite who arrived yesterday? I have seen him wandering about, and considered inviting him to come for a talk. And dinner, perhaps," Pele added in a flick of humor, "abundant though the servings must be."

"I can introduce him to you, milady. May I tell you the story?"

He gave her an account of Axor's quest, succinct because that should whet her appetite for details. "—In Olga's Landing he acquired a guide, a vagabond by the name of Diana Crowfeather—"

Pele raised his hand. "Wait. Is that the dark-haired ragamuffin girl who was strolling at his side?"

"Who else?" Targovi observed her grow thoughtful, and at the same time seem a bit amused. He continued: "Diana and I are old acquaintances. I decided to do her a kindness and provide passage to Daedalus, where I thought it likelier they would find relics such as they sought than on Imhotep. If naught else, here they would have access to records of whatever may have been discovered but never really publicized. Furthermore, Diana should enjoy this planet, more congenial and almost new to her. And, to be sure, Axor would pay me." Slipping fast by that bit of mendacity: "Unfortunately, as I said, the outbreak of hostilities left us stranded. In fact, we were arrested and interrogated.

"Upon release, Axor and Diana spent a while in Aurea searching for information about Ancient relics. What they learned made them decide to fare downstream. They might as well. I stayed behind, striving to wheedle a clearance for return to Imhotep. Nothing availed. Finally I took a boat to Lulach myself. It was an express, therefore it arrived nearly as soon." Considering the number of such craft and their short turnaround times, Targovi didn't anticipate anyone would attempt verification of his narrative.

"An intriguing story," Pele said, "but what significance has it to me?"

"Much, I trust, milady," he replied. "May I ask a question? Are there mysterious remnants on Zacharia?"

She gave him a close look. "No."

"Truly not?"

"We have occupied the island for centuries and modified every square centimeter of it. We would know."

Targovi sighed. "Then the clues that my comrades came upon are false. Ah, I hate the prospect of disappointing them. Their hopes were so high."

"It was always inevitable that all sorts of unfounded rumors would go about, concerning us. Why should I lie to you?" Pele stroked her jaw. "I have, myself, heard of huge, inexplicable walls and the like—but afar in the mainland jungles or glaciers. It may be nothing more than travelers' tales. Your associates should inquire further."

"That may be less than easy, donna; for their purses have grown lank too. What has occured to me is this. You yourself know naught certain about Ancient relics, aside from their existence on some other planets. The subject has not interested you. However, during the centuries that Zacharians have dwelt on Daedalus, their explorers and factors must have ranged over the whole globe, as well as distant worlds. There must be ample records, and mayhap even individuals, to tell what is or is not real. It would save us—Axor—an effort that could prove hopelessly great."

"Do you wish me, then, to make a search of our database?" The woman pondered before continuing genially, "Well, I can. You have roused my curiosity."

"*Ng-ng,* milady is most generous," Targovi said, "but that is not truly what I had in mind. Could we come to Zacharia in person and pursue our inquiries? You know that printed words and pictures, valuable though they be, are not everything. There is no substitute for discourse, for the interplay of brains."

Pele sat straight. Her gaze sharpened. "Are you in search of free food and lodging?"

Targovi chuckled. "Plainly, yes, that is my chief motivation. Give me several standard days without pressure, perchance a week or two, and I can devise some means of keeping myself alive on Daedalus. I might even make trade arrangements with you Zacharians, or at any rate get your kind of help in persuading the Navy to let me flit home. You have influence."

"I told you we are not a charitable organization."

"Nor am I a beggar, donna. My humble goods may prove worthless to you, but at the moment my stock in trade includes Axor himself. Think. He is likely the first Wodenite ever to betread Daedalus. Certainly none else have come here in living memory. Not only can he tell your savants much about his world and his folk—the sort of facts that do not get into dry dispatches—but he has roamed throughout the Empire. Not only is he a leading authority on the fascinating Ancients, he has experience of many and many contemporary societies. Let us admit that this entire sector is provincial, marginally touched by the currents of civilization. Axor will come like a breath of fresh air. I assure you, as a person he is delightful." Targovi interposed a few seconds of strategic silence. "And . . . the total situation in the galaxy has become totally fluid. Aught can happen, whether mortal danger or radiant opportunity. Axor is no political scientist or seeker of wealth and advantage. But he is widely traveled and he has thought deeply about the things he has witnessed—from his nonhuman, non-Cynthian, non-Merseian perspective. Who knows what clues toward action or precaution lie in what he has to tell? Dare you refuse yourselves the input he can give you?"

The quietness that fell again grew lengthy. At last Pele asked, "What does the girl want of us?"

"Why, simply the thrill of newness. Whatever you care to show her. She is young and adventurous . . . We three travel together, you understand."

Pele looked beyond him. "She *is* attractive," she murmured.

Targovi knew the reputation of Zacharian men. They practically never married outside their society; that meant exile. They did, though, spread their superior genes through the lesser breeds of humanity whenever they got the chance; and they had a way of creating frequent chances for themselves. Pele must be thinking she could put her brethren on the track of some fun.

To a degree, Targovi had taken this into his calculations. He didn't feel he was betraying Diana. She should be capable of reaching her own decisions and enforcing them. If not—well, she'd likely enjoy herself anyway, and bear no permanent scars.

Zacharian women were different, he recalled. They took occasional outsider lovers, whose later accounts of what had happened were awestruck and wistful. But they never became pregnant by such men. At most, if they thought someone was worthy, they would donate an ovum for *in vitro* fertilization. Their womb time they kept for their own kind.

Pele emerged from her reverie. "I'll call home and inquire," she said crisply. "I may well recommend a positive answer. You do make a plausible case for yourself. They'll send someone to investigate closer before they decide. He will want to talk with each of you. Where are you staying?"

"At the Inn of Tranquil Slumber. That is where my friends are, and I will take a room there too."

"You should find this house more hospitable when we summon you," Pele said. Conviviality provides openings for the probing of character. "At present I have my work to do. Good day."

Diana sped to meet him, over the cobblestones of the hostel courtyard. "Oh, Targovi, old dear!" She hugged him till his firmly muscled ribs creaked. The fragrance of her hair and flesh filled his tendrils. "Welcome, welcome!"

"How have you two fared?" he asked.

She let him go and danced in the sunlight. "Wonderful," she caroled. "Listen. We went parleyin' around, and right away we heard about what's *got* to be Ancient ruins, with inscriptions, in the jungle south of Ghundrung."

"The Donarrian settlement? But that's far downstream, and then you'd have to outfit an expedition overland. Where's the money coming from?"

"Oh, we'll earn it. Axor already has an offer from a lumberin' company. He can snake a log through the woods cheaper'n any gravtrac can airlift it. And me, I've lived off odd jobs all my grown-up life. I won't have any trouble gettin' by. This is a live town." Diana sobered. "I'm sure we can find somethin' for you as well, if you want."

"But you'd take months, a year or more, to save what you will need!" Targovi exclaimed. "Meanwhile the war goes on."

She cocked her head and stared at him. "What's that got to do with us? I mean, sure, it's terrible, but we can't do anything about it. Can we?"

Chapter 15

He drew a long breath. "Come aside with me and let us talk," he said.

Her jubilation died away as she sensed his uneasiness. "Of course." She tucked an arm beneath his and led him off. "I've found a trail out of town, through the woods, where nobody'll overhear us." Her smile was a trifle forlorn. "I want to learn what you've been up to anyway, and how you figure to stay out of jail, and, oh, everything."

"You shall, as much as is safe for you to know."

She bridled. "Now wait a minute! Either you trust me or you don't. I've let you rush me along this far, and conned Axor for you, because you didn't have a chance to explain. Or so you claimed. Not any more, fellow."

He raised his ears. "Ah, you are your father's child—and your mother's—eh, little friend? . . . Well, you leave me no choice. Not that I had much left me, after today. My thought was that you, being an honest young person, could best play the part I need played if you believed it was genuine."

"Hmf! You don't know me as well as you

think." Diana frowned. "We might have to shade the truth for Axor. I'll hate that, but we might have to."

"Did I indeed underestimate your potential, all these years?" Targovi purred.

They said no more until they were well into the forest east of town. The trail ran along the river, a short way in from the high bank, so that water could be seen agleam beyond tree boles and canebrakes. Underneath canopies of darkling leaves, sun-flecked shadow was somewhat cooler than air out in the open, though still subtropical. It was full of unfamiliar odors, sweet, rank, spicy, or indescribable in Anglic or Toborko. Tiny, pale wings fluttered about. No songs resounded, but now and then curious whistles and glissandos went among the boughs above. The sense of ruthless fecundity was overwhelming. You understood what a war it had been, and was yet, to keep terrestroid life going on this—unusually Terra-like—world.

Diana remarked as much. "Makes you wonder how firm a grip we've got on any place, doesn't it?" she added. Her tone was hushed. "On our whole Empire, or civilization itself."

"The Merseians have long been trying to pry us loose from existence," Targovi snarled.

She gave him a troubled glance. "They can't be that bad. Can they? It's natural for a Tigery to think of them as purely evil. They'd've let your whole race, and the Seafolk's, die with Starkad. That plan of theirs depended on it. Only, well, it wasn't 'they,' not their tens of billions plottin' together, it was their government—a few key people in it, nobody else havin' any inklin'."

"Granted. I overspoke myself. Humans are too many, too widespread for extermination. But they can be diminished, scattered, conquered, rendered powerless. That is the Merseian aim."

"Why?" she wondered in hurt. "A whole galaxy, a whole universe, a technology that could make every last livin' bein' rich—why are we and they locked in this senseless feud?"

"Because both our sides have governments," Targovi said, calming down.

Presently: "Yet Terra's did rescue enough of my people that we have a chance to survive. I am not ungrateful, nor unaware of where Imhotep's best interest lies. I actually dream of serving Terra in a wider field than any one planet. What a grand game of play!"

"I'd sure like to get out there too." Diana shook herself. "S'pose we stop talkin' like world-weary eighteen-year-olds—"

"Sound counsel, coming from a seventeen-year-old."

She laughed before she went on: "All right, down to business. You're a secret agent of the Navy, no matter how low in grade. You're onto somethin' havin' to do with the fight for the throne. You need some kind of help from Axor and me. That's about the whole of what I know."

"I know not a great deal more myself," Targovi confessed. "What I have is a ghosting of hints, clues, incongruities. They whisper to me that naught which has been happening is what it pretends to be—that we are the victims of a gigantic hoax, like an ice bull which a hunter stampedes toward a cliff edge. But I have no proof. Who would listen to me, an outlaw?"

Diana squeezed his hand. The fur was velvety under her fingers. "I will."

"Thank you, small person who is no longer so small. Now, you too will find it hard to think ill of Admiral Sir Olaf Magnusson."

"What?" For an instant she was startled, until she remembered the Tigery touching on this matter before. "Oh, maybe he has let his ambition, his ego run away with him. But we did get a rotten deal out in this sector. He alone kept the Merseians from overrunin' us—"

"The crews of his ships had somewhat to do with it. Many died, many live crippled."

"Sure, sure. That doesn't change the fact that Sir Olaf provided the leadership that saved us. 'Twasn't the first time he'd done that sort of thing, either. And still he wants peace. A strong and honest man on the throne, a man who's dickered with the Merseians in the past and made them respect him—maybe he really can give us what nobody else can, a lastin' peace. Maybe that really is worth all the blood and sorrow that Gerhart's resistance is costin'."

"And mayhap not."

"Who can tell? *I* can't. The Empire's had succession crises before. It'll prob'ly have them again in the future. What can we ordinary people do except try to ride them out?"

"This crises may be unique." Targovi marshalled his words before he proceeded:

"Let me give you the broad outlines first, details afterward. Terran personnel are not the only ones whom last year's clash left embittered. The Mersian captains were wholly inept. It wasn't like them in the least. Nor were the issues worth fighting over, save as a pretext for launching a total war against Terra, and everybody who has studied the matter knows Merseia isn't ready for that. Seemingly the eruption happened because their diplomats blundered, their lines of communication became tangled, and some hotheaded officers took more initiative than proper.

"But once conflict was rolling, the Merseians should have won. They did have superior strength in these parts. Altogether like them would have been to break our defense, take this sector over, then call for a cease-fire; and at the conference table, they would have held higher cards than Terra. They would have come out greatly advantaged.

"But they lost in space. Magnusson's outnumbered fleet cast them back with heavy casualties. We hear this was due his brilliance. It was not. It was due stupidity in the Merseian command.

"Or was it?"

They walked on mute for a spell, in the shadowy, steamy, twittering jungle.

"Later will I explain how I collected this information from the Merseians themselves," Targovi said at length. "Some was readily available, if anybody had directed that statements made by war prisoners should be recorded and collated. Nobody did. Strange, *ng-ng?* The gathering of more exact, higher-level data put me to a fair amount of trouble. You may find the story entertaining.

"Now I had also, in my rovings, picked up tales of things seen—spacecraft, especially, coming and going oftener than erstwhile—around Zacharia. This struck me as worthy of further investigation. No doubt the Zacharians have ever used their treaty-given privileges to carry on a bit of smuggling. Their industries need various raw materials and parts from elsewhere. In return, they have customers beyond the Patrician System. Why pay more taxes on the traffic than is unavoidable? The Zacharians never, m-m, overindulged in contraband. Rather, the slight measure of free trade benefited Daedalus in general. But of recent months, folk on the mainland or out at sea—on this horizonless planet—have marked added landings and takeoffs, ofttimes of ships that belong to no class they recognized. They thought little of it. I, who put their accounts together, thought much."

"You're worried about the Zacharians? Those cloned people? Why, how many of them ever set foot off their island?"

"Not cloned, precisely," he reminded. Having rarely been on this globe before, and then as a child, she had the ignorance which follows from lack of interaction. She had better get rid of it. "They reproduce in the common fashion. But they are genetically near-identical, apart from sex. A hermit society, theirs, despite its far-flung enterprises. Nobody really knows what goes on inside it, unless they be other Zacharians dwelling elsewhere in the Empire."

"Well, but, Targovi," Diana protested, "an individualist like you should be the last to think somebody's up to no good, just because they're different and value their privacy."

"In times of danger—and the winds were foul with danger, already then—you cannot afford to assume that anyone is trustworthy. Certainly not ere you've investigated them. A shame, from the moral viewpoint; but secret agents cannot afford morals, either."

"What'd you do?"

"What doctrine called for, my dear. Having found all this spoor, I reported to my superior. As it happens, he was at top of Intelligence operations on Daedalus, Captain Jerrold Ronan. That was logical, when the Patrician System had never hitherto required surveillance of the truly intensive kind. What was *not* logical was Ronan's reaction. He forbade me to follow the trail any farther or bespeak it to anybody whatsoever, and ordered me straight back to Imhotep, despite the fact that this was an implausible move for a trader whose cargo was half unsold."

"And you didn't give up!" Diana cried. "You took it on yourself to keep on trackin'. Oh, you are a Tigery!"

"Well, it was irresistible," he said. "I had not flatly been barred from Daedalus, simply warned that I might be marooned—which was, itself, queer, for why should the sector command await any new emergency? In you and Axor, I found what seemed the perfect—stalking horses, is that your human phrase? Gently nudged this way or that on your innocent quest, you would draw attention off me. Never meant I to endanger you—"

"Though you didn't hesitate to take a chance with us." Diana caught his hand again. "Don't you mind. I don't. And who'd want to shoot at gentle old Axor? Killin' him would be a contract job anyway."

Fangs flashed as Targovi grinned. "What a waste, him a pacifist!" Soberly: "Well, the rebellion began—not a complete surprise to us—as we were approaching Daedalus. Needs must I pounce on my decision. We could return to Imhotep and abide there, safe and impotent, while events played themselves out. Or we could plunge forward and land. Did we do so, then belike a computer program had my meddlesome self listed for indefinite detention. I chose to risk that. If I decamped, you and Axor should not suffer worse than inconvenience.

"The rest of the story you know, until this day."

They walked on. The trail bent out of the woods, toward the verge of the riverbank. Long green blades rustled under a slow breeze. They resembled grass, but were not. A few boats traversed the water. The absence of aircraft overhead had begun to seem eerie. Patricius was declining toward mists that it turned sulfurous, that veiled the distant sea. Although this was summer, and Daedalus has an axis more tilted then Terra's, daylight is always brief; or else, if you reckon the sun-ring, it is never absent.

"Tell me about today," Diana said softly.

Targovi did. She clapped hands together in glee. "Hey, what a stunt, what a stunt!"

"Let us hope nobody looks too closely at the *mise-en-scène*." Targovi had acquired a good many-tag-ends of human languages other than Anglic. "I think your main part in the act will be to divert thoughts away from it."

She squinted westward. "You aim to get us to Zacharia, then?"

"Yes, and snoop about."

"What do you think you might find?"

Targovi shrugged with his tendrils. "It is a capital mistake to theorize in advance of the data. I have my suspicions, naturally. Clear does it seem, the Zacharians have close connection to Magnusson. For example, the lady Pele casually mentioned bringing in another person soon—which means by air, at a time when air traffic is restricted. Mayhap they've decided Magnusson will be the best Emperor, from their viewpoint. In any case, what support have they been giving him? Unmistakably, it's of importance. What hope they to gain? I doubt they nourish any mystique of the Terran Empire as an end in itself."

"Who does, any more?" Diana mumbled.

"Some of us deem its survival the lesser evil. But no matter that." Targovi paused. "Here is where I fall silent. Did I tell you my guess, you could well become tense, nervous, wary—and the Zacharians would see. They are not stupid. Ai, they are not stupid! For that matter, I seldom voice my thoughts to myself. They could be mistaken. I hope to arrive open-minded, no blinkers upon my senses."

"How about me?" Diana asked slowly.

"Relax and enjoy," he answered. "That will be your best service."

"And keep ready." She touched the haft of her Tigery knife.

"And, aye, prevent Axor from blurting out awkward information," Targovi said. "Can you?"

She deliberated. "M-m-m . . . well, he scarcely knows any more than you want him to. The main inconsistency, I think, is that you say you sold him passage to Daedalus—you bein' a huckster with an eye for any credits you could make—while he thinks you carried us out of benevolence. I'll slip him a hint that I paid you, from a bigger money stash than I'd admitted havin', for the sake of the trip. Not that anybody's likely to quiz him, but if they do, that should satisfy them. Otherwise . . . m-m-m . . . he did see you run from arrest in Aurea—Yes. Got it. You panicked because Tigeries can't stand long imprisonment. You were embarrassed to tell Pele Zachary that, because in fact the patrol soon caught you. Havin' been cleared anyhow and released, you followed us on an express boat the way you said." Laughter. "Yay, that should make you out to be the kind of half-civilized bumbler you want to seem!"

His gaze drew downright respectful. "You have it, I believe." Just the same, he felt compelled to add: "Remember, do not let yourself get caught up in this. Play calm, play safe. The last thing we want is an uproar."

"I understand," she said, "though I'll bet we get one regardless."

Chapter 16

The aircar came from the *east.*

That meant, almost surely, from Aurea; and that in turn could mean trouble—fight, flight, outlawry proclaimed across the entire planet. Ordinarily Targovi would have felt no such forebodings. A number of vehicles still flew, some of them touching at Lulach, and they weren't all military. Not even a majority were. Civilian needs must still be served, if Daedalus was to continue providing Magnusson with the stuff of war.

But Pele went to meet this arrival.

At first Targovi knew no cause for apprehension. Rather, his blood flowed quick when she emerged from her building and strode off toward the airfield. He had grown weary of waiting. His stakeout had degenerated into routine, which never took long to bore him.

For a large part of each fair-weather rotation period he settled down under a shading kura tree beside a main street. There he eked out his dwindled exchequer by telling Toborko folk tales to whomever would stop, listen, and eventually toss him a coin or two. It was quite plausible that he would do this, and the fact that his position gave him a view of Zacharia House signified nothing, did it? At other times he wandered idly about; when nobody was looking, he might scramble onto untenanted boughs from whose leafage he could invisibly observe; he seldom left the place out of his sight, and then it was by prearrangement with Diana.

The girl passed her time in "a lot of pokin' around and people-watchin'," so it was no surprise that she occasionally lounged beneath the kura and followed the passing scene. Cynthians often paused to exchange banter with her. Several male human residents did likewise, and tried to get her to accompany them elsewhere. She accepted a few of their invitations, but just for times when Targovi would be on watch and—as they discovered—just to go sightseeing or canoeing or to a tavern for a little drinking and dancing.

She had persuaded Axor to postpone acceptance of the job he was offered, in hopes of something better. He took rambles or swims that covered a great many kilometers, and else usually sprawled in front of a terminal screening books from the public database. When Diana asked him if he wasn't lonely, he replied, "Why, no. You are kind to think of me. However, I always have God, and am making some splendid new friends. All of yesterday I visited with Montaigne." She didn't inquire who that was, not having hours in which to sit and hear him.

Since Targovi kept most of the vigils, it was only probable that Pele should set forth under his gaze. That was on an overcast afternoon, when odors of wilderness lay rank and dank in windless heat. Yet a tingle went through him. She had frequently emerged on errands that proved to be commonplace, or else to saddle a horse she kept at the inn and ride it away in the night, down game trails through the forest. He had been unable to track her then, and didn't believe it mattered. Today she walked fast, an eagerness in her gait that he thought he also glimpsed on her face; and the path she took among the trees wound toward the airfield.

Targovi had been yarning to half a dozen adult Cynthians and the young they had brought. He was becoming popular in that regard. "—And so," he said hastily, "the warrior Elgha and her companions heard from the wise female Dzhannit that they must make their way to the Door of the Evil Root. Ominous though that sounded, Dzhannit assured them that beyond it lay wisdom—not money, as Terrans might suppose, but knowledge of many new things. Long and hard would the road be, with more adventures upon it than can now be told." To a chorus of protests: "No, no. I must not keep you past your sleeptimes. Besides, it looks like rain, and better to stop here than in the middle of, say, a thrilling combat with the horrible, ravenous Irs monster. Tomorrow, my dears, I will resume."

As he bounded off at the speed which high-gravity muscles made possible, he wondered whether he would in fact ever finish the story. Well, if not, maybe someday one of those cubs, grown up, would hear it on Imhotep and remember him; or, a fonder hope, another Tigery would come to Lulach and get a request for it.

Pele had disappeared from view. That was desirable. She mustn't know she was being trailed. Targovi's tendrils picked the faint traces of her individual scent-complex out of the air. Yes, she was definitely bound for the field. He turned his pace into a soundless, casual-looking saunter that kept him in every shadow or behind every bole he could find. The intermingling of town and woods was a blessing to detectives.

It was also the reason why cars did not lower themselves at their destinations, but required a landing field like larger vehicles. That was a paved hectare on the outskirts, with a couple of hangars and a repair shop for whoever had need. A wire mesh fence surrounded it against stray wild animals. Periodic charges of poison kept the Daedalan jungle at bay. Everywhere yonder mass crowded murky beneath the low gray sky.

Pele Zachary waited at the gate. Hardly anyone else was in sight. The last part of the way here had been deserted. Nobody had reason to come nowadays, except to meet a specific flight. She must have gotten a call about this one. Targovi sidled into a thicket.

The teardrop shape of a car glinted downward. He bared his teeth. It was coming not from the west but the east!

It braked in racer style and dropped into a parking stall. A man got out, carrying a suitcase. He proceeded to the gate, where he and the woman kissed briefly before trading words. Side by side, they started toward the settlement.

When they had gone by Targovi, he stole after them through the brush that walled the street. The turf that made a tough surface for traffic was genetically engineered to kill any invading growth.

He required all his hunter's skill to move without rustle or crackle. It would have been easier at home. The dense Imhotepan atmosphere carried sound more loudly, but also let him hear better, providing added feedback. In Terran-like air he had often slipped small amplifiers into his ears. Those were in the secret compartments of *Moonjumper*, along with the rest of his specialized gear. He must make do with what nature had provided him.

That was not a gross handicap. He heard almost as well as a normal human; and his tendrils picked up vibrations too, which gave him useful cues. They whom he stalked were speaking Anglic. The accent was unique, but Targovi was accustomed to a variety of dialects. He caught most of what reached him and could deduce the rest. It was not the sort of conversation that called for whispers. Whoever accidentally overheard a part would make nothing special of it.

"I expected someone like Ares or Cernunnos," Pele was saying, "and sooner."

The man shrugged. He was her male counterpart, aside from being apparently younger. His height was greater by some ten centimeters, shoulders more broad, hips narrow, build generally muscular and masculine; but as athletic as she likewise was, the difference became less striking than it might have been. The same smooth olive complexion contrasted with brief white garments, the same brown hair clustered on a similarly brachycephalic head. His visage was distinctive, but almost entirely because of being a version of hers—larger, bonier, yet just as regular. When he spoke, his baritone had a harmoniousness of its own.

"They didn't delay consideration of your word on Zacharia," he said, "but inasmuch as I was in Aurea, they decided to have me stop on my way home and do the further investigating. If nothing else, I might have picked up some relevant information."

Targovi's pelt stood on end. The information could include those data he had been at such pains to suppress locally.

Well, if so, he'd be forewarned, and would hurry off to make what escape arrangements he was able for himself and his comrades. That was what justified the risk he took in this shadowing.

"Did you?" Pele asked.

Straining to hear, Targovi blundered. A withe whipped past him and smote a stand of cane. Leaves swished, stalks clacked. The man halted, as instantly alert as any Tigery. "What was that?" he barked.

Targovi was bound up the nearest tree. No human could have done it that fast. Besides his strength, he had agility, reaction time, and claws on his feet. Bark and vines alike he seized. A leathery-winged creature croaked alarm and fluttered out of the foliage.

"It was only—" The woman went unheard. The man left the path and thrust into the brush, peering about, a hand on the grip of the pistol belted at his waist. Zacharians had various legal privileges. . . . Targovi flattened himself on a branch.

"You are too nervous, Kukulkan," Pele said. "We always hear animals blundering around. They aren't edible, you see, and they don't devour crops, so they're hardly ever hunted."

The man satisfied himself. "No doubt you're right," he said. "I admit I am rather on edge."

"Why?"

He and she resumed walking. In a minute they would be beyond earshot. Targovi gauged his chances. He was no Cynthian, to try arboreal feats, but—He crouched and sprang. Soaring above the humans, he caught a limb ahead of them and did his best to blend with it.

This time they paid no heed to whatever they heard. "—may have to start Phase Two earlier than planned," Kukulkan Zachary said. "If only interstellar communications were faster! All they had to show me was a single message, though it came directly from Magnusson. In any event, *we* could find ourselves suddenly very busy."

"Hm." Pele tugged her chin. "Then you don't think we should invite those three outsiders?"

"That doesn't follow. I didn't mean we'll inevitably come under high pressure in the near future. If it does happen, we can dump them back on the mainland fast enough. They do sound interesting, and—who knows?—they might provide us with some extra cover."

Pele snickered. "I know what you'd like to cover."

Kukulkan grinned. "Those recordings you took of the girl are attractive. I was busy my entire time in Aurea."

"I've been busy but solitary too," Pele murmured.

He laughed in his turn and laid an arm about her waist. "Let's do something about that." They went on close together.

Targovi stayed behind. It was manifest that they would utter nothing more of any importance until well after they were safely inside their building. Also, they were entering habitation, and soon a Cynthian was bound to notice him aloft. That might cause gossip.

He returned to the ground and ambled lazily. Within him flickered fires. He had learned as much as he dared hope for. The Zacharians had no suspicions of him . . . thus far. They actually liked the idea of bringing his party to their island. What would come of that, only the gods knew, and maybe not they either. Javak the Fireplayer might once again take a hand in what would otherwise have been the working out of fate.

Chapter 17

Three hundred kilometers west of the mainland lifted Cliffness, the prow of Zacharia. Thence the island reached another two hundred, and from north to south eighty at its widest. Diana first saw it as the vehicle bearing her came into clear air. It still lay well ahead and below, but spread in its entirety by the strange perspectives of Daedalus. "O-o-oh-h," she breathed.

"A beautiful sight, true?" Kukulkan Zachary said. She barely noticed at first how his arm slipped around her waist, and later she didn't mind. "How glad I am that the seeing conditions were right for you."

Together with Axor and Targovi, they stood in an observation lounge. Since a good-sized craft was needed to carry the Wodenite in comfort, Kukulkan had gone all-out and summoned a first class passenger cruiser. It wasn't plying the global lanes anyway in wartime. Only ribs of metal crossed this section of the hull; the rest was vitryl, thick and strong but totally transparent. Apart from bulkheads fore and aft, you stood above the world in the middle of heaven.

Given the swift spin of Daedalus, Patricius did not much affect the doings of humans. This was a night flight because the hour chanced to be convenient. The sky ranged from deep violet-blue overhead, where a few stars glimmered, to berylline near the waters. Eastward towered clouds, their peaks and ridges frosted by the moon they hid, their lower steeps and canyons amethyst, their rains gleaming bronze and silver from the sun-ring. That lay around the rest of the Phosphoric Ocean, not as a boundary but as a shiningness unimaginably remote, within which the curve of the planet lost itself in its own vastness. There the sea gleamed like damascened steel; inwardly it shaded through turquoise to jet. Upon those darknesses swirled and sparked green fire, the light of tiny life that rode the surges.

Amidst all else, Zacharia was splendor and enigma. Most of it showed dimly verdant, the contours making intricate patterns, argent-threaded with rivers, lakes, and mists. Not far from the north coast a mountain range ran east to west, its snowpeaks now roseate, its flanks falling down into valleys which were mazes of blue-black. Light from dwellings sprinkled diamond dust across the island and several outlying cays. Movable motes betokened travelers in the air or down on the water.

The transport throbbed and the deck tilted subtly underfoot as it began descent toward the wonder.

Kukulkan slightly tightened his embrace while he steered Diana toward a sideboard.

"Lacking a spaceship's acceleration compensators, we shall soon have to take seats for our landing," he said, his voice livelier than the words. "Let us enjoy a glass of champagne first—and many afterward."

"You're so, so, uh, kind," she stammered.

His exotic features lofted a smile. "Elementary courtesy, donna," he said, lips close to her ear; his breath stirred her hair. "Although in your case—" He let her go in a hand-gliding fashion and poured into both their goblets, with a glance toward Axor and Targovi. That was *pro forma,* when neither of them cared for the wine. But it was typical of him, Diana thought.

He could not have been more gracious back in Lulach. Nor, granted, could Pele Zachary have been, his—sibling?—but she was reserved and formal while Kukulkan had laid himself out.

Oh, yes, Diana knew full well when a man was undertaking to be charming. The question was whether he could manage it or not, and the answer depended on him, on how much thoughtfulness was behind the fine manners. For instance, no matter the skill with which he flattered her, she would have understood him entirely and scornfully if he had neglected her friends. Instead he gave them, if anything, more attention, and not just time but obvious concentration, real listening. Especially to Axor—Sure, he did have the responsibility of deciding whether to import such an odd pilgrim. However, he could have gone about it like some kind of personnel officer, brisk and overbearing. After all, it was the wanderers who were asking to be taken there, not the other way around.

Kukulkan had not. He'd arranged a lovely lunch at Pele's house and been marvelous to everybody. Diana had not yet sorted out her memories of the conversation. They were too dazzling. Kukulkan had been *out*, across the Empire, to world after world. . . . At the same time she was haunted by one remark. "Oh, yes, we need newness, we Zacharians, more than ever in this year of enclosure; we need it as we need food and air and light. I begin to believe that you can provide some, and so put us in your debt."

That was all. Talk had slipped elsewhere. She found herself yearning to know what he meant. Had she the right to abet spying on him, to violate his hospitality and trust? But she had given Targovi her promise, Targovi her brotherling, the son of Dragoika who had been like a mother to her after Maria her blood-mother died—and if he found no evidence of wrongdoing, what harm would she have done?

How could she say? How dared she say?

Kukulkan's glass clinked against hers. "Happy morrows," he toasted. She smiled back and tossed off a longer draught than was sophisticated. Tartness danced down her throat, bubbles tickled her nostrils. Presently she felt almost at ease—aware, without any belligerence, of the muscles beneath her skin and the Tigery knife at her belt. She hoped that whatever happened would indeed be happy; but whatever it turned out to be, surely an adventure awaited her.

Nacre Bay was a broad half-circle cut into the north coast. The Mencius Hills formed an inner arc, with a narrow flatland between them and the water. Through them flowed the Averroes River, glacier-fed by the Hellas Mountains farther south. Janua occupied the shore and the slopes behind.

It was not a town. Kukulkan had explained that Zacharia bore none. Most buildings stood by themselves, usually rather far apart. Aircars and telecommunications linked them as well as if they formed a village. However, it was most practical to have certain things close together—the small spaceport, a large airfield, a harbor for surface vessels, associated facilities— and in the course of time various industries and institutions had naturally located in the same area—which meant more homes and service enterprises—The region of relatively concentrated population got the name Janua. By ordinary standards it was dispersed enough, sprawling without official boundaries across more than two hundred square kilometers. As their pilot brought the cruiser down, Diana saw the same blend of forest and housing as at Lulach.

No, she realized, not the same at all. The hills were landscaped into terraces, ridgeways, contoured hollows, graceful sweeps of greensward. Gardens abounded. Trees grew orderly along roads or in bowers or groves. Some of the latter were quite large, but had clearly been planted and tended. They, like vegetation everywhere, were Terran, as near as she could judge. That was not very near, when she knew the life of the mother planet mostly from pictures, but Kukulkan had told her that the original settlers eradicated everything native and reshaped their new home according to their will.

Such houses as she glimpsed were unique in her experience. They seemed to be of stone or a stonelike synthetic, rectangular in plan, peak-roofed, fronted or surrounded by porticos, their colors subdued when not plain white. Even the large utilitarian structures down close to the shore followed that general style. She thought it was pretty—doubtless gorgeous when you got a close look—but already wondered if it might not prove monotonous. A frowning, rough-walled compound on the heights was well-nigh a relief to her eyes.

The spaceport was probably a standard model. She couldn't be certain, because she got only the most fleeting sight of it during approach. It was on the untenanted southern slope of the range, opposite the fortress-like place, as if to keep such inelegance from intruding on vision. The airfield, on the eastern rim of the bay, was screened by tall hedges below which ran flowerbeds.

They landed. Passengers unsnapped their harnesses and rose from their seats. "Welcome to Zacharia," said Kukulkan gravely, and offered Diana his arm. She didn't recognize the gesture. He chuckled and, his free hand taking hers, demonstrated what he had in mind. A delicious shiver went through her.

"Tomorrow we'll start showing you about," he said.

Axor cleared his throat, somewhat like a volcano. "We should not unduly impose on your generosity," he boomed. "If I may meet the appropriate persons and make use of the appropriate materials—"

"You shall, you shall," Kukulkan promised. "But first we must get you settled into your quarters, and let you rest after your journey."

The flight had been neither long nor taxing. Nevertheless Diana confessed a degree of weariness to herself. So incredibly much excitement!

Kukulkan escorted her into the terminal. A wall displayed a mural which puzzled her. It depicted a male and female human, nude, of the variant she had heard called "Mongoloid," emerging from clouds wherein drifted hints of stars, like a galaxy a-borning. "An ancestral creation myth," the man told her. "To us it symbolizes—Ah, but here is the greeting committee."

Almost the only folk present at this hour, they were four and, like the pilot, not as precisely similar in appearance as Kukulkan and Pele were, to that pair or to one another. While the gene pool in the population was fixed, homozygosity for every desired trait—including some that were not sex-linked—had proven to be a biological impossibility. Discrete combinations appeared in each generation; if you counted the slightest of the changes that were rung, they were manyfold. Yet the "family" resemblance overrode any minor variations in height, coloring, cast of features. Sex and age and the marks left by life were the principal differences between Zacharians. These were all older than the new arrivals, and, over and above the basic pridefulness of their breed, bore an air of distinction.

Their garb was what Diana would learn was formal: sandals on the feet, wreaths on the brows, the two men in tunics and the two women in flowing but constraining wraparound gowns, white with colored borders. Their names were foreign to her, Vishnu and Heimdal male, Kwan Yin and Isis female. The latter woman took the word, her gaze on Axor:

"Welcome. It is an honor and will be a pleasure to receive an outstanding scholar. I shall be your introducer to the Apollonium, since I am the one among us most familiar with the subject in which we hear you are interested. But my colleagues in general anticipate learning much from you."

"*Ochla,* I came to, to beg knowledge of you," the Wodenite faltered. "Although—no, I will not discuss religion more than is necessary, unless you desire, but the exchange of . . . ideas, information—" An earthquake quiver of avidity went through him from snout to tailtip. His dorsal plates moved like a saw, the light rippled off his scales.

Heimdal said to Targovi, on a note of polite skepticism: "Being in offplanet trade, I am willing to discuss possibilities with you. I cannot encourage optimism. The local market for Imhotepan curiosities was saturated long ago."

"We can at least talk," the Tigery replied, "and then mayhap I can, by your leave, look about this neighborhood. Something may occur to me, whereby we can both profit." Diana could sense the watchfulness beneath his affability.

"Come," Kukulkan murmured in her ear. "If you have no set purpose of your own among us, I'll be delighted to be your dragoman—provided I can fend off my envious brethren."

"Don't you have work to do?" she asked, anxious not to overreach her self.

He shrugged and smiled. "My work is somewhat special, and at present I am, shall we say, on standby."

They went from the terminal. After the heat and damp of the valley, sea breezes were a benediction. A flatbed vehicle waited for Axor, in which Isis joined him; the rest got into a ground limo. Diana was aware of a boulevard flanked by trees and abstract sculpture, of windows aglow, of other cars but not many, of pedestrians and occasional horseback riders— handsome, physically perfect, eerily alike— The ride ended at a house which stood on what appeared to be a campus, to gauge by lawns, trees, and larger neighbor buildings.

The muted sunlight of night showed that the portico columns were fluted, their capitals running out in pleasing geometrical shapes. A frieze overhead depicted individuals of assorted sophont species, coming from right and left to a Zacharian who sat enthroned at the center. Diana couldn't make out whether the Zacharian was man or woman. Within, a mosaic anteroom gave on a spacious chamber with comfortable furniture, luxurious drapes, well-chosen pictures, laden bookshelves, archaic fireplace, everything meant for conversation.

"This is a hospice for visiting scholars," Kwan Yin explained. "Ordinarily they come from elsewhere on the island or the cays, to confer in person or to use specialized equipment. But we have lodged outsiders." Her courtesy remained intact as she added, "You will understand that it is beneath our dignity to be servants. Besides, we assume you will prefer some privacy. Therefore, this house is yours for the duration of your stay. We will conduct you through it and demonstrate the appliances. They are completely robotic, no menial work required. A selection of meals that we hope you will enjoy, when you are not dining with colleagues, is ready for heating. Supplements needed for Wodenite and Starkadian health are included. Should anything be lacking, you have only to call the service department of the Apollonium. Additional communicator codes are in the directory program. Please feel free to ask any questions and make any requests at any time."

A saying of her mother's, that Maria had said she got from Dominic Flandry, who had gotten it from somebody else, came back to Diana. *"This is Liberty Hall. You can spit on the mat and call the cat a bastard."* She felt guilty, ungrateful, about the irreverence.

"We have modified two rooms as best we could for our xenosophont guests," Vishnu added. "I trust they will prove satisfactory."

The four finally left Diana alone in the boudoir assigned her. It was pleasant. The pictures on the walls were conventional scenes and historic portraits, but a hospice should stay neutral and the sight of the Hellas peaks from her south window was breathtaking. A bath adjoined. Closet and drawers held a variety of garments closer to her exact size than she could reasonably have expected. Also set forth were tobacco cigarettes, which she would not use; marijuana smokes, which she might; and a bottle of excellent whisky, which she immediately did.

Wallowing in a tubful of hot water, prior to a small supper and a long sleep, she found it unbelievable that Targovi should imagine evil of these people. Or at least, she forced herself to admit, she did not want to find it believable.

Heimdal would call on the Tigery and Isis on the Wodenite, for preliminary sightseeing and getting acquainted. Diana's guide would be Kukulkan. She gulped her brunch, marginally noticing that it was tasty, and had nothing but mumbles for her tablemates, before she returned to her room to dress for the occasion.

How? It was a problem new to her. While her mother lived, boys had begun shyly inviting her to picnics or dances or toboggan parties, that kind of thing; but they were her sort, from families stationed in an outpost where finery was rare. Since then she'd been encountering grown men and learning considerable wariness of them. Some were decent, of course, and she could have been safely married by now if she had wanted. The stars beckoned too brilliantly, though.

And for Kukulkan Zachary, the stars were reachable.

"Easy, lass, easy," she warned herself. Nevertheless her hand shook a bit while she combed luster back into her hair and secured it with a silver headband. After agonizing, she had chosen a white frock, knee-length, suitable for a broad leather belt; sturdy sandals, good to walk distances in; and a hooded blue cloak with a bronze-and-ruby snake brooch. Given such an outfit she could wear her knife as a very natural accessory. Not that she expected trouble. What she did need to do, in the middle of this overwhelmingness, was proclaim—to herself as much as anybody else—that she remained her own woman.

Kukulkan waited in the living room. He rose and bowed in Imperial court style. He himself wore everyday Terran-type shirt (saffron, open halfway down the chest), slacks (dark blue, form-hugging), and shoes (sturdy, scuffed, lots of hiking behind them). "Good day, milady," he greeted. "We're lucky. Magnificent weather, and nothing to hurry for."

"Good day," she replied, annoyed that her voice fluttered like her pulse. "You're so kind."

He took her hand. "My pleasure, I assure you. My joy." How white his teeth were, how luminous his slanty eyes.

"Well, I—I'm at your call, I reckon. Uh, what were you thinkin' of for today?"

"M-m, the afternoon is wearing on. We might start with a stroll up to Falconer's Park on the western headland. The name comes from a tremendous view. Later—well, the night will be clear again, and things stay open around the clock. Things like museums and art galleries, I mean. We don't have the ordinary sort of public entertainments or restaurants or anything like that. But automated food and drink services aren't bad, and eventually—well, if we happen to end at my home, I scramble a mean egg, and all we Zacharians keep choice wine cellars."

She laughed, more consciously than was her wont. "Thanks very much. Let's see what I can do before I collapse."

They left. A fresh breeze blew over the campus, smelling of grass lately mown. It soughed through silvery trembling of poplars, dark stoutness of chestnuts. A few persons were afoot among the ivied buildings. They wore ordinary clothes, and for the most part were getting along in years. But . . . scholars, scientists, lords and ladies of the arts, whose minds ranged beyond this heaven—?

"You've built yourselves a real paradise, haven't you?" Diana ventured.

The response surprised her. "There are those who would consider it a hell. This is ours, as water is for the fish and air for the bird. Each is forever denied the environment of the other."

"Humans can go into both," she said, mostly to show that she too had a brain. "You Zacharians get around on Daedalus, yes, throughout the Empire, don't you?" Smitten by realization, she hesitated before adding: "But we, the rest of us, we couldn't live here, could we? Even if you allowed us."

"We have special needs," he answered soberly. "We have never claimed to be . . . common humans. Foremost among our needs is the conserving of our heritage. Only here is it secure. Elsewhere our kind exists as individuals or nuclear families, all too susceptible to going wild."

"Uh, 'goin' wild'?"

"Outbreeding. Outmarrying, if you will. Losing themselves and their descendants in the ruck."

She stiffened. He saw and went on quickly. "Forgive me. That sounded more snobbish than I intended. It's a mere phrase in the local dialect. If you reflect upon our history you'll understand why we are determined to maintain our identity."

Interest quelled umbrage. Besides, he was intelligent and good-looking and they were bound along a stately street, downhill toward a bay whose minute planet life made the water shine iridescent. Persons they passed gave her glances—marvelling from children, knowing from adults, admiring and desiring from young men. Often the latter hailed Kukulkan and moved close in unmistakable hopes of an introduction. He gave them a signal which she guessed meant, "Scram. I saw her first." The compliment was as refreshing as the wind off the sea."

"Frankly, I'm ignorant of your past," she acknowledged. "I'm a waif, remember, who'd heard little more than the name of your people."

"Well, that can be remedied," said Kukulkan cordially, "though not in an hour, when our origins lie almost a thousand years back in time, on Terra itself."

"I know that, but hardly any more, not how or why it happened or anything. Tell me, please."

Pride throbbed through the solemnity of his tone. He was a superb speaker.

"As you wish. Travel beyond the Solar System was just beginning. Matthew Zachary saw what an unimaginably great challenge it cast at humankind, peril as well as promise, hardihood required for hope, adaptability essential but not at the cost of integrity. A geneticist, he set himself the goal of creating a race that could cope with the infinite strangeness it would find. Yes, machines were necessary; but they were not sufficient. *People* must go into the deeps too, if the whole human adventure were not to end in whimpering pointlessness. And go they would. It was in the nature of the species. Matthew Zachary wanted to provide them the best possible leaders."

Kukulkan waved his left hand, since Diana had his right arm. "No, not 'supermen', not any such nonsense," he continued. "Why lose humanness in the course of giving biological organisms attributes which would always be superior in machines? He sought the optimum specimen—the all-purpose human, to use a colloquialism. What would be the marks of such a person? Some were obvious. A high, quick, wide-ranging intelligence; psychological stability; physical strength, coordination, organs and functions normal or better, resistance to disease, swift recuperation from any sickness or injury that did occur and was not irreversible—you can write the list yourself."

"I thought a lot of that had already been done," Diana said.

"Of course," Kukulkan agreed. "Genetic treatment was in process of eliminating heritable defects. To this day, they seldom recur, in spite of ongoing mutation and in spite of the fact that comparatively few prospective parents avail themselves of genetic services. Many can't, where they are. I daresay your conception was entirely random, 'natural.' But thanks to ancestors who did have the care, you are unlikely to come down with cancer or schizophrenia or countless other horrors that you may never even have heard named.

"Still, this does not mean that any zygote is as good as any other. The variations and combinations of the genes we accept as normal make such an enormous number that the universe won't last long enough to see every possibility realized. So we get the strong and the feeble, the wise and the foolish, *ad infinitum*. Besides, Zachary understood that that optimum human is unspecialized, is excellent at doing most things but not apt to be the absolute champion at any one of them.

"What is the optimum, except the type which can flourish under the widest possible range of conditions? Zachary acquired a female associate, Yukiko Nomura, who influenced his thinking. She may be responsible for the considerable proportion of Mongoloid traits in us. For example, the eyefold is useful in dry, cold, windy climes, and does no harm in others. By way of contrast, a black skin is ideal in the tropics of Terra under primitive conditions, or today on a planet like Nyanza; and it does not prevent its owner from settling in a different environment; but it does require more dietary iodine than a lighter complexion, and iodine shortages are not uncommon in nature. I could go on, but no matter now. And I admit that a number of the choices were arbitrary, perhaps on the basis of personal preference, when *some* choice had to be made.

"In the end, after years of labor and frequent failure, Zachary and Nomura put together the cell that became ancestral to us. It is not true what a derogatory legend says, that they supplied all the DNA. Their purpose was too grand for vanity. What they gave of their own was that small fraction they knew to be suitable. The rest they got elsewhere, and nearly everything underwent improvement before going into the ultimate cell.

"That cell they then caused to divide into two. For one X chromosome they substituted a Y, thus making the second cell male. They put both in an exogenetic apparatus and nurtured them to term. The infants they adopted, and raised to maturity and their destiny. Those were Izanami and Izanagi, mother and father of the new race.

"Ever afterward, we have guarded our heritage."

There was a long silence. Man and girl left the street for a road that swung out between trees and estates, toward the western promontory. Patricius declined, its light going tawny. The wind blew cooler, with a tang of salt.

"And you marry only amongst yourselves?" Diana asked finally.

"Yes. We must, or soon cease to be what we are. Permanent union with an outsider means excommunication. M-m—this is not boastfulness, it is realism—we do consider our genes a leaven, which we are glad to provide to deserving members of the general species. You are a rather extraordinary young lady, yourself."

Her face heated. "And not yet ready for motherhood, thanks!"

"Oh, I would never dream of distressing you."

She switched the subject back in a hurry. "Doesn't inbreedin' make for defective offspring?"

"Not when there are no defects in the parents. As for the inevitable mutations, tests for those are routine, early in pregnancy. You may find our noninvasive DNA-scanning technique interesting. The equipment for it is an export of ours, but protective restrictions on trade have kept it out of the inner Empire. No clinic on Imhotep has felt it could afford the cost."

Diana grimaced. "And any embryo that isn't 'perfect' you—terminate, is that the nice word?"

"As a matter of fact, seldom; only if the prospects for a satisfying life are nil. True, the mother usually elects to have the zygote removed. But it's brought to term externally . . . or in the womb of an ordinary Daedalan volunteer. We always find couples eager to adopt such a baby. Remember, it's not born with any serious handicap; as a rule, nothing undesirable is evident at all. It's still a superior human being. It is simply not a Zacharian."

"Well, that's better." Diana shook her head and sighed. "You're right, this is an almighty peculiar place. How'd it get started, anyway?"

Kukulkan scowled. "What the Founders did not foresee was the effect of an unpleasant characteristic of the species; and before you point this out yourself, I concede that Zacharians aren't free of it either. Perhaps, if we had had the upper hand, we would have developed into an oppressive master caste. As it was, we were a tiny minority, inevitably but annoyingly exclusive. Astarte Zachary, let us say, might be a loyal shipmate of Pierre Smith; she might take him for a lover; but never would she consider marrying him, or his brother, or anybody except a fellow Zacharian. The reasons were plain, and they were . . . humiliating. The ordinaries retaliated, more and more, with exclusionism of their own. Here and there, discrimination turned into outright persecution. 'Incest' was almost the least ugly of the words thrown at us. The collapse of the Polesotechnic League removed the last barrier against intolerance—not individual intolerance, which we could deal with, but institutionalized intolerance, discriminatory laws in society after society. Many among us found it easier to give up the struggle and merge into the commonality. The need for a homeland became ever more clear.

"Zacharia Island was the choice. At the time, settlement on Daedalus was young, small, embattled against nature. Our pioneers found this real estate unclaimed and saw the potential. They were workers and fighters. They took a leading role in defending against bandits, barbarians, eventually Merseians, during the Troubles. The price they demanded was a treaty of autonomy. When at last the Terran Empire extended its sway this far, the treaty was only slightly modified. Why should we not continue to govern ourselves as we wished? We caused no dissension, we paid our tribute, we made a substantial contribution to the regional economy. As you've seen, the rest of the Daedalans accept us on our traditional terms; and by now, elsewhere in the Empire, we are merely people who carry on some enterprises of business, exploration, or science. In short, having forsaken old dreams of leadership, we are just one more ethnic group within a domain of thousands."

"What sort of government do you have?" Diana asked.

Kukulkan's intensity yielded to a smile. "Hardly recognizable as such. Adults generally handle their private affairs and earn their livelihoods however they see fit. In case of difficulties, they have plenty of helpful friends. In case of serious disputes, those same friends act as arbitrators. What public business we have is in charge of a committee of respected elders. When it becomes more than routine, telecommunications bring all adults into the decision-making process. We are not too numerous for that. More important, consensus comes naturally to us."

Again, silence. The road climbed heights above the bay. There water shimmered quiet, but from up ahead Diana began to hear the crash of surf on rocks.

"What are you thinking, rare lady?" Kukulkan prompted.

"Oh, I—I don't know how to say it. You're bein' generous to me. I'd hate to sound, oh, ungracious."

"But?"

She let it out: "But isn't this life of yours awfully lonely? Everybody a copy of yourself, even your wife, even your kids—How do you stand it? It's not as if you were dullards. No! I think if I had to be by myself, for always, I'd want it to be on an empty planet, me and nobody else—no second and third me to keep feedin' back my thoughts, my feelin's, and, and everything."

"Fear not," he said quietly. "I expected your question and take no offense. A full answer is impossible. You must be a Zacharian before you can understand. But use that fine mind of yours and do a little logical imagining. We are not identical. Similar, yes, but not identical. Besides the genotypal variations, we have our different lives behind us, around us. That happens to multiple-birth children of ordinaries, too. They never tread out the same measure. Often they go widely separate ways. Recall that Pele is currently taking her turn as a factor, while her principal career is in industrial administration. Isis is a planetary archaeologist, Heimdal a merchant, Vishnu a xenologist, Kwan Yin a semantician . . . and thus it goes, as diverse as the cosmos itself.

"And we have our constant newness, our ever-changing inputs, here on our island. We are in touch with the outside universe. News comes in, books, dramas, music, arts, science, yes, fashions, amusements. Each individual perceives, evaluates, experiences this in his or her particular way, and then we compare, argue, try for a synthesis—Oh, we do not stagnate, Diana, we do not!"

In a corner of her consciousness she was unsure whether to be pleased or warned by so early a first-name familiarity from him. Mainly she struggled to define her response. "Just the same—somethin' you mentioned before, and your whole attitude toward us, your takin' in three raggedy castaways, when for centuries it's been a scarce privilege for any outsider to set foot here—Believe me, we appreciate your help and everything. But I can't keep from wonderin' if—what with the war cuttin' off that flow of information from the stars—if you aren't desperate already for anything fresh."

"You are wise beyond your years," he answered slowly. " 'Desperate' is too strong a word. Father Axor is in fact very interesting, and his comrades come in the package. Deeper motivations—but only a Zacharian would understand. In your own right, Diana, you are more than welcome."

Still she saw around her a Luciferean isolation, and puzzled over how it had worked on the community, lifetime by lifetime. Targovi seemed abruptly less alien than this man at her side.

But then they reached land's end and stopped. He swept an arm across the sight. She gasped. Cliffs dropped down to skerries where breakers roared, white against blue, violet, green. The ocean went on beyond, without limit, finally dimming away in weather; at that distance, stormclouds were not rearing monsters but exquisitely sculptured miniatures. The bay sheened opalescent, the terrain rose in changeable play of golden light and blue-black shadow over its emerald richness. Westward, Patricius was beginning to reach out wings. Southward, vision was bounded by the Hellene snowpeaks, softly aflame.

When Kukulkan took her hand, it was natural to clutch his tightly. He smiled anew and pursued his thought: "Humankind needs your genes. They are valuable. It is your duty to pass them on."

Chapter 18

Admiral and self-proclaimed Emperor Sir Olaf Magnusson gave safe conduct to the ship from Terra, on condition that her crew surrender their arms and let his men take over. It was not that she posed any serious threat in herself, being an unescorted light cruiser stripped down and fine-tuned for speed. It was, perhaps, because the chief of the delegation she bore was Fleet Admiral Sir Dominic Flandry.

The trip was short from the rendezvous star to the sun of Sphinx, the planet on which Magnusson currently maintained his headquarters. That was a shrewd selection. Besides its location, strategic under present conditions, it was humanly habitable and the center of formidable industries occupying that entire system. It was not humanly inhabited; the name had been bestowed in a mood of despair at ever comprehending the natives. They simply paid the Empire its tribute and went about their inexplicable business. When Magnusson arrived, they were equally unemotional, offering him no resistance, providing him what he demanded, accepting his promises of eventual compensation, but volunteering nothing. This suited him well. He neither needed nor wanted another set of societies to fit into a governance still thinly spread and precariously established.

Those were relative terms. Throughout the space he controlled—by now a wedge driven into more than ten percent of the volume claimed by the Empire—life went on in most places with little change, except where curtailment of interstellar trade had repercussions. The same authorities carried out essentially the same tasks as before. The difference was that they reported, when they did, to his Naval commissioners rather than Gerhart's satraps. They saw to the filling of any requisitions. They gave no trouble; had they done so, they would soon have been overthrown by their subordinates, with the heartfelt cheers of populaces that might otherwise have suffered nuclear bombardment.

As yet, few had openly embraced the Olafist cause. The basic requirement laid on everybody was to refrain from resisting it. Should Gerhart's side prevail, you could explain that there had been no choice. Should Magnusson's, there would be ample time to switch loyalty.

Thus fared, in broad and oversimplified outline, the civilians. Some Navy officers took their oaths with antique seriousness, and led such personnel as would follow them into space or into the hills, to wage guerilla warfare on behalf of the Molitor dynasty. They were more than counterbalanced by those who swore allegiance to the new claimant. Seldom were the latter mere opportunists. Many bore old anger against a regime that they saw as having starved their service and squandered lives to no purpose. Others saw the revolution as a chance for public honesty, fairness, firmness—and even, by whatever means the leader selected, an end to the grindstone half-war with Merseia.

Thus Magnusson's grip on his conquests was secure enough as long as he suffered no major reversal. The moment it slackened, they would fall apart in his fingers. More closely knit, the inner Empire that Gerhart's faction held was less vulnerable. Yet once pierced, it could soon tear asunder: as interdependent nations, worlds, races hastened to yield before civil war destroyed their sacrosanct prosperity.

Hence Magnusson did not risk overextending himself. Instead, he directed his vanguard forces to make fast what they had captured and seek no further battle. Meanwhile he consolidated the guardianship of his rearward domains. This released squadron after squadron for front-line duty in his next great onslaught.

For their part, Gerhart's commanders were not anxious to fight again soon. They had taken a bad beating. Repairs and replacements were necessary, not least where morale was concerned. The total strength on their side remained hugely superior, but only a fraction was available for reinforcements, if the rest of the Empire was to be kept safe—especially against a surprise flank attack. Collecting the data, making the decisions, issuing the calls, obtaining the means, reorganizing the fleets and support corps, all this would take time.

So the conflict dwindled for the nonce into random skirmishes. Magnusson sent a message proposing negotiations. Rather to his surprise, an acceptance came back. Emperor Gerhart would dispatch several high-ranking officers and their aides to conduct exploratory talks. Almost on the heels of this word, Flandry followed.

"Why are you here?" Magnusson asked.

Flandry grinned. "Why, because his Majesty cherishes a statesmanlike wish for peace, reconciliation, and the return of his erring children to righteous ways and his forgiveness."

Magnusson glared. "Are you trying to make fun of me?"

They sat alone in what had been a room of the Imperial resident's house. It was small and plainly furnished, as befitted a person who had had little to do. A full-wall one-way transparency gave a view of surrounding native structures. They were like gigantic three-dimensional spiderwebs. Now that the orange sun was down, lights twinkled throughout them, changing color at every blink. Magnusson had dimmed interior illumination so his visitor might better see the spectacle. Unfiltered, the air was a bit cold, with a faint ferrous odor. Sometimes a deep hum penetrated the walls. And sometimes a cluster of sparks drifted across the sky, an atmospheric patrol or a space unit in high orbit, sign of power over foreignness.

Flandry reached in his tunic for a cigarette case. "No, I am quoting news commentaries I heard as I was preparing for departure. Unless the government buried all reports of your offer, which would have been hard to do, it must needs explain its response, whether positive or negative. I daresay your flacks use similar language."

Magnusson's big frame eased back into his chair. "Ah, yes. I was forgetting how sardonically superior you like to make yourself out to be. It's been years since we last met, and that was just in passing."

Flandry drew a cigarette from the silver box, tapped it on his thumbnail, ignited it and trickled smoke across his lean features. "You ask why I am here. I might ask you the same."

"Don't play your games with me," Magnusson snapped, "or I'll send you packing tomorrow. I invited you to talk privately because I had hopes the conversation would be meaningful."

"You don't expect that of the official discussions between my group and whatever staff members you appoint?"

"Certainly not. This was a charade from the beginning."

Flandry raised the glass of neat whisky at his elbow and sipped. "You initiated it," he said mildly.

"Yes. As a token of good will. You'd call it propaganda. But you must know I have to demonstrate the truth over and over—that I have no other aim than the safety and well-being of the Empire, which the corruption and incompetence of its rulers have been undermining for dangerously long." Magnusson, who had had no refreshment set out for himself, growled forth a laugh. "You're thinking I've started believing my own speeches. Well, I do. I always did. But I'll grant you, maybe I've been giving so many that I've gotten in the habit of orating."

He leaned forward. "I did expect that, at this stage, my proposal would be rebuffed," he said. "Apparently Gerhart decided to try sounding me out. Or, rather, his chief councillors did; he hasn't that much wit. Now it's hardly a secret that he—or, at any rate, the Policy Board—listens closely to whatever Dominic Flandry has to say. I suspect this mission was your idea. And you are leading it in person." His forefinger stabbed toward the man opposite. "Therefore my question really was, 'Why are *you* here?' Answer it!"

"That is," Flandry drawled, "on the basis of my presence you assume I have more in mind than a jejune debate?"

"You wouldn't waste your time on any such thing, you fox."

"Ah, you've found me out. Yes, I did urge that we accept your invitation, and believe me, I had to argue hard before I got agreement to such an exercise in futility. Not that the people with me unanimously know it is. Apart from a couple of leathery old combat commanders and one tough-minded old scholar, to keep the rest from going completely off into Cloud Cuckoo Land, they're career civil officials with excellent academic backgrounds. They believe in the power of sweet reason and moral suasion. I suggest that to meet with them you assign whatever officers of yours are in need of amusement."

"If I bother. You admit this has been an excuse to get you into play—which I'd already guessed. What do you intend?"

"Exactly what is happening."

Magnusson's heavy countenance stiffened. He clenched a fist on the arm of his chair. Behind him, the star-points in the spiderwebs blinked, changed, blinked, changed.

Flandry sat back, crossed shank over knee, inhaled and sipped. "Relax ," he said. "You've nothing to fear from a solitary man, aging and unarmed, when a squad of guards must stand beyond that door. You spoke of us trying to sound you out. That means nothing around the conference table. What is anyone going to do—what can anyone do?—but bandy clichés? However, I've a notion that it may be possible for me to sound you out, as man to individual man." He made an appeasing gesture. "In return, I can tell you things, give you a sense of what the situation is on Terra and inside the Imperium, such as would be unwise to utter in the open."

"Why should I believe you?" Magnusson demanded hoarsely.

Again Flandry grinned. "Belief isn't compulsory. Still, my remarks are input, if you'll listen, and I think you'll find they accord with facts known to you. What is to keep you from lying to me? Nothing. Indeed, I take it for given that you will, or you'll refuse to respond, when words veer in inconvenient directions. Usually, though, you should have no reason not to be frank." His gray gaze caught Magnusson's and held on. "It's lonely where you are, isn't it, Sir Olaf?" he murmured. "Wouldn't you like to slack off for this little while and talk ordinary human talk? You see, that's all I'm after: getting to know you as a man."

"This is fantastic!"

"No, it's perfectly logical, if one uses a dash of imagination. You realize I'm not equipped to draw a psychomathematical profile of you, which could help us predict what you'll do next, on the basis of an evening's gab. I am not Aycharaych."

Magnusson started. "Him?"

"Ah," said Flandry genially, "you've heard of the late Aycharaych, perhaps had to do with him, since you've spent most of your time on the Merseia-ward frontier. A remarkable being, wasn't he? Shall we trade recollections of him?"

"Get to the point before I throw you out," Magnusson rasped.

"Well, you see, Sir Olaf, to us on Terra you're a rather mysterious figure. The output of your puffery artists we discount. We've retrieved all the hard data available on you, of course, and run them through every evaluation program in the catalogue, but scarcely anything has come out except your service record and a few incidentals. Understandable. No matter how much you distinguished yourself, it was in a Navy whose officers alone number in the tens of millions, operating among whole worlds numbering in the tens of thousands. Whatever additional information has appeared about you, in journalistic stories and such over the years, that's banked on planets to which you deny us access. As for your personality, your inner self, we grope in the dark."

Magnusson bridled. "And why should I bare my soul to you?"

"I'm not asking you to," Flandry said. "Tell me as much or as little, as truthful or false, as you like. What I am requesting is simply talk between us—that you and I set hostility aside tonight, relax, be only a couple of careerists yarning together. Why? Because then we on Terra will have a slightly better idea of what to prepare ourselves for. Not militarily but psychologically. You won't be a faceless monster, you'll be a human individual, however imperfectly we still see you. Fear clouds judgment, and worst when it's fear of the unknown.

"Wouldn't you like to make yourself clear to us? Then maybe a second round of negotiations could mean something. Suppose you're being defeated, the Imperium might well settle for less than the extermination of you and your honchos. Suppose you're winning, you might find us more ready to give you what you want, without further struggle." Flandry dropped his voice. "After all, Sir Olaf, you may be our next Emperor. It would be nice to know beforehand that you'll be a good one."

Magnusson raised his brows. "Do you seriously think an evening's natter can make that kind of difference?"

"Oh, no," Flandry said. "Especially when it's off the record. If I reach any conclusions, they'll be my own, and I wouldn't look for many folk at home to take my naked word. But I am not without influence. And every so often, a small change does make a big difference. And, mainly, what harm to either of us?"

Magnusson pondered. After a time: "Yes, what harm?"

Dinner was Spartan, as suited the master's taste. He took a single glass of wine with it, and afterward coffee. Flandry had two glasses, plus a liqueur from the resident's stock, sufficient to influence his palate and naught else. Nevertheless, that dining room witnessed speech more animated than ever before. In the main it was noncontroversial, reminiscent, verging on the friendly. Both men had had many odd experiences in their lives.

Flandry was practiced at keeping vigilance behind a mask of bonhomie. Magnusson was not; when he felt such a need, he clamped down a poker face. It appeared toward the end of things, after the orderly had cleared the table of everything except a coffeepot and associated ware. The hour was late. A window showed the spiderweb constellations thinning out as their lights died. Warm air rustled from a grille, for the nights here were cold. It wafted the smoke of Flandry's cigarettes in blue pennons. His brand of tobacco had an odor suggesting leaves on fire in a northern Terran autumn.

He finished his account of a contest on a neutral planet between him and a Merseian secret agent: "Before you object, I agree that poisoning him wasn't very nice. However, I trust I've made it clear that I could not let Gwanthyr go home alive if there was any way of preventing it. He was too able."

Magnusson scowled, then blanked his visage and said flatly, "You have the wrong attitude. You regard the Merseians as soulless."

"Well, yes. As I do everybody else, myself included."

Magnusson showed irritation. "Belay that infernal japing of yours! You know what I mean. You look on them as inevitable foes, natural enemies of humans, like a—a strain of disease bacteria." He paused. "If it weren't for your prejudice, I might seriously consider inviting you to join me. We could make a pretext for your wife to come out before you declared yourself. You claim your purpose is to hold off the Long Night—"

"As a prerequisite for continuing to enjoy life. Barbarism is dismal. The rule of self-righteous aliens is worse."

"I'm not sure but what that's another of your gibes, or your lies. No matter. Why can't you see that I'd bring an end to the decadence, give the Empire back strength and hope? I think what's blinkering you is your sick hatred of Merseians."

"You're wrong there," Flandry said low. "I don't hate them as a class. Far more humans have earned my malevolence, and the one being whose destruction became an end in itself for me didn't belong to either race." He could not totally suppress a wince, and hastened on: "In fact, I've been quite fond of a number of individual Merseians, mostly those I encountered in noncritical situations but sometimes those who crossed blades with me. They were honorable by their own standards, which in many respects are more admirable than those of most modern humans. I sincerely regretted having to do Gwanthyr in."

"But you can't see, you're constitutionally unable to see or even imagine, that a real and lasting peace is possible between us and them."

Flandry shook his head. "It isn't, unless and until the civilization that dominates them goes under or changes its character completely. The Roidhun could make a personal appearance singing 'Jesus Loves Me' and I'd still want us to keep our warheads armed. You haven't had the chance to study them, interact with them, get to know them from the inside out, that I've had."

Magnusson lifted a fist. "I've fought them—done them in, as you so elegantly put it, by the tens of thousands to your measly dozen or two—since I enlisted in the Marines thirty years ago. And you have the gall to say I don't know them."

"That's different, Sir Olaf," Flandry replied placatingly. "You've met them as brave enemies, or as fellow officers, colleagues, when truces were being negotiated and in the intervals of so-called peace that followed. It's like being a player on one of two meteor ball teams. I am acquainted with the owners of the clubs."

"I don't deny hostility and aggressiveness on their part. Who does? I do say it's not been unprovoked—from the time of first contact, centuries ago, when the Terran rescue mission upset their whole order of things and found ways to get rich off their tragedy—and I do say they have their share of good will and common sense, also in high office—which are utterly lacking in today's Terran Imperium. It won't be quick or easy, no. But the two powers can hammer out an accommodation, a peace—an alliance, later on, for going out together through the galaxy."

Flandry patted a hand over the beginnings of a yawn. "Excuse me. I've been many hours awake now, and I must confess to having heard that speech before. We play the recordings you send our way, you know."

Magnusson smiled grimly. "Sorry. I did get carried away, but that's because of the supreme importance of this." He squared his blocky shoulders. "Don't think I'm naive. I do know Merseia from the inside. I've been there."

Flandry lounged back. "As a youngster? The data we have on you suggested you might have paid a couple of visits in the past."

Magnusson nodded. "Nothing treasonable about that. No conflicts were going on at the time. My birthworld, Kraken, has always traded freely, beyond the Terran sphere as well as within it."

"Yes, your people are an independent lot, aren't they? Do go on, please. This is precisely the sort of personal insight I've been trying for."

Magnusson went expressionless. "My father was a space captain who often took cargoes to and from the Roidhunate, sometimes to Merseia itself. That was before the Starkad incident caused relations to deteriorate entirely. Even afterward, he made a few trips, and took me along on a couple of them. I was in my early teens then—impressionable, you're thinking, and you're right, but I was also open to everything observation might show me. I got chummy with several young Merseians. No, this didn't convince me they're a race of angels. I enlisted, didn't I? And you know I did my duty. But when that duty involved getting together with Merseians in person, my senses and mind stayed open."

"It seems a pretty fragile foundation for a consequential political judgment."

"I studied too, investigated, collected opinions, thought and thought about everything."

"The Roidhunate is as complex as the Empire, as full of contradictions and paradoxes, if not more so," Flandry said in a level tone. "The Merseians aren't the sole species in it, and members of some others have been influential from time to time."

"True. Same as with us. What of it?"

"Why, we know still less about their xenos than we do about our own. That's caused us rude surprises in the past. For example, my long-time antagonist Aycharaych. I got the impression you also encountered him."

Magnusson shook his head. "No. Never."

"Really? You seem to recognize the name."

"Oh, yes, rumors get around. I'd be interested to hear whatever you can tell."

Flandry bit his lip. "The subject's painful to me." He dropped his cigarette down an ashtaker and straightened in his chair. "Sir Olaf, this has been a fascinating conversation and I thank you for it, but I am genuinely tired. Could I bid you goodnight? We can take matters up again at your convenience."

"A moment. Stay." Magnusson reflected. Decision came. He touched the call unit on his belt. A door slid aside and four marines trod through. They were Irumclagians, tall, slim, hard-skinned, their insectlike faces impassive.

"You are under arrest," Magnusson said crisply.

"I beg your pardon?" Flandry scarcely stirred, and his words came very soft. "This is a parley under truce."

"It was supposed to be," Magnusson said. "You've violated the terms by attempting espionage. I'm afraid you and your party must be interned."

"Would you care to explain?"

Magnusson snapped an order to the nonhumans. It was clear that they knew only the rudiments of Anglic. Three took positions beside and behind Flandry's chair. The fourth stayed at the door, blaster unholstered.

Magnusson rose to stand above the prisoner, legs widespread, fists on hips. He glowered downward. Wrath roughened his voice: "You know full well. I was more than half expecting it, but let you go ahead in hopes you'd prove to be honest. You didn't.

"For your information, I learned three days ago that the Terran spies specially sent to Merseia were detected and captured. I suspect they went at your instigation, but never mind; you certainly know what they were up to. The leading questions you fed me were part and parcel of the same operation. No wonder you came yourself. Nobody else would've had your devil's skill. If I hadn't been warned, I'd never have known—till the spies and you had returned home and compared notes. As it is, I now have one more proof that the God looks after His warriors."

Flandry met the fire-blue stare coolly and asked, "Won't our captivity be a giveaway?"

"No, I think not," Magnusson said, calming. "Nobody will expect those agents of yours to report back soon. Besides, the Merseians will start slipping the Terrans disinformation that seems to come from them. You can imagine the details better than I can. As for your mini-diplomatic corps here, won't the Imperium be happy when it does not return at once? When, instead, courier torps bring word that things look surprisingly hopeful?"

"The Navy isn't going to sit idle because of that," Flandry cautioned.

"Of course not. Preparations for the next phase of the war will go on. All my side has done is stop an attempt by your side that could have been disastrous if it had succeeded. Yes, I'm sure there are people back there whom you've confided your suspicions to; but what value have they without proof? After fighting recommences in earnest, who'll pay them any further attention?"

Magnusson sighed. "In a way, I'm sorry, Flandry," he said. "You're a genius, in your perverse fashion. This failure is no fault of yours. What a man you would have been in the right cause! I bear you no ill will and have no wish to mistreat you. But I dare not let you continue. You and your entourage will get comfortable quarters. When the throne is mine, I will . . . decide whether it may eventually be safe to release you."

He gave orders. Unresisting, Flandry rose to be led away. "My compliments, Sir Olaf," he murmured. "You are cleverer than I realized. Goodnight."

"Goodnight, Sir Dominic," replied the other.

Chapter 19

The climax was violent.

It began with delusive smoothness. "How I shall regret leaving this place," Axor mused at supper. "Though I will always thank God for the privilege of having encountered wonder here."

Targovi pricked up his ears. "Leaving?"

"Well, we cannot expect our hosts to maintain us forever—especially me, bearing in mind what my food must cost them. Working together with the lady Isis Zachary and her colleagues at the Apollonium in these past days, I have learned things of supreme value, and perhaps contributed some humble moiety in return, but now we seem to have exhausted our respective funds of information and the conclusions which discussion has led us to draw therefrom."

"Apollonium?" Targovi's question was absent-minded, practically a reflex. His thoughts were racing away.

Axor waved a tree-trunk arm around the room where he sprawled and the Tigery sat at table. He was really indicating the nighted campus beyond the hospice walls. "This center of learning, research, philosophy, arts. They do not call it a university because it has no teaching function. Being what they are, Zacharians require no schools except input to their homes, no teachers except their parents or, when they are mature, knowledgeable persons whom they can call when explanation is necessary."

"Oh, yes, yes. You've finished, you say?"

"Virtually. Dear friend," Axor trumpeted, "I cannot express my gratitude for your part in bringing me to this haven. While they have never undertaken serious investigation of the Foredwellers, the Zacharians are insatiably curious about the entire cosmos. Their database contains every item ever reported or collected by such of their people as have gone to space. I retrieved scores of descriptions, pictures, studies of sites unknown to me. Comparison with the facts I already possessed began to open portals. Isis, Vishnu, and Kwan Yin were those who especially took fire and produced brilliant ideas. I would not venture to claim that we are on the way to deciphering the symbols, but we have identified regularities, recurrences, that look highly significant. Who knows where that may lead future scholarship? To the very revelation of Christ's universality, that will in time bring all sentient beings into his church?"

The crocodilian head lifted. "I should not lament my departure," the Wodenite finished. "Ahead of me, while this mortal frame lasts, lie pilgrimages to those planets about which I have learned, to the greater glory of God."

"Well, good," mumbled Targovi. "Know you when we must leave?"

"No, not yet. I daresay they will tell me at the next session. You might be thinking where we should ask them to deposit us on the mainland. They have promised to take us anyplace we like."

"Diana will be sad, I suppose. She's had a fine time. Where is she this eventide?"

Though Axor's visage was not particularly mobile, somehow trouble seemed to dim his brown eyes, and assuredly it registered in his basso profundo: "I cannot say. I have seldom seen her throughout our stay. She goes about in company with that man—what is his name?"

"Kukulkan, if she hasn't swapped escorts."

"Ah." Fingers that could have snapped steel bars twiddled with the spectacles hanging from the armored neck. "Targovi, I—this is most embarrassing, but I must speak—Well, I am not human, nor versed in human ways, but lately I . . . I have begun to fear for that maiden's virtue."

The Tigery choked back a yowl of laughter.

"You know her well," Axor continued. "Do you think, before it is too late—I pray it be not too late—you could advise her, as an, an elder brother?"

Opportunity! Targovi pounced. "I can try," he said. "Truth to tell, I too have fretted about her. I know humans well enough to understand what Kukulkan's intentions are. If we are bound away soon—what one Zacharian knows, they all seem to know—he'll press his suit."

"Oh, dear. And she so young, innocent, helpless." Axor crossed himself.

"I'll see if I can find them," Targovi proposed. "She may not thank me tonight, but afterward—" Despite an urgency which had become desperate, he must still hold down his merriment. Oh, aye, wouldn't Diana Crowfeather be overjoyed at having her business minded for her? His tail dithered. "Wish me luck."

Axor bowed his head and silently invoked a saint or two. Targovi shoved the rest of his meal aside and left.

The whole farce might have been unnecessary. He didn't know whether the hospice was bugged; lacking equipment hidden aboard *Moonjumper*, he had no way of finding out. Therefore he assumed it was, and furthermore that there was a stakeout—not a flesh-and-blood watcher, nothing that crude, but sensors in strategic locations. His going forth should, now, arouse no more misdoubts than his feckless wanderings about in the area appeared to have done.

At most, whoever sat monitoring might flash Kukulkan word that Targovi meant to deboost any seduction, and Kukulkan might thus do best to take the girl for a romantic ride over the mountains . . . if he had not already done so . . . The Zacharians did indeed stick together. No, more than that. They were almost a communal organism, like those Terran insectoids they had introduced to the island ecology—ants—though ants with individual intelligence far too high for Targovi's liking upon this night.

He went out the door. A breeze lulled cool, smelling of leaves and sea, ruffling his fur; he wore nothing but his breechcloth, belt, and knife. Lawns dreamed empty beneath a sky where clouds drifted, tinged argent by Icarus and bronze by the sun-ring. That band was blocked off in the south by the peaks, in places elsewhere by distant weather, but it and the moon gave ample light for humans to see by. He had been waiting for fog or rain to lend comparative darkness in which his vision would have the advantage.

Well, he could wait no longer.

Leaving the campus behind, he followed a street at a trot which should look reasonable under the circumstances, until it passed by a park. There he cut across. Trees roofed grass. He vanished into the gloom. At its farther edge he went on his belly and became a ripple of motion that could easily have been a trick of wind-blown cloud shadows.

From there on he was a Tigery hunter a-stalk, using every scrap of cover and every trick in the open, senses tuned to each least flicker, shuffling, whiff, quivering, clues and hints for which human languages lacked words. Often he froze for minutes while a man or a woman walked by, sometimes close enough to touch. Had dogs been about, he would perforce have left a number of the abominable creatures dead, but fortunately the Zacharians had better taste than to keep any. As was, he took more than an hour to approach his goal.

It stood high in the hills, on the fringe of settlement. A five-meter wall, thirty meters on a side, surrounded an area forbidden to visitors. When Heimdal was showing him about, Targovi had inquired what was within. "Defense," his guide answered. "You may not know it, but under the treaty we take responsibility for the defense of this island—not out into space, of course; that's the job of the Navy; but against whatever hostile force might break through or might come over the surface. We maintain our own installations. This one guards Janua."

Guards, aye. Flattened on the ground, Targovi felt a faint shudder. Something had passed beneath. Well, he had already eye-gauged that the spaceport—from which outsiders were also banned—lay just opposite, on the far side of the range. A connecting tunnel was logical.

His glance roved. Above the stony bulk of the wall, the Mencius ridge made a grayness beyond which glimmered the Hellene peaks. Sculptured slopes fell downward, multiply shadowed, frostily highlighted. The Averroes River was brokenly visible, agleam. It plunged into the sheening of the bay. Phosphorescence traced runes over the ocean. Beneath him were soil, pebbles, prickly weeds, dew.

Attention went back to the fortress. No, he realized, it wasn't any such thing as St. Barbara's had been part of. It must be a command post for missiles, energy projectors, aircraft, and whatever else laired in the vicinity. He doubted there was much. Daedalus had long been under Imperial protection. Now it was under Magnusson's, but that should make no immediate difference. Likewise, Targovi conjectured, security was lax. The Zacharians would have had no cause to be strict, not for centuries, and if requirements had changed overnight, organization and training could hardly have done the same.

Still, all it took was a single alarm, or afterward a single bullet or ray or flying torpedo. . . .

Hence he never considered the gate from which a road wound off. Instead, he slithered to a point well away, where he could stand in shadow and examine the wall. It sloped upward, as was desirable for solidity. The material was unfinished stone, perhaps originally to keep anyone from climbing on vacsoles—or was that notion too ridiculous? Erosion had blurred the roughness of the blocks but also pitted the mortar. A human could never have gone up, but a Tigery might, given strength and claws and eyesight adaptable to dim light. He found no indications of built-in warning systems. Why should they exist? Who, or what, would be so crazy as to attempt entry?

Being of the species he was, Targovi did not stop to wonder about his saneness. He had little more to go on than a hunter's hunch. What lay behind the wall, he could barely guess. What he could do after he found it was unknowable beforehand. He sorely missed the weapons and gear stowed in his ship. Yet he did not consider himself reckless. He went ahead with that which he had decided to do.

After long and close study, he had a way picked out. He crawled backward until he judged the distance sufficient for a running start. Lifting eyes, ears, and tendrils above the shrubs, he searched for possible watchers. None showed. Then better be quick, before any did! He sprang to his feet and charged.

Well-conditioned Tigeries under a single standard gravity can reach a sprint speed which outdoes their Terran namesake. Sheer momentum carried Targovi far up the barrier. Fingers and claws did the rest; he needed only an instant's purchase to thrust himself onward, too fast to lose his grip and fall. Over the top he went, fell, landed on pads that absorbed much of the shock, took the rest in rubbery muscles, and promptly dived for cover.

That was behind a hedge. It would do him scant good if someone had noticed. After a minute, having heard and smelled nothing, he hazarded a look. The grounds were deserted. His readiness flowed from fight-or-flight back to stealth.

A garden surrounded a fair-sized building. While not neglected, it showed signs of perfunctory care. That bore out Targovi's estimate, that this post had seen little use until quite recently, and was still weakly and slackly manned. Why not? What need had the Zacharians had for military skills since Daedalus came under the Pax Terrana? What reason had they, even now, to worry about intruders? Nonetheless Targovi continued cautious. His venture was wild at best.

First establish lines of retreat. A couple of big oaks offered those. A human could not leap from their upper boughs to the top of the wall, but a Tigery could. Avoiding paths, he eeled from hedge to bush. The building loomed ahead, darkling in the half-light of heaven. It too was old, weather-worn; it had the same peaked roof as those downhill but lacked their gracefulness, being an unrelieved block, though with ample windows and doors. Toward the rear, two of those windows glowed.

They were plain vitryl. Targovi slipped alongside and peered around an edge. Breath hissed between his fangs. The hair erected over his body. This was the total and stunning confirmation of his—fears?—expectations? —guesses?—The quarry he had been tracing stood terrible before him.

The windows gave on a room bare-walled and sparsely furnished, with a bath cubicle adjoining. Most of its space went to a computer. While engineering imposes basic similarity on all such machines, Targovi could see that this one had not been manufactured in the Terran Empire. Black-uniformed, blaster at belt and rifle grounded, on guard through the night watch, was a Merseian.

For a long spell, the Tigery stood moveless. Ring-gleam and cloud shadows, wind-sough in leaves, odors of green life, grittiness of masonry under his palms, seemed abruptly remote, things of dream, against the reality which confronted him. What to do?

The sensible thing was to withdraw unobserved, keep silence, let the Zacharians return him to the mainland, contact Naval Intelligence. . . .

Which would be the absolute in lunacy, he

thought. What had happened when he just hinted that certain matters might rate investigation? And that was before Magnusson openly rebelled. How far today would a nonhuman outlaw get on his raw word?

The overwhelming majority of Daedalans and, yes, members of the armed forces desired the survival of the Empire. What else was there for them? But they'd need proof, evidence that nobody could hide or explain away.

"When we hunted the gaarnokh on Homeworld," Dargoika often said, "and he stood at bay, to spear him in the heart we must needs go in between his horns."

Targovi slipped along the wall to the next-nearest door. It was unlocked. Nobody came through the gate or up from the spaceport tunnel unless the leaders had complete confidence in him. Targovi entered a short hall which led to a corridor running the length of the building. Unlighted at this hour of rest, it reached dusky along rows of closed chambers—offices mainly, he assumed, long disused. Some must lately have been seeing activity, as must the weapon emplacements, wherever they were: but not much, because the Zacharians did not await any emergency. They *knew* Merseia wasn't going to attack the Patrician System.

Chiefly, Targovi decided, this strongpoint housed a few officers and their aides from the Roidhunate, observers, liaison agents, conveyors of whatever orders their superiors issued. Ships traveled to and fro, bringing replacements for those who went back to report. That traffic wouldn't be hard to keep secret. It was infrequent; its captains knew the right recognition codes; Planetary Defense Command would assign sentry vessels to orbits that never gave them a good look at such arrivals; and private landing facilities waited on the island.

The gatortails must have quarters under this roof. A smell of them reached Targovi as he neared. It was warm, like their blood, but neither Tigery-sweet nor human-sour—bitter. He bristled.

Partly by scent, partly by keeping track of direction and distance, he identified the door to his goal. It was closed. Unfortunate, that. He'd have to proceed without plan. But if he stood here hesitating his chances would rapidly worsen. Dawn drew nigh. Though most people's sleeptime might last later, many would soon be astir throughout Janua—must already be—and full sunlight upon wayfarers.

He thumbed the "open" plate and stepped aside. As the door slid back, the Merseian would look this way and wonder why nobody trod through. He'd likely come closer to see—Now Targovi heard click of boots on the floor, now the sound stopped but he caught a noise of breathing—not quickened, the guard didn't imagine an enemy at hand, he was probably puzzled, maybe thinking a collywobble had developed in these ancient circuits—

Targovi came around the jamb and sprang.

As he appeared, he saw what was needful, pivoted on his claws, and launched himself, in a single storm-swift movement. Driven by the muscles of his race, he struck faster than the Merseian could lift weapon. They tumbled down together. The rifle clattered aside. Targovi jammed his right forearm into a mouth that had barely started to gape in the green-skinned face. Only a stifled gurgle got around it.

He could have killed a human with a karate chop, but had not studied Merseian anatomy and dared not suppose it was that similar. His left hand darted to catch the opponent's right arm before the holstered blaster could be drawn. Strength strained against strength. Meanwhile he hooked claws into the thick tail, which would else be a club smashing upon him or thumping a distress signal. The boots, which might have done likewise, he pinned between his calves.

The Merseian was powerful, less so than him but surging against his pressure, sure to break free somewhere. Targovi released the gun wrist. His own arm whipped around behind the neck of the foe. Low and blunt, unlike Axor's, the spinal ridge nevertheless bruised him—as his right arm shoved the head back over that fulcrum.

The Merseian clutched his blaster. Targovi heard a *crack*. The head flopped. The body shuddered, once, and lay still.

Whatever their variations, Merseian, Tigery, and human are vertebrates.

Targovi jumped off the corpse, snatched the rifle, crouched to cover the doorway. If the noise had roused someone, he'd have to try shooting his way free.

Minutes crawled by. Silence deepened. Light grew stronger in the windowpanes.

Targovi lowered the weapon. Nobody had heard. Or, if anybody did, it had been so briefly that the being sank back into sleep. After all, he had taken just seconds to kill the guard.

How much time remained before reveille, or whatever would reveal him? It was surely meager. Targovi got to work.

Having closed the door, he examined the computer. Aye, Merseian made, and he was ignorant of the Eriau language. Not entirely, though. Like most mentally alive persons in this frontier space, he had picked up assorted words and catchphrases. His daydream of operating among the stars had also led him to learn the alphabet. Moreover, Merseia had originally acquired modern technology from Terra; and logic and natural law are the same everywhere.

When they first arrived here, the gatortails must have brought this as their own mainframe computer. Not only would they be most familiar with it, they need not fear its being tampered with, whether directly or from afar. Besides making active use of it, they'd keep their database within. . . . Yes. Targovi believed he had figured out the elementary instruction he wanted.

He touched keys. "Microcopy everything."

The machine had rearranged molecules by the millions and deposited three discus-shaped containers on the drop shelf before Targovi finished the rest of his job. Yet what he did went swiftly. He stripped the tunic from the

Merseian, who now resisted him with mere weight, and slashed it in places until he could tie it together as a package. The weapons would go in, as well as the data slabs and—He set things out of the way while his knife made the next cuts, and afterward fetched a towel from the bathroom. It wouldn't do to have his bundle drip blood.

Ready for travel, he opened the door a crack, peered, opened it wide, stepped through, closed it again. Quite possibly no one would be astir for another hour or two. Merseians tended to be early risers, but had no good reason to reset their circadian rhythms according to the short Daedalan period. In fact, they had good reason to refrain. The effort was lengthy and demanding; meanwhile they'd be at less than peak efficiency.

It was likewise possible that, whenever the rest of his mission got up, the sentry would not be immediately due for relief, and no other occasion would arise for them to pass this door.

Targovi couldn't count on any of that. Thus far his luck had been neither especially fair nor especially foul. Most of it he had made for himself. Had he come upon a different situation, he would have acted according to it as best he was able. Throughout, he had exploited surprise.

How much longer could he continue to do so? Not very!

He stole down corridor and hall. At the exit, he dropped to a belly-scraping all fours and crept, dragging his burden in his teeth. Up a tree—a flying leap to the outer wall and a bounce to the ground beyond—snake's way through brush till a dip of terrain concealed him—He rose and ran.

Zacharians stared at the carnivore form that sped unhumanly fast down their streets, a bundle under an arm. With his spare hand, he waved at them. They had gotten used to seeing the poor itinerant huckster around, his hopes of business gone, aimlessly adrift. If today he bounded along, why, he must be stretching his legs. He looked cheerful enough.

The sun-ring had contracted to a broad, incandescent arc in the east. The sky above was nearly white; a few clouds hung gilded. Westward the blue deepened. Dew sparkled on grass. Songbirds twittered. A red squirrel flamed along a bough. Here and there, savants passed from hall to ivy-covered hall. It would have been hard to imagine a scene more innocent.

When Targovi let himself into the hospice, he missed the scent of Diana. He went to her room and peeked in. The bed stood unused. For a second he stood irresolute. Should he try to find her? The loss of time could prove fatal. On the other hand, a third member of his party might tip the scales, and the gods knew that most weight now lay in the wrong pan. . . . And what of his sisterling herself? Ought he make her share his danger? Would she be safest staying behind? Maybe. The Zacharians might be satisfied with a straightforward interrogation and do her no harm. If she had been romping with the man Kukulkan, he should have the decency to use his influence on her behalf. . . . But maybe the Zacharians would work ghastliness upon her, in fear or in spite. Maybe none of them felt in any way honor-bound to an outsider lover.

Decision. Targovi couldn't hunt over Janua for her. But if she was where he thought was likely, it might not be too distant. He sought the infotrieve and keyed the area directory. Kukulkan's home address appeared on the screen. Houses lacked numbers, but streets had names, and coordinates on a grid indicated each location. Acacia Lane—yes—Targovi's disconsolate wanderings while Axor conferred and Diana flirted had had the purpose of learning the geography. Acacia Lane was south of here, not really out of the way when you were trying to escape.

He entered the Wodenite's room. Axor filled it, curled on a seat of mattresses. His breathing was like surf below the sea cliffs. Targovi slipped past the scaly body, bent over the muzzle, took hold of its nostrils. Those, he had discovered, were the most sensitive point. He tweaked them. Horny lids flipped back under craggy brow ridges. A row of teeth, meant for both ripping and crushing, gleamed into view. *"Ochla, hoo-oo, ksyan ngunggung,"* rolled between them. "What's this, eh, what, what?"

"Quick!" Targovi said. "Follow me. I've come on something unique. It won't last. You'll want to see it."

"Really. I was awake late, reading."

"Please. I beg you. You'll not regret it."

"Ah, well, if you insist." Hoofs banged, the floor creaked, Axor's tail scraped a wall. He followed Targovi out and across the greensward. Such people as were in sight gave them looks but continued on their own paths. The xenosophonts were no longer a novelty.

Where a pair of majestic trees shaded a bench, Targovi stopped. "This will be an unpleasant surprise," he warned. "Hold fast to your emotions. Reveal naught."

"What?" The Wodenite blinked. "But you said—"

"I lied. Here is the truth. Curl around. I want you to screen off what you're about to see."

Squatting, Targovi pulled his bundle from under the bench where he had left it and undid its knots. Three data slabs, two firearms on non-Technic make, and something wrapped in a wet red towel appeared. He unfolded the cloth. Axor failed to suppress a geyserish gasp. Beneath his gaze lay the severed head of a Merseian.

Chapter 20

A few times in the past, Diana had felt she was being well and thoroughly kissed. Now she found her estimates had been off by an order of magnitude. Kukulkan's body pressed hard and supple. When she opened her eyes she saw his blurrily, but gold-brown, oblique, brilliant. The man-scent of him dizzied her. She felt his heartbeat against hers. She clung tight with her left arm and let her right fingers go ruffling through his hair.

His hand slid from her hip, upward, inside her half-opened blouse. It went under her brassiere. Sweetness exploded.

Wait! rang through. Dragoika's voice purred across the years: "Give yourself to the wind, but first be sure 'tis the wind of your wish." The loneliness of Maria Crowfeather—

Diana pulled back. She must exert force. "Hold on," she said with an unsteady laugh. "I need to come up for air."

"Oh, my beautiful!" His weight thrust her downward on the sofa where they sat.

She resisted. A gentle judo break, decisive since unawaited, freed her. She sprang from him and stood breathing hard, flushed and atremble but back in charge of herself.

"Easy, there," she said, smiling, because warmth still pulsed. She found occupation in pushing back her tousled locks. "Let's not get carried away."

He rose, too, himself apparently unoffended, though ardency throbbed in his tone: "Why not? What harm? What except love and joy?"

He refrained from advancing, so she stayed where she was, and wondered if she could really resist the handsomeness that confronted her. "Well, I—Oh, Kukulkan, it's been wonderful." And it had been, culminating in this night's flight above the Hellenes to a lake where they swam while the reflection of the sun-ring flashed everywhere around them, as if they swam in pure light; and ate pheasant and drank champagne ashore; and danced on a boat dock to music from the car's player, music and a dance she had never known before, a waltz by somebody named Strauss; and finally came back to his place, where one thing led to another. "I thank you, I do, I do. But soon I'll be gone."

"No, you won't. I'll see to that. You'll stay as long as you want. And I'll take you all over this planet, and eventually beyond, to the stars."

Did he mean it? Suppose he did!

She had no intention of remaining a virgin for life, or until any particular age. Pride, if nothing else, forbade becoming somebody's plaything or, for that matter, making a toy of a man. But she liked Kukulkan Zachary—more than liked him—and she must be a little special to him, or why would he have squired her around as he did? What an ingrate she was, not to trust him.

If only she'd had a reversible shot. She wanted neither a baby in the near future nor an abortion ever; but living hand-to-mouth on Imhotep, as often as not among the Tigeries, she just hadn't gotten around to the precaution. She *thought* this week was safe for her—

"I'd better go," she forced herself to say. "Let me think things over. Please don't rush me."

"At least let me kiss you goodbye until later," he replied in that melodious voice of his. "A few hours later, no more, I beg you."

She couldn't refuse him so small a favor, could she, in common courtesy?

He gathered her in. She responded. Resolution wobbled.

Whether or not it would have stood fast, she never knew. The front door, unlocked on the crimeless island, opened. Targovi came in. Behind him reared the dragon head of Axor.

Diana and Kukulkan recoiled apart. "What the flickerin' hell!" ripped from her. He snarled and tensed.

Targovi leveled the blaster he carried. "Don't," he said.

"Have you two jumped your orbits?" Diana yelled, and knew freezingly that they had not.

Kukulkan straightened. His features stiffened. "Drop that thing," he said as if giving a routine order to a servant. "Do you want the girl killed in a firefight?"

"Who is to start one?" Targovi retorted. He gestured at a window. Leafage turned young daylight to gold-spattered green. Like most local homes, this was tucked into its garden, well back from the street, screened by trees and hedges. It was obvious that the intruders had entered unseen.

Axor crowded in. He went to Diana, laid his enormous arms about her, drew her to his plated breast, as tenderly as her mother. "My dear, my dear, I am sorry," he boomed low. "Horror is upon us. Would that you could be spared."

For a minute she clung tight. It was as though strength and calm flowed out of him, into her. She stepped back. Her gaze winged around the scene and came to rest on Targovi. "Explain," she said.

His scarlet eyes smoldered back at her. "The spoor I followed proved true," he answered. "I followed it into the lair of the beast. Axor, show her what I brought back."

The Wodenite visibly shuddered. "Must I?"

"Yes. Didn't diddle about. Every tailshake we wait, the odds mount against us."

While Axor took a package from a carrier bag and untied it, Targovi's words trotted remorseless: "The Zacharians are in collusion with the Merseians. This means they must be with Magnusson. The Merseians must be! You understand what this betokens."

"No," she protested, "please, no. Impossible.

How could they keep the secret? Why would they do such a thing?"

Axor completed his task, and It stared sightlessly up at her.

"They are not like your folk," Targovi reminded. Struggling out of shock, she heard him dimly. "We must bring this evidence back."

"How?" challenged Kukulkan. Diana regarded him, which hurt like vitriol to do. He stood shaken but undaunted. "Would you steal a car and fly off? You might succeed in that, even committing another murder or two in the process. But missiles will come after you, rays, warcraft if necessary, to shoot you down. Meanwhile, whatever transmissions you attempt will be jammed—not that they'd be believed. A waterboat is merely ludicrous. Surrender, and I'll suggest clemency."

"You'll not be here." Targovi aimed the blaster. He had set it to narrow beam. Kukulkan never flinched.

"No!" shouted Diana and bellowed Axor together. She pursued with a spate of words: "D'you mean to silence him? What for? The alarm'll go out anyhow, when they find that poor headless body. Tie him up instead."

"You do it, then," the Tigery growled. "Be quick, but be thorough. Meanwhile, think whether you want to join us. Axor, stow the goods again."

"Into the bedroom," Diana directed. The irony smote her. "Oh, Kukulkan, this is awful! You didn't know anything about it, did you?"

Under the threat of Targovi's gun, he preceded her, turned, and said in steeliness: "I did. It would be idiotic of me to deny that. But I intended you no harm, lovely lass. On the contrary. You could have become a mother of kings."

She wiped away tears, drew her knife, slashed a sheet into bonds. "What do you want, you people? Why've you turned traitor?"

"We owe the Terran Empire nothing. It dragooned our forebears into itself. It has spurned our leadership, the vision that animated the Founders. It will only allow us to remain ourselves on this single patch of land, afar in its marches. Here we dwell like Plato's man in chains, seeing only shadows on the wall of our cave, shadows cast by the living universe. The Merseians have no cause to fear or shun us. Rather, they will welcome us as their intermediaries with the human commonality. They will grant us the same boundless freedom they desire for themselves."

"Are you s-s-certain about that? Lie down on the b-b-bed, on your stomach."

He obeyed. She began fastening his hands behind his back. Would he twist about, try to seize her for shield or hostage? She'd hate slashing him; but she stayed prepared. He lay passive, apart from speech: "What do *you* owe the Empire, Diana, this shellful of rotting flesh? Why should you die for it? You will, if you persist. You have nowhere to flee."

Instantly, almost involuntarily, she defied him. "We've got a whole big island where we can live off the farms and wildlife, plenty of hills and woods for cover. We'll survive."

"For hours; days, at most. In fear and wretchedness. Think. I offer you protection, amnesty. My kin will not be vindictive. They are above that. I offer you glory."

"He may intend it, or he may just want the use of you," Targovi said from the doorway. "In either case, sisterling, belike it's your safest trail. If we bind you, too, somebody will come erelong to see what's happened, and none should blame you."

"Naw." Diana secured Kukulkan's ankles. "I stay by my friends."

"A forlorn hope, we."

She hitched the strips to the bedframe, lest the prisoner roll himself off and out into the street. Straightening, she happened to spy and open closet. Hanging there were clothes for both man and woman.

Well, sure, she thought, Zacharians didn't marry. No point in it, for them. He had admitted as much, and mentioned children raised in interchangeable households, and she had wondered how lonesome he was in his heart and whether that was what drew him to her, and then they had gone on with their excursion. But, sure, Zacharians would have sex for other reasons than procreation. Interchangeable people? The idea was like a winter wind.

She stooped above the bonny face. He gave her a crooked smile. "Goodbye," she said to the alien.

Seeking Targovi: "All right, let's scramble out o' here."

* * *

"—state secrets. Almost as dangerous are their persons, for they are armed and desperate. While capture alive is desirable for purposes of interrogation, killing them on sight is preferable to any risk of allowing them to continue their rampage—"

Targovi heard the announcement out before he switched off the audio transceiver he had brought from the hospice. It was a natural thing to put in Axor's carrier, along with food, after they had voiced their decision to go on a long tramp through the hills, for the benefit of any electronic eavesdroppers. While the Wodenite recorded a message apologizing for thus cancelling his next appointment with Isis, explaining that he wished to savor the landscape and this was his last chance, his comrade had surreptitiously added a hiking outfit for Diana to the baggage.

Being a Tigery, Targovi skipped banalities like, "Well, now they know." He did murmur, "Interesting is how they phrase it, the scat about 'state secrets'. I should think most Zacharians will realize at once what this means. The rest should cooperate without questions."

"I s'pose the words're for the benefit of whatever outsiders may catch the broadcast," said Diana around a mouthful of sandwich. "F'r instance, on watercraft passin' within range. Not that they'd investigate for themselves."

The three rested in a hollow in the heights above Janua, well away from settlement. Its peacefulness was an ache in them. Birch stood around, leaves dancing to a breeze in the radiance of westbound Patricius. Prostrate juniper grew among the white trunks, itself dark blue-green and fragrant. A spring bubbled from a mossy bank. Somewhere a mockingbird trilled.

"The Zacharians will be out like a swarm of *khrukai*—swordwings," Targovi said. "They'll use aircraft and high-gain sensors. We'll need all the woodcraft that is ours. And . . . we are not used to forest such as this."

Diana smote fist on ground. "Be damned if we'll die for naught, or skulk around useless till Magnusson's slaughtered his way to the throne!" Her head and voice drooped. "Only what can we do?"

Axor cleared his throat. "I can do this much, beloved ones," he said, almost matter-of-factly. "My size and lack of skill at concealment will betray us even before my bodily need has exhausted the rations. Let me angle off and divert pursuit while you two seek the mountains." He lifted a hand against Diana's anguished cry. "No, no, it is the sole sensible plan. I came along because, much though I abhor violence, as a Christian should, yet there seemed to be a chance to end the war before it devours lives by the millions. Also, while I cannot believe the Merseians are creatures of Satan, they would deprive many billions of whatever self-determination is left. It is a worthy cause. Afterward, if you live, pray that we be forgiven for the harm we have done our opponents, and for the repose of their souls, as I will pray." His neck swayed upward from where he lay till light caught the crest of his head and made a crown of it. "Let me serve in the single way I am able. Lord, watch over my spirit, and the spirits of these my friends."

This time the girl could not stem tears. "Oh, Axor—!"

"Quiet, you two blitherers," Targovi grated. "What we want is less nobility and more thinking."

He jumped and paced, not man-style but as a Tigery does, weaving in and out among the trees and around the bushes. His right hand stroked the blade of his great knife over the palm of the left, again and again. Teeth gleamed when he muttered on the track of his thought.

"I led us hither because I dared not suppose my deed at the command post would go undetected enough longer for us to rustle transportation and reach the mainland. In that I was right. My hope was that the Zacharians would show such confusion at the news, being inexperienced in affairs like this, that we could double back and find means of escape—mayhap forcing the owner of a vehicle to cover for us. After all, they had not been well organized at the post. The hope was thin just the same, and now is not a wisp. I think their . . . oneness . . . makes them able to react to the unforeseen as coolly as an individual, not with the babble and cross purposes of an ordinary human herd taken by surprise. You heard the broadcast. Every car and boat will stay in a group of three or more, under guard. Every movement from the island will be stopped for inspection. This will prevail until we are captured or slain.

"Shall we yield? They might be content to shoot me, and the imprisonment of you two might not be cruel.

"You signal a no."

"My mother passed on an ancient sayin' to me," Diana told them. "Better to die on your feet than live on your knees."

"Ah, the young do not truly understand they *can* die," Axor sighed. "Yet if any possibility whatsoever is left us, what can we in conscience do other than try it?"

Still the Tigery prowled. "I am thinking, I am thinking—" Abruptly he halted. He drove the knife into a bole so that the metal sang. "Javak! Yes, it was on my horizon—a twisted path—But we must needs hurry, and not give the foe time to imagine we are crazy enough to take that way."

The south side of the Mencius range dropped a short distance before the land resumed its climb. This was unpeopled country, heavily wooded save where the canyon of the Averroes River slashed toward the sea, and on the higher flanks of the mountains. Kukulkan had told Diana it was a game and recreational preserve. The location of the spaceport here dated from troubled early days, when it might have become a target, minor though it was. Perhaps its isolation had been a factor in the conceiving of the Merseian plot.

Despite everything, the girl caught her breath at the sight. Clear, apart from a slight golden fleece of clouds, the sky was pale below, deepening in indigo at the zenith; but still night cast a dusk over the reaches around her. Heights to north and south walled in the world. Only at the ends of the vale did the sun-ring shine, casting rays that made the bottom a lake of amber. Where trees allowed glimpses, the hills above were purple-black, the snowcaps in the distance moltenly aglow. Air was cool on her brow. Quietness towered.

Wonder ended as Targovi pointed ahead.

Beyond the last concealment the forest afforded was a hundred-meter stretch, kept open though overgrown with brush and weeds. A link fence, to hold off animals, enclosed a ferrocrete field. Her pulse athrob but her senses and judgment preternaturally sharp, she gauged its dimensions as five hundred by three hundred meters. Service buildings clustered and a radionic mast spired at the farther end. Of the several landing docks, two were occupied. One craft she identified as interplanetary, a new and shapely version of *Moonjumper.* The other was naval—rather small as interstellar ships went, darkly gleaming, gun turret and launcher tubes sleeked into her leanness—akin to the Comet class, but not identical, not designed or wrought by humans—What ghost in her head blew a bugle call?

Huge and vague in the shadows, Axor whispered hoarsely, "We take the Zacharian vessel, of course."

"No, of course not," Targovi hissed. His eyes caught what light there was and burned like coals. "I was right in guessing the islanders are as militarily slovenly here as at the centrum, and have armed no watch. The thought of us hijacking a spaceship is too warlike to have occurred to them. But the Merseians are bound to have a guard aboard theirs. I know not whether that's a singleton or more, but belike whoever it is knows how to dispatch a seeker missile, or actually lift in chase." Decision. "However, we may well dupe them into supposing we are after the easier prey, and thus catch them off balance. The dim light will help—"

When he burst from concealment, Axor carried Diana in the crook of an arm, she would otherwise have toiled far behind him and Targovi. The pounding of his gallop resounded through her. She leaned into his flexing hardness, cradled her rifle, peered after a mark.

It was an instant and it was a century across the clearing, until they reached the fence. Axor's free arm curved around to keep torn strands off her while he crashed through. Nevertheless, several drew blood. She barely noticed.

Men ran from the terminal, insectoidal at their distance, then suddenly near. She saw pistols in the hands of some. She heard a buzz, a thud. Axor grunted, lurched, went on. Diana opened fire. A figure tumbled and lay sprattling.

Targovi bounded alongside. The cargo carrier was straight ahead. He raised his arm, veered, and went for the Merseians. Diana's vision swooped as Axor came around too. She glanced past his clifflike shoulder and saw the Zacharians in bewilderment. They numbered perhaps a dozen.

Targovi mounted the entry ramp of the dock. An airlock stood shut against him. He shielded his eyes with an arm and began to cut his way in with the blaster. Flame spurted blue-white, heat roiled, air seethed, sparks scorched his fur. A light ship like this relied on her forcefields and interceptors for protection in space. Nobody expected attack on the ground.

The Zacharians rallied and pelted toward him. They had courage aplenty, Diana thought in a breath. Axor went roaring and trampling to meet them. She threw a barrage. The men scattered and fled, except for one wounded and two shapeless.

Diana's trigger clicked on an empty magazine. Above her, Targovi's blaster sputtered out, its capacitors exhausted.

Axor thundered up the ramp. "Diana, get down!" he bawled. "Both of you, behind me!"

They scrambled to obey. He hammered his mass against the weakened lock. At the third impact it sagged aside.

Four Merseians waited. Their uniforms revealed them to be soldiers, unqualified to fly the craft they defended. Rather than shut the inner valve and risk it being wrecked too, they had prepared to give battle. Merseians would.

Axor charged. Beams and bullets converged on him. That could not check such momentum. Two died under his hoofs before he collapsed, shaking the hull. Targovi and Diana came right after. The Tigery threw his knife. A handgun rattled off a bulkhead. He and the Merseian went down together, embraced. His fangs found the green throat. Diana eluded a shot, got in close, and wielded her own blade.

Targovi picked himself up. "They'll've sent for help," he rasped out of dripping jaws. "Lubberly warriors though Zacharians be, I give us less than ten minutes. While I discover how to raise this thing, you close the portal." He whisked from sight.

The lock gave her no difficulty; the layout resembled that of *Moonjumper*. With the ship sealed, she made her way across a slippery deck to Axor. He lay breathing hard. Scorch marks were black over his scales. Redness oozed from wounds, not quite the same hue as hers, which was not quite the same as the Merseians', but it was all blood—water, iron, life. . . . "Oh, you're so hurt," she keened. "What can I do for you?"

He lifted his head. "Are you well, child?"

"Yes, nothin' hit me, but you, darlin', you—"

Lips drew back in a smile that others might have found frightening. "Not to fear. A little discomfort, yes, I might go so far as to say pain, but no serious injury. This carcass has many a pilgrimage ahead of it yet. Praises be to God and thanks to the more militant saints." The head sank. Wearily, soberly, he finished, "Now let me pray for the souls of the fallen."

A shiver went through Diana's feet. Targovi had awakened the engines.

* * *

Atmospheric warcraft zoomed over hills and mountains. He did not try keying in an order to shoot. Instead, he outclimbed them. Missiles whistled aloft. By then he had learned how to switch on the deflector field.

And after that he was in space. The planet rolled beneath him, enormous and lovely, burnished with oceans, emblazoned with continents, white-swirled with clouds. Once more he saw stars.

He could only take a moment to savor. Single-handing, he hadn't a meteorite's chance against attack by any Naval unit. "Diana," he said over the intercom, "come to the bridge, will you?" and devoted himself to piloting. He couldn't instruct the autosystem the unfamiliar manual controls responded clumsily to him, and the navigational instruments were incomprehensible; he must eyeball and stagger his way. At least he'd managed to set a steady interior field of about a gee. Otherwise his comrades would be getting thrown around like chips in a casino.

Well, if he and they could walk from the landing, that was amply good—if they walked free.

The girl entered and took the copilot's seat. "I hope to bring us down at Aurea port," he told her. "No doubt the Zacharians will call frantically in, demanding the Navy blow us menaces out of the sky, and no doubt there are officers who will be happy to oblige. I lack skill to take us away on hyperdrive. You are the human aboard. What do you counsel?"

She considered, hand to smoke-smudged

cheek—tangle-haired, sweaty, ragged, begrimed. Glancing at her, scenting her, knowing her, he wished he could be, for some hours, a male of her species.

"Can you set up a strong audiovisual transmission, that'll punch through interference on the standard band?" she asked.

He studied the console before him. "I think I can."

"Do." She closed her eyes and sagged in her harness.

But when he was ready, she came back to strength. To the computer-generated face in the screen she said: "I have a message for Commandant General Cesare Gatto. It's not crank, and it is top priority. If it don't get straight to him, courts martial are goin' to blossom till you can't see the clover for 'em. The fact I'm in a spacecraft you'll soon identify as Merseian should get you off your duffs. He'll want a recognition code, of course. Tell him Diana Crowfeather is bound home."

Chapter 21

The database contained much that became priceless to the Navy in its operations against the revolt. Some continued valuable afterward, to Terran Intelligence, until the Merseians had completed necessary changes of plan and organization—an effort which, while it went on, kept them out of considerable mischief abroad. A part of the record dealt with Sir Olaf Magnusson. From previous experience and knowledge, Flandry reconstructed more of the story, conjecturally but with high probability.

A man stern and righteous lived under an Imperium effete and corrupt. Emperor Georgios meant well, but he was long a-dying, and meanwhile the favorites of the Crown Prince crowded into power. After Josip succeeded to the throne, malfeasance would scarcely trouble to mask itself, and official after official would routinely order atrocities committed on outlying worlds entrusted to them, that wealth might be wrung into their coffers. Erik Magnusson, space captain and trader of Kraken, forswore in his heart all allegiance to the Empire that had broken faith with him.

Somehow a Merseian or two, among those

whom he occasionally met, sensed the unhappiness in him and passed word of it on to those who took interest in such matters. Upon his next visit to their mother planet, he received baronial treatment. In due course he met the great lord—not the Roidhun, who has more often been demigod than ruler, but the chief of the Grand Council, the day-by-day master of that whole vast realm, insofar as any single creature could ever be.

This was Brechdan Ironrede, the Hand of the Vach Ynvory, an impressive being whose soul was in many respects brother to the soul of Captain Magnusson. Well did he know what would appeal. There were humans by race who were Merseian subjects, just as there were Merseians by race who were Terran subjects —tiny minorities in either case, but significant on many levels. Those whom Brechdan summoned must have joined their voices to his. Why should Kraken pay tribute to an Imperium which enriched toadies, fettered commerce, and neglected defenses? The law of the Roidhun was strict but just. Under him, men could again be men. United, the two civilizations would linger no more in this handful of stars on a fringe of the galaxy; they would fare forth to possess the cosmos.

Erik Magnusson was converted. Perhaps Aycharaych, the telepath, confirmed it.

The man must have realized how slight the chance was that he could ever be of important service. He might or might not recruit a few others, he might or might not sometimes carry a message or an agent, but basically he was a reservist, a silent keeper of the flame. At home he could not even declare openly his love for Merseia.

But the time came when he gave Merseia his son.

The boy Olaf accompanied him there and remained. Nobody on Kraken suspected aught amiss when Erik returned within him. Olaf's mother was dead, his father had not remarried, his siblings had learned to refrain from pestering with questions. "I got him an apprentice's berth on a prospector ship. He'll learn more and better than in any of our schools."

The secret school he did enter was neither human or humane. High among its undertakings was to strengthen the strong and destroy the weak. Olaf survived. He learned science, history, combat, leadership, and tearlessness. Toward the end, Aycharaych took him in charge, Aycharaych the Chereionite, he of the crested eagle countenance and the subtle, probing intellect. Merseian masters had laid a foundation in the boy: knowledge, physique, purpose. Upon it Aycharaych now raised the psychosexual structure he wanted.

The Golden Face, the uttered wisdom, the Sleep and the Dreams and the words that whispered through them . . . carefully orchestrated pleasures of flesh, mind, spirit . . . dedication to a God unknowable—

Young Olaf Magnusson reappeared on Kraken after some years, taciturn about his adventures. He soon enlisted in the Imperial marines. From then on, he carried out his orders.

They were the directives of his superiors. Never was he a spy, a subversive, or anything but a bold, bright member of the Terran armed services—enlisted man, cadet on transfer, Navy officer. The commandment of the Merseians was to do his utmost, rise as fast and high as possible, and inwardly stand by for an opportunity that might well never come.

What action he saw at first was against barbarians, bandits, local rebels and recalcitrants, nothing to stir inner conflict. But when crisis erupted into combat at Syrax, he fought Merseians. What agony this cost him—and perhaps that was little, for he had been taught that death in battle is honorable, and an individual is only a cell in the bloodstream of the Race—was eased when a secret agent brought him praise and told him that henceforward he would be in the minds of the Roidhunate's mighty.

He had also called himself to the attention of the Empire's. His career plunged ahead like a comet toward its sun. If Merseia or its cat's paws made trouble, that was frequently in regions where he was stationed, and he distinguished himself. Knowing Eriau and two other major Merseian languages, he served on negotiating commissions, and gained still greater distinction. Beginning as an aide, he proffered such excellent suggestions that presently he was in charge; and under his direction, the Terrans got terms more advantageous to themselves than they had really hoped for.

True, these were all *ad hoc* arrangements, concerning specific, spatially limited issues of secondary concern. Nonetheless Olaf Magnusson proved that he understood the Merseians and could get along with them. Manifestly, they did not hold his combat career against him; rather, they respected his ability and determination.

The Navy did likewise. Aloofness and austerity became advantageous traits in the reformist reign of Emperor Hans; they showed Magnusson to be no mere uniformed politician. He was a spit-and-polish disciplinarian, but always fair, and, given a deserving case, capable of compassion. Where he held office, morale rose high, also among civilians, especially after his broadcast speeches. Thus it became logical to make him responsible for the defense of an entire, strategically critical sector, bordering on the debatable spaces between Empire and Roidhunate.

Terra later had cause to give the High Command thanks for so wise a choice. What seemed like another quarrel between the powers, ugly but resolvable, abruptly escaped control. It flared into the worst emergency since Syrax. There was no rhyme or reason to that; but how often is there with governments? Once again a Merseian task force moved toward an undermanned Terran frontier "to restore order, assure the safety of the Race and its client species, and make possible the resumption of meaningful diplomatic discussions."

The meaning of those discussions would be obvious, when Merseia held a sizeable chunk ripped out of the Empire's most vulnerable side. The concessions demanded would not be such to provoke full-scale war; but they would leave Terra sorely weakened. Time was lacking in which to send adequate reinforcements. Against the threat, Olaf Magnusson's fleet orbited alone.

"We will pay the price," the Merseian envoy had said in the hidden place. "You must it exact it ruthlessly. Spare us no blow that you can deal. Your duty is to become a hero."

The Imperials at Patricius met the foe and broke him. His shattered squadrons reeled back into the darkness whence they came. Merseian representatives called for an immediate reconvening of the high-level conference, and suddenly what they asked and offered was reasonable. Jubilation billowed through the Empire, yes, even on jaded Terra. Magnusson went there to receive a knighthood at the hands of the Emperor.

He returned to folk who adored him and felt cheated by their Imperium—almost as embittered as were many Merseians who had seen comrades die and ships lost because of unprecedented ineptitude. Sir Olaf began to speak out against the decadence of the state, of the entire body politic. He spoke both publicly and privately. Given his immense prestige and his remoteness from the center of things, no one ventured to quell him . . . until he proclaimed himself master of all, and his legions hailed him; and then it was too late.

"This is the day for which we have prepared

throughout your lifetime," said the envoy in the hidden place.

"I am to reach the throne?" Magnusson asked, amazed in spite of having guessed what his engineered destiny was. "Why? To undermine the Empire till it lies ready for conquest? I—do not like that thought. Nor do I really believe it's a possibility. Too many unforeseeables, too many whole worlds."

"Khraich, *no. Victory shall be as quick and clean as we can make it. You are to come not as the executioner, but the savior."*

"Hard to do."

"Explain why."

"Well—Hans Molitor had it easier. The Wang dynasty was extinct, aside from a few idiots who could raise no following. Everybody wished for a strong man and the peace he would impose. Hans was the ablest of the contending war lords. From the first, he had the most powerful forces behind him. Yet the struggle dragged on for bloody years. Gerhart may be unpopular, but he is a son of Hans, and people hope for better things from his son. I would not expect very much of the Navy, besides the units I lead, to support me, nor any large part of the populations. Most will see me as a disturber of their lives."

"You shall have our *support. Abundant war material will flow to you through this sector, once you have achieved an initial success. Later, 'volunteers' will appear, in organized detachments drawn from subject species of ours. They need not be many or conspicuous; you can employ them with care, while affirming your loyalty to your own civilization. We will furnish*

proof of that, border incidents wherein your partisans show they continue ready to hold the foreign threat off.

"As soon as you seem clearly in the ascendant, you should find more and more Terrans—Navy officers included—embracing your cause. Your triumph should be total, and at relatively low cost. You will thereupon set about binding up the wounds of war, pardoning opponents but punishing evildoers, reforming, cleansing, strengthening, just as you promised. You should become the most widely beloved Emperor Terra has had since Pedro II."

"But what then? How does this serve the Race? You must be aware that the power of the Emperor is only absolute in theory. I couldn't decree submission to the Roidhun; I'd be dead within the hour."

"Assuredly. But you will call for a genuine peace, wherein both sides bargain honestly, and see to it that your side does so bargain. You will make appropriate appointments, first to the Policy Board and High Command, afterward elsewhere; the names will be furnished you. From time to time questions will arise, political, economic, social, where you, the forceful and incorruptible Emperor, will make yourself arbiter. The list goes on. I will not weary you with it now. Your imagination can write much of it already.

"Fear not, Olaf Magnusson. You should end your days old and honored. Your inheriting son should follow in your tracks. By then Mersiean advisors will sit in his councils, and Mersiean virtue be the ideal extolled by his intellectuals,

and if certain edicts are nevertheless so distasteful as to cause revolts, Merseia will come to the help of the good Emperor. . . . Your grandsons will belong to the first generation of the new humanity."

Chapter 22

Lieutenant General Cesare Gatto, Imperial Marine Corps, Commandant for the Patrician System, issued his orders immediately. An escadrille of corvettes left Daedalus orbit and accelerated downward. At the speed wherewith they hit atmosphere, it blazed and blasted about them, behind them.

They were too late by minutes, and buzzed back and forth over Zacharia like angry hornets. The interplanetary freighter which had been in port on the island had taken off. She could never have escaped pursuit, except by the means chosen. Rising several hundred kilometers, she nosed over and crash-dived. Under full thrust and no negafield protection, she became a shooting star. Afterward, Merseians would sing a ballad in praise of those comrades of theirs who had died such a death.

No Zacharians attempted flight. "Our people tried to stop them, but they were armed and resolved on immolation," their spokesman said over the eidophone. "We are staying together."

"You will destroy no evidence and make no

resistance when his Majesty's troops land," Gatto snapped.

Tangaroa Zachary shrugged. His smile was as sorrowful a sight as the general had ever beheld. "No, we realize we are trapped, and will not make the situation worse for ourselves. You will find us cooperative. We are not conditioned to secrecy, thus hypnoprobing should be unnecessary; I suggest narcoquizzing a random sample of us."

"Behave yourselves, and I may put in a word on your behalf when the time comes for dealing out penalties. I may—provided you can explain to me what in God's name made you commit mass treason."

"We are that we are."

Gatto's broadcast ended a week of uncertainty and unease. Nobody but the most trusted members of his staff knew more than that he had let a Merseian vessel land at Aurea, and had had the crew hurried away in an opaque vehicle; that he had thereupon put the defense forces on alert against possible Merseian action; and that for reasons unspecified, a brigade occupied Zacharia and held it incommunicado. He needed the week to prepare forestalling measures, while his Intelligence agents feverishly studied three data slabs.

At the appropriate moment, various officers were surprised when placed under arrest. Their detention was precautionary; he could not be sure they would be able to instantly accept the truth about their idol Sir Olaf. Then Gatto went on the air.

From end to end of the system, that which he had to tell cut through the tension like a sword. Recoil came next, a lashing of outrage and alarm. Yet a curious quiet relief welled up underneath. How many folk had really wanted to undergo hazard and sacrifice for a change of overlords? Now, unless the Merseians took an ungloved hand in matters, the requirement upon them was just that they muddle through each day until the *status quo* could be restored.

By the hundreds, recordings of the announcement, together with copies and analyses of the proof, went off in message torpedoes and courier boats to the Imperial stars.

Gatto's image was not alone there. After his speech, the uptake had gone to a woman. She stood very straight against a plain red backdrop. A gray robe draped her slenderness. A white coif framed dark, fine features. Behind her stood two half-grown boys and a little girl. They wore the same headgear. On the planet Nyanza, it is the sign of mourning for the dead.

"Greeting," she said, low and tonelessly. "I am Vida Lonwe-Magnusson, wife of Admiral Sir Olaf. With me are the children we have had. Many of you sincerely believed in the rightfulness of his cause. You will understand how we four never thought to question it, any more than we question sunlight or springtime.

"Tonight we know that Olaf Magnusson's life has been one long betrayal. He would have delivered us into the power of our enemies—no, worse than enemies; those who would domesticate us to their service. I say to you, disown him, as we do here before you. Cast down him and his works, destroy them utterly, send the dust of them out upon the tides of endless space. Let us return to our true allegiance. No, the Empire is not perfect; but it is ours. *We* can better it.

"As for myself, when we have peace again I will go back to the world of my people, and bring my children with me. May all of you be as free. And may you be ready to forgive those who were mistaken. May those of you who are religious see fit to pray for the slain in this most abominable of wars. Perhaps a few of you will even find it in your hearts to pray for the soul of Olaf Magnusson.

"Thank you."

The task finished, she gathered her sons and her daughter to her, and they wept.

Winter night lay over the South Wilwidh Ocean. Waves ran black before a harrying wind, save where their white manes glimmered fugitively in what light there was. That came from above. The moon Neihevin seemed to fly through ragged clouds. So did a tiny, lurid patch, the nebula expanding from the ruin of Valenderay; and across more than a parsec, its radiation unfolded aurora in cold hues. Several speeding glints betokened satellites whose forcefields must still, after half a millennium, guard Merseia against the subatomic sleetstorm the supernova had cast forth. Hazy though it was, this luminance veiled most stars.

Those that blinked in vision were far apart and forlorn.

Seas crashed, wind shrilled around the islet stronghold from which Tachwyr the Dark spoke with his Grand Council. The images somehow deepened his aloneness in the stony room where he sat.

"No, I have as yet no word of what went wrong," he told them. "Searching it out may require prolonged efforts, for the Terrans will put the best mask they can upon the facts. And it may hardly matter. Some blunder, accident, failure of judgment—that could well be what has undone us." Starkly: "The fact is that they have learned Magnusson was ours. Everywhere his partisans are deserting him. If they do not straightaway surrender to the nearest authorities, it is because they first want pardons. The enterprise itself has disintegrated."

"You say Magnusson *was* ours," Alwis Longtail murmured. "How do you know his fate? Might he be alive and bound hitherward?"

"That is conceivable," Tachwyr replied; "but I take for granted that the crew of his flagship mutinied too, when the news came upon them. We shall wish they killed him cleanly. He has deserved better than trial and execution on Terra—yes, better than dragging out a useless existence as a pensioner on Merseia."

"Likewise," said Odhar the Curt, "your statement that his followers are giving up must be an inference."

"True. Thus far I have only the most preliminary of reports. But think."

"I have. You are certainly correct."

"What can we do?" asked Gwynafon of Brightwater.

"We will not intervene," said Tachwyr to the dull member of the Council. "What initial gains we might make while the Terran Navy is trying to reorganize itself would be trivial, set next to the consequences. Much too readily could the militant faction among the humans, minority though it is, mobilize sentiment, seize control, and set about preparing the Empire for total confrontation with us.

"No, Merseia denies any complicity, blames whatever may have happened upon overzealous officers—on both sides, and calls for resumption of talks about a nonaggression pact. My lords, at this conference we should draft instructions to Ambassador Chwioch. I have already ordered the appropriate agencies to start planning what to feed the Imperial academies, religions, and news media."

"Then we might yet get two or three beasts out of this failed battue?" Alwis wondered.

"We must try," Odhar said. "Console yourselves with the thought that we invested little treasure or effort in the venture. Our net loss is minor."

"Except for hope," Tachwyr mumbled. He drew his robe close about him; the room felt chill. "I dreamed that I would live to behold—" He straightened. "By adversity, the God tempers the steel of the Race. Let us get on with our quest."

Chapter 23

Imhotep spun toward northern autumn. Dwarfed Patricius burned mellower in skies gone pale. When full, the big moon Zoser rose early and set late; with its lesser companions Kanofer and Rahotep it made lambent the snowpeaks around Mt. Horn. Sometimes flakes dusted off them, aglitter, vanishing as they blew into the streets of Olga's Landing. Dead leaves scrittled underfoot. In Old Town crowds milled, music twanged, savory odors rose out of foodstalls and Winged Smoke houses; for this was the season when Tigery caravans brought wares up from the lowlands.

Fleet Admiral Sir Dominic Flandry had time to prowl about. Things had changed a good deal since last he was here, but memories lingered. One hour he went to the Terran cemetery and stood quiet before a headstone. Otherwise, mostly, he enjoyed being at liberty, while hirelings flitted in search of the persons he wanted.

After the loyalists—the Navy of Emperor Gerhart—reoccupied Sphinx and released him, he had set about learning just what had been going on. His connections got him more information than would ever become public. On that basis, he decided to send Banner a reassuring message but himself, before returning home, visit Daedalus. There he spent an especially interesting while on Zacharia. However, those individuals he most desired to see had gone back to Imhotep. Flandry followed, to learn that Diana Crowfeather and Father F.X. Axor were at sea on an archaeological expedition, while Targovi was off in the asteroid belt chaffering for precious metals. Like everything else, thc minerals industry was in a fluid state, and would remain thus until the aftermath of the recent unpleasantness had damped out. A smart operator could take advantage of that.

Having called on Dragoika in Toborkozan, Flandry engaged searchers. In Olga's Landing he took lodgings at the Pyramid and roved around the city.

Almost together, his detectives fetched his guests. Flandry bade them a cordial welcome over the eidophone, described the credit to their accounts in the bank, and arranged a date for meeting. Thereafter he commandeered an official dining room and gave personal attention to the menu and wine list.

From this high level, a full-wall transparency looked far over splendor. Westward the city ended at woods turned scarlet, russet, amber. Beyond the warm zone were boulders and crags, hardy native bush, thinly frozen rivulets and ponds, to the dropoff of the summit. Beyond the depths, within which blue shadows were rising, neighbor mountains waited for the sun. Their snows had come aglow; glaciers gleamed nebula-green.

In air, weight, warmth, the room was Terra. Recorded violins frolicked, fragrances drifted. It made the more plain what an enclave this was, and how much the more dear for that.

Flandry leaned back, let cigarette smoke trail, regarded his daughter through it. A charming lass, he thought. Granted, the outfit she had bought herself was scarcely in the latest Imperial court fashion—crimson minigown, leather sandals, bracelet and headband of massive silver set with raw turquoises, spotted gillycat pelt from right shoulder to left hip, where her Tigery knife rested—but it might well have ignited a new style there, and in any event the Imperial court was blessedly distant.

As he hoped, cocktails were bringing ease between him and her. But Targovi, to whom the drinking of ethanol was not a social custom and who had not started to inhale what was set before him, persisted in hunting down what he wanted to know. The Tigery had vanity enough to wear a beaded breechcloth and necklace of land pearls; a colloidal spray had made his fur shine. Still— "And so you, sir, you caught the same suspicions as I?" he inquired.

In the background Axor rested serene along the floor, listening with one bony ear while contemplating the sunset. He was clad merely in his scales and scutes, unless you counted the purse, rosary, and spectacles hung from his neck.

"Why, yes," Flandry said. "Magnusson's being a sleeper, as we call it in the trade—that possibility occurred to me, although an undertaking such as his would be the most audacious ever chronicled outside of cloak-and-blaster fiction. I thought of comparing his account of his early life with what various Merseians recalled. They could not all have been vowed to secrecy; and as for those who had been, a percentage would be susceptible .... Blatant inconsistencies would give me a strong clue. Unfortunately, Merseian counter-intelligence nailed our agents before they could accomplish anything worthwhile. Fortunately, you had the same intuition, and this trio here in front of me carried out a coup more dramatic and decisive than I had dared fantasize."

"What's the latest news about the war?" Diana asked. "The truth, I mean, not that sugar puddin' on the screens."

Flandry's grin was wary. "I wouldn't dignify it with the name of war. Not as of weeks and weeks ago. Mainly, everything is in abeyance while Imperium and bureaucracy creak through the datawork. People who, in good faith, fought for Magnusson—they're too many to kill or imprison. Punishments will have to range from reprimands, through fines and reductions in rank, to cashiering. The scale and the chaos of making it all orderly defies imagination; beside it, the accretion disc of a black hole is as neat as a transistor. But it'll settle down eventually."

"Magnusson. Any word about him?"

Flandry frowned. "He died at the hands of his men. Do you really want to hear the details? I gather there are no plans to release them. Why risk rousing sympathy for him?"

"And I suppose," Targovi put in slowly, "the tale of how the conspiracy came to light, that will also stay secret?"

Flandry sighed. "Well, it wouldn't make the government look so terribly efficient, would it? Besides, my sources inform me that Merseia had indicated its release would make Merseia equally unhappy. It could jar the peace process . . . Not that you're forbidden to talk. The Empire is big, and you have no particular access to the media."

"What of the Zacharians?" came like surf from Axor. "Is mercy possible for those tormented souls?"

"Tormented, my foot!" cried Diana, and stamped hers. She checked herself, drank of her martini, and said, while a slight flush played across her cheekbones: "Not that I'm after genocide on them or any such thing. Javak, no! But what will happen? You got any notion, Dad?"

"Yes, I do," Flandry replied, glad to steer conversation into softer channels. "Not that a final decree has been issued; but I've been studying the situation, and . . . my word is not without leverage."

He likewise sipped, drew breath and smoke, before he continued: "They're unique. No other population, at least no other human population, could have kept a secret the way theirs did. Virtually every adult was privy to it. Let's eschew quibbles about what 'human' really means.

"Their children, of course, are innocent, had no idea of what was going on. Can we kill them? The Merseians might, to 'purge the Race.' Whatever its entropy level, the Empire has not yet sunk to that.

"Pardons, amnesties, and limited penalties are going to be the order of the day. They must, if we want to shore up this social structure of ours so it might last another century or two.

"I think the punishment of the Zacharians will be the loss of their country. They'll be forced to vacate—scatter—find new homes wherever they can. I'd not be surprised but what Merseia offers them a haven, and many of them accept. The rest—will have to make their way among the rest of us."

"And what will come of that?" Targovi mused.

Flandry spread his hands. "Who knows? We play the game move by move, and never see far ahead—the game of empire, of life, whatever you want to call it—and what the score will be when all the pieces at last go back into the box, who knows?"

He tossed off his drink, tossed away his cigarette, and stood up. "My friends," he said, "dinner awaits. Let us go in together and rejoice in what we have.

"But first—" his glance swooped about—"I'd like to give you three some extra reason for rejoicing. Diana, Targovi . . . are you really heart-bent on faring out yonder? I'm prepared to arrange that for you, however you choose. Trader, explorer, scientist, artist, or, God help you, Intelligence operative—I can see to it that you get the schooling and the means you'll need. I only ask that first you think hard about what you truly want."

The girl's and the Tigery's spirits fountained radiance.

"As for you, Father Axor," Flandry went on, "if you wish, I'll obtain adequate funding for your research. Shall I?"

"God bless you, whether you like it or not," the Wodenite replied, ocean-deep. "What you endow goes beyond space or time." He crossed his hands on his forelegs and smiled, as a being may who is winning salvation for himself and his beloved.

Lycon was the greatest of the beast hunters
who fed the bloody maw of Rome's Coliseum.
How was he to know that the creature
he sought this time was not only as cunning
as he...but came from a world
more vicious than he could imagine?

288 pp. • $2.95

Distributed by Simon & Schuster
Mass Merchandise Sales Company
1230 Avenue of the Americas • New York, N.Y. 10020